DITTE: GIR
BY
MARTIN ANDERSON NEXÖ

CHAPTER I
DITTE'S FAMILY TREE

It has always been considered a sign of good birth to be able to count one's ancestors for centuries back. In consequence of this, Ditte Child o' Man stood at the top of the tree. She belonged to one of the largest families in the country, the family of Man.

No genealogical chart exists, nor would it be easy to work it out; its branches are as the sands of the sea, and from it all other generations can be traced. Here it cropped out as time went on—then twined back when its strength was spent and its part played out. The Man family is in a way as the mighty ocean, from which the waves mount lightly towards the skies, only to retreat in a sullen flow.

According to tradition, the first mother of the family is said to have been a field worker who, by resting on the cultivated ground, became pregnant and brought forth a son. And it was this son who founded the numerous and hardy family for whom all things prospered. The most peculiar characteristic of the Man family in him was that everything he touched became full of life and throve.

This boy for a long time bore the marks of the clinging earth, but he outgrew it and became an able worker of the field; with him began the cultivation of the land. That he had no father gave him much food for thought, and became the great and everlasting problem of his life. In his leisure he created a whole religion out of it.

He could hold his own when it came to blows; in his work there was no one to equal him, but his wife had him well in hand. The name Man is said to have originated in his having one day, when she had driven him forth by her sharp tongue, sworn threateningly that he was master in his own house, "master" being equivalent to "man." Several of the male members of this family have since found it hard to bow their pride before their women folk.

A branch of the family settled down on the desert coast up near the Cattegat, and this was the beginning of the hamlet. It was in those times when forest and swamp still made the country impassable, and the sea was used as a highway. The reefs are still there on which the men landed from the boats, carrying women and children ashore; by day and by night white seagulls take turns to mark the place—and have done so through centuries.

This branch had in a marked degree the typical characteristics of the family: two eyes—and a nose in the middle of their faces; one mouth which could both kiss and bite, and a pair of fists which they could make good use of. In addition to this the family was alike in that most of its members were better than their circumstances. One could recognize the Man family anywhere by their bad qualities being traceable to definite causes, while for the good in them there was no explanation at all: it was inbred.

It was a desolate spot they had settled upon, but they took it as it was, and gave themselves up patiently to the struggle for existence, built huts, chopped wood and made ditches. They were contented and hardy, and had the Man's insatiable desire to overcome difficulties; for them there was no bitterness in work, and before long the result of their labors could be seen. But keep the profit of their work they could not; they allowed others to have the spending of it, and thus it came about, that in spite of their industry they remained as poor as ever.

Over a century ago, before the north part of the coast was discovered by the land folk, the place still consisted of a cluster of hunch-backed, mildewed huts, which might well have been the originals, and on the whole resembled a very ancient hamlet. The beach was strewn with tools and drawn-up boats. The water in the little bay stank of castaway fish, catfish and others which, on account of their singular appearance, were supposed to be possessed of devils, and therefore not eaten.

A quarter of an hour's walk from the hamlet, out on the point, lived Sören Man. In his young days he had roamed the seas like all the others, but according to custom had later on settled himself down as a fisherman. Otherwise, he was really more of a peasant and belonged to that branch of the family which had devoted itself to the soil, and for this had won much respect. Sören Man was the son of a farmer, but on reaching man's estate, he married a fisher girl and gave himself up to fishing together with agriculture—exactly as the first peasant in the family had done.

The land was poor, two or three acres of downs where a few sheep struggled for their food, and this was all that remained of a large farm which had once been there, and where now seagulls flocked screaming over the white surf. The rest had been devoured by the ocean.

It was Sören's, and more particularly Maren's foolish pride that his forefathers had owned a farm. It had been there sure enough three or four generations back; with a fairly good ground, a clay bank jutting out into the sea. A strong four-winged house, built of oak—taken from wrecks—could be seen from afar, a picture of strength. But then suddenly the ocean began to creep in. Three generations, one after the other, were forced to shift the farm further back to prevent its falling into the sea, and to make the moving easier, each time a wing was left behind; there was, of course, no necessity for so much house-room, when the land was eaten by the sea. All that now remained was the heavy-beamed old dwelling-house which had prudently been placed on the landward side of the road, and a few sandhills.

Here the sea no longer encroached. Now the best had gone, with the lands of Man, it was satiated and took its costly food elsewhere; here, indeed, it gave back again, throwing sand up on to the land, which formed a broad beach in front of the slope, and on windy days would drift, covering the rest of the field. Under the thin straggling downs could still be traced the remains of old plowland, broken off crudely on the slope, and of old wheeltracks running outwards and disappearing abruptly in the blue sky over the sea.

For many years, after stormy nights with the sea at high tide, it had been the Man's invariable custom each morning to find out how much had again been taken by the sea; burrowing animals hastened the destruction; and it happened that whole pieces of field with their crops would suddenly go; down in the muttering ocean it lay, and on it the mark of harrow and plow and the green reflection of winter crops over it.

It told on a man to be witness of the inevitable. For each time a piece of their land was taken by the sea with all their toil and daily bread on its back, they themselves declined. For every fathom that the ocean stole nearer to the threshold of their home, nibbling at their good earth, their status and courage grew correspondingly less.

For a long time they struggled against it, and clung to the land until necessity drove them back to the sea. Sören was the first to give himself entirely up to it: he took his wife from the hamlet and became a fisherman. But they were none the better for it. Maren could never forget that her Sören belonged to a family who had owned a farm; and so it was with the children. The sons cared little for the sea, it was in them to struggle with the land and therefore they sought work on farms and became day-laborers and ditchers, and as soon as they saved sufficient money, emigrated to America. Four sons were farming over there. They were seldom heard of, misfortune seemed to have worn out their feeling of relationship. The daughters went out to service, and after a time Sören and Maren lost sight of them, too. Only the youngest, Sörine, stayed at home longer than was usual with poor folks' children. She was not particularly strong, and her parents thought a great deal of her—as being the only one they had left.

It had been a long business for Sören's ancestors to work themselves up from the sea to the ownership of cultivated land; it had taken several generations to build up the farm on the Naze. But the journey down hill was as usual more rapid, and to Sören was left the worst part of all when he inherited; not only acres but possessions had gone; nothing was left now but a poor man's remains.

The end was in many ways like the beginning. Sören was like the original man in this also, that he too was amphibious. He understood everything, farming, fishing and handicraft. But he was not sharp enough to do more than just earn a bare living, there was never anything to spare. This was the difference between the ascent and the descent. Moreover, he—like so many of the family—found it difficult to attend to his own business.

It was a race which allowed others to gather the first-fruits of their labors. It was said of them that they were just like sheep, the more the wool was clipped, the thicker it grew. The downfall had not made Sören any more capable of standing up for himself.

When the weather was too stormy for him to go to sea, and there was nothing to do on his little homestead, he sat at home and patched seaboots for his friends down in the hamlet. But he seldom got paid for it. "Leave it till next time," said they. And Sören had nothing much to say against this arrangement, it was to him just as good as a savings bank. "Then one has something for one's old days," said he. Maren and the girl were always scolding him for this, but Sören in this as in everything else, did not amend his ways. He knew well enough what women were; they never put by for a rainy day.

CHAPTER II
BEFORE THE BIRTH

The children were now out of their care—that is to say, all the eight of them. Sören and Maren were now no longer young. The wear and tear of time and toil began to be felt; and it would have been good to have had something as a stand-by. Sörine, the youngest, was as far as that goes, also out of their care, in that she was grown up and ought long ago to have been pushed out of the nest; but there was a reason for her still remaining at home supported by her old parents.

She was very much spoiled, this girl—as the youngest can easily be; she was delicate and bashful with strangers. But, as Maren thought, when one has given so many children to the world, it was pleasant to keep one of them for themselves; nests without young ones soon become cold. Sören in the main thought just the same, even if he did grumble and argue that one woman in the house was more than enough. They were equally fond of children. And hearing so seldom from the others they clung more closely to the last one. So Sörine remained at home and only occasionally took outside work in the hamlet or at the nearest farms behind the downs. She was supposed to be a pretty girl, and against this Sören had nothing to say: but what he could see was that she did not thrive, her red hair stood like a flame round her clear, slightly freckled forehead, her limbs were fragile, and strength in her there was none. When speaking to people she could not meet their eyes, her own wandered anxiously away.

The young boys from the hamlet came wooing over the downs and hung round the hut—preferably on the warm nights; but she hid herself and was afraid of them.

"She takes after the bad side of the family," said Sören, when he saw how tightly she kept her window closed.

"She takes after the fine side," said the mother then. "Just you wait and see, she will marry a gentleman's son."

"Fool," growled Sören angrily and went his way: "to fill both her own and the girl's head with such rubbish!"

He was fond enough of Maren, but her intellect had never won his respect. As the children grew up and did wrong in one way or another, Sören always said: "What a fool the child is—it takes after its mother." And Maren, as years went on, bore patiently with this; she knew quite as well as Sören that it was not intellect that counted.

Two or three times in the week, Sörine went up town with a load of fish and brought goods home again. [Pg 12] It was a long way to walk, and part of the road went through a pine wood where it was dark in the evening and tramps hung about.

"Oh, trash," said Sören, "the girl may just as well try a little of everything, it will make a woman of her."

But Maren wished to shelter her child, as long as she could. And so she arranged it in this way, that her daughter could drive home in the cart from Sands farm which was then carrying grain for the brewery.

The arrangement was good, inasmuch as Sörine need no longer go in fear of tramps, and all that a timid young girl might encounter; but, on the other hand, it did not answer Maren's expectations. Far from having taken any harm from the long walks, it was now proved what good they had done her. She became even more delicate than before, and dainty about her food.

This agreed well with the girl's otherwise gentle manners. In spite of the trouble it gave her, this new phase was a comfort to Maren. It took the last remaining doubt from her heart: it was now irrevocably settled. Sörine was a gentlefolks' child, not by birth, of course—for Maren knew well enough who was father and who mother to the girl, whatever Sören might have thought—but by gift of grace. It did happen that such were found in a poor man's cradle, and they were always supposed to bring joy to their parents. Herrings and potatoes, flounders and potatoes and a little bacon in between—this was no fare for what one might call a young lady. Maren made little delicacies [Pg 13] for her, and when Sören saw it, he spat as if he had something nasty in his mouth and went his way.

But, after all one can be too fastidious, and when at last the girl could not keep down even an omelet, it was too much of a good thing for Maren. She took her daughter up to a wise woman who lived on the common. Three times did she try her skill on Sörine, with no avail. So Sören had to borrow a horse and cart and drove them in to the homeopathist. He did it very unwillingly. Not because he did not care for the girl, and it might be possible, as Maren said, that as she slept, an animal or evil spirit might have found its way into her mouth and now prevented the food from going down. Such things had been heard of before. But actually to make fools of themselves on this account—rushing off with horse and cart to the doctor just as the gentry did, and make themselves, too, the laughing stock of the whole hamlet, when a draught of tansy would have the same effect—this was what Sören could not put up with.

But, of course, although the daily affairs were settled by Sören Man, there were occasions when Maren insisted on having her way—more so when it seriously affected *her* offspring. Then she could—as with witchcraft—suddenly forget her good behavior, brush aside Sören's arguments as endless nonsense, and would stand there like a stone wall which one could neither climb over, nor get round. Afterwards he would be sorry that the magic word which should have brought Maren [Pg 14] down from her high and mightiness, failed him at the critical moment. For she *was* a fool—especially when it affected her offspring. But, whether right or wrong, when she had her great moments, fate spoke through her mouth, and Sören was wise enough to remain silent.

This time it certainly seemed as if Maren was in the right; for the cure which the homeopathist prescribed, effervescent powder and sweet milk, had a wonderful effect. Sörine throve and grew fat, so that it was a pleasure to see her.

There can be too much of a good thing, and Sören Man, who had to provide the food, was the first to think of this. Sörine and her mother talked much together and wondered what the illness could be, could it be this or could it be that? There was a great to-do and much talking with their heads together; but, as soon as Sören appeared, they became silent.

He had become quite unreasonable, going about muttering and swearing. As though it was not hard enough already, especially for the poor girl! He had no patience with a sick person, beggar that he was; and one day it broke out from him with bitterness and rage: "She must be—it can be nothing else."

But like a tiger, Maren was upon him.

"What are you talking about, you old stupid? Have *you* borne eight children, or has the girl told you what's amiss? A sin and a shame it is to let her hear such talk; but now it is done, you might just as well ask her [Pg 15] yourself. Answer your father, Sörine—is it true, what he says?"

Sörine sat drooping by the fireplace, suffering and scared. "Then it would be like the Virgin Mary," she whispered, without looking up. And suddenly sank down, sobbing.

"'There, you can see yourself, what a blockhead you are," said Maren harshly. "The girl is as pure as an unborn child. And here you come, making all this racket in the house, while the child, perhaps, may be on the point of death."

Sören Man bowed his head, and hurried out on to the downs. Ugh! it was just like thunder overhead. Blockhead she had called him—for the first time in the whole of their life together; he would have liked to have forced that word home again and that, at once, before it stuck to him. But to face a mad, old wife and a howling girl—no, he kept out of it.

Sören Man was an obstinate fellow; when once he got a thing into his three-cornered head, nothing could hammer it out again. He said nothing, but went about with a face which said: "Ay, best not to come to words with women folk!" Maren, however, did not misunderstand him. Well, as long as he kept it to himself. There was the girl torturing herself, drinking petroleum, and eating soft soap as if she were mad, because she had heard it was good for internal weakness. It was too bad; it was adding insult to injury to be jeered at—by her own father too. [Pg 16]

At that time he was as little at home as possible, and Maren had no objection as it kept him and his angry glare out of their way. When not at sea, he lounged about doing odd jobs, or sat gossiping high up on the downs, from where one could keep an eye on every boat going out or coming in. Generally, he was allowed to go in peace, but when Sörine was worse than usual, Maren would come running—piteous to see in her motherly anxiety—and beg him to take the girl in to town to be examined before it was too late. Then he would fall into a passion and shout—not caring who might hear: "Confound you, you old nuisance—have you had eight children yourself and still can't see what ails the girl?"

Before long he would repent, for it was impossible to do without house and home altogether; but immediately he put his foot inside the door the trouble began. What was he to do? He had to let off steam, to prevent himself from going mad altogether with all this woman's quibbling. Whatever the result might be, he was tempted to stand on the highest hill and shout his opinion over the whole hamlet, just for the pleasure of getting his own back.

One day, as he was sitting on the shore weighting the net, Maren came flying over the downs: "Now, you had better send for the doctor," said she, "or the girl will slip through our fingers. She's taking on so, it's terrible to hear."

Sören also had himself heard moans from the hut; [Pg 17] he was beside himself with anger and flung a pebble at her. "Confound you, are you deaf too, that you cannot hear what that sound means?" shouted he. "See and get hold of a midwife—and that at once; or I'll teach you."

When Maren saw him rise, she turned round and ran home again. Sören shrugged his shoulders and fetched the midwife himself. He stayed outside the hut the whole afternoon without going in, and when it was evening he went down to the inn. It was a place within which he seldom set his foot; there was not sufficient money for that; if house and home should have what was due to it. With unaccustomed shaking hand he turned the handle, opened the door with a jerk and stood with an uncertain air in the doorway.

"So, that was it, after all," said he with miserable bravado. And he repeated the same sentence over and over again the whole evening, until it was time to stumble home.

Maren was out on the down waiting for him; when she saw the state he was in, she burst into tears. "So, that was——" he began, with a look which should have been full of withering scorn—but suddenly he stopped. Maren's tears moved him strangely deep down under everything else; he had to put his arms round her neck and join in her tears.

The two old people sat on the down holding each other until their tears were spent. Already considerable [Pg 18] evil had fallen in the path of this new being; now fell the first tears.

When they had got home and busied themselves with mother and child and had gone to rest in the big double bed, Maren felt for Sören's hand. So she had always fallen asleep in their young days, and now it was as if something of the sweetness of their young days rose up in her again—was it really owing to the little lovechild's sudden appearance, or what?

"Now, perhaps, you'll agree 'twas as I told you all along," said Sören, just as they were falling asleep.

"Ay, 'twas so," said Maren. "But how it could come about ... for men folk...."

"Oh, shut up with that nonsense," said Sören, and they went to sleep.

So Maren eventually had to give in. "Though," as Sören said, "like as not one fine day she'd swear the girl had never had a child." Womenfolk! Ugh! there was no persuading them.

Anyhow, Maren was too clever to deny what even a blind man could see with a stick; and it was ever so much easier for her to admit the hard truth; in spite of the girl's innocent tears and solemn assurances, there was a man in the case all the same, and he moreover, the farmer's son. It was the son of the owner of Sands farm, whom Sörine had driven home with from the town—in fear of the dark forest.

"Ay, you managed it finely—keeping the girl away [Pg 19] from vagabonds," said Sören, looking out of the corners of his eyes towards the new arrival.

"Rubbish! A farmer's son is better than a vagabond, anyway," answered Maren proudly.

After all it was she who was right; had she not always said there was refinement in Sörine? There was blue blood in the girl!

One day, Sören had to put on his best clothes and off he went to Sands farm.

"'Twas with child she was, after all," said he, going straight to the point. "'Tis just born."

"Oh, is it," said the farmer's son who stood with his father on the thrashing-floor shaking out some straw. "Well, that's as it may be!"

"Ay, but she says you're the father."

"Oh, does she! Can she prove it, I'd like to know."

"She can take her oath on it, she can. So you had better marry the girl."

The farmer's son shouted with laughter.

"Oh, you laugh, do you?" Sören picked up a hayfork and made for the lad, who hid behind the threshing-machine, livid with fear.

"Look here," the boy's father broke in: "Don't you think we two old ones had better go outside and talk the matter over? Young folk nowadays are foolish. Whatever the boy's share in the matter may be, I don't believe he'll marry her," began he, as they were outside.

"That he shall, though," answered Sören, threateningly.

"Look you, the one thing to compel him is the law—and that she will not take, if I know anything about her. But, I'll not say but he might help the girl to a proper marriage—will you take two hundred crowns once and for all?"

Sören thought in his own mind that it was a large sum of money for a poor babe, and hurried to close the bargain in case the farmer might draw back.

"But, no gossip, mind you, now. No big talk about relationship and that kind of thing," said the farmer as he followed Sören out of the gate. "The child must take the girl's name—and no claim on us."

"No, of course not!" said Sören, eager to be off. He had got the two hundred crowns in his inner pocket, and was afraid the farmer might demand them back again.

"I'll send you down a paper one of these days and get your receipt for the money," said the farmer. "It is best to have it fixed up all right and legal."

He said the word "legal" with such emphasis and familiarity that Sören was more than a little startled.

"Yes, yes," was all Sören said and slipped into the porch with his cap between his hands. It was not often he took his hat off to any one, but the two hundred crowns had given him respect for the farmer. The people of Sands farm were a race who, if they did break down their neighbor's fence, always made good the damage they had done.

Sören started off and ran over the fields. The money was more than he and Maren had ever before possessed. All he had to do now was to lay out the notes in front of her so as to make a show that she might be impressed. For Maren had fixed her mind on the farmer's son.

CHAPTER III
A CHILD IS BORN

There are a milliard and a half of stars in the heavens, and—as far as we know—a milliard and a half of human beings on the earth. Exactly the same number of both! One would almost think the old saying was right,—that every human being was born under his own star. In hundreds of costly observatories all over the world, on plain and mountain, talented scientists are adjusting the finest instruments and peering out into the heavens. They watch and take photographic plates, their whole life taken up with the one idea: to make themselves immortal with having discovered a new star. Another celestial body—added to the milliard and a half already moving gracefully round.

Every second a human soul is born into the world. A new flame is lit, a star which perhaps may come to shine with unusual beauty, which in any case has its own unseen spectrum. A new being, fated, perhaps, to bestow genius, perhaps beauty around it, kisses the earth; the unseen becomes flesh and blood. No human being is a repetition of another, nor is any ever reproduced; each new being is like a comet which only once in all eternity touches the path of the earth, and for a brief time takes its luminous way over it—a phosphorescent body between two eternities of darkness. No doubt there is joy amongst human beings for every newly lit soul! And, no doubt they will stand round the cradle with questioning eyes, wondering what this new one will bring forth.

Alas, a human being is no star, bringing fame to him who discovers and records it! More often, it is a parasite which comes upon peaceful and unsuspecting people, sneaking itself into the world—through months of purgatory. God help it, if into the bargain it has not its papers in order.

Sörine's little one had bravely pushed itself into the light of day, surmounting all obstacles, denial, tears and preventatives, as a salmon springs against the stream. Now she lay in the daylight, red and wrinkled, trying to soften all hearts.

The whole of the community had done with her, she was a parasite and nothing else. A newly born human being is a figure in the transaction which implies proper marriage and settling down, and the next step which means a cradle and perambulator and—as it grows up—an engagement ring, marriage and children again. Much of this procedure is upset when a child like Sörine's little one is vulgar enough to allow itself to be born without marriage.

She was from the very first treated accordingly, without maudlin consideration for her tender helplessness. "Born out of wedlock" was entered on her certificate of birth which the midwife handed to the schoolmaster when she had helped the little one into the world, and the same was noted on the baptismal certificate. It was as if they all, the midwife, the schoolmaster and the parson, leaders of the community, in righteous vengeance were striking the babe with all their might. What matter if the little soul were begotten by the son of a farmer, when he refused to acknowledge it, and bought himself out of the marriage? A nuisance she was, and a blot on the industrious orderly community.

She was just as much of an inconvenience to her mother as to all the others. When Sörine was up and about again, she announced that she might just as well go out to service as all her sisters had done. Her fear of strangers had quite disappeared: she took a place a little further inland. The child remained with the grandparents.

No one in the wide world cared for the little one, not even the old people for that matter. But all the same Maren went up into the attic and brought out an old wooden cradle which had for many years been used for yarn and all kinds of lumber; Sören put new rockers, and once more Maren's old, swollen legs had to accustom themselves to rocking a cradle again.

A blot the little one was to her grandparents too—perhaps, when all is said and done, on them alone. They had promised themselves such great things of the girl—and there lay their hopes—an illegitimate child in the cradle! It was brought home to them by the women running to Maren, saying: "Well, how do you like having little ones again in your old days?" And by the other fishermen when Sören Man came to the harbor or the inn. His old comrades poked fun at him good-naturedly and said: "All very well for him—strong as a young man and all, Sören, you ought to stand treat all round."

But it had to be borne—and, after all, it could be got over. And the child was—when one got one's hand in again—a little creature who recalled so much that otherwise belonged to the past. It was just as if one had her oneself—in a way she brought youth to the house.

It was utterly impossible not to care for such a helpless little creature.

CHAPTER IV
DITTE'S FIRST STEP

Strange how often one bears the child while another cares for it. For old Maren it was not easy to be a mother again, much as her heart was in it. The girl herself had got over all difficulties, and was right away in service in another county; and here was the babe left behind screaming.

Maren attended to it as well as she could, procured good milk and gave it soaked bread and sugar, and did all she could to make up for its mother.

Her daughter she could not make out at all. Sörine rarely came home, and preferably in the evening when no one could see her; the child she appeared not to care for at all. She had grown strong and erect, not in the least like the slender, freckled girl who could stand next to nothing. Her blood had thickened and her manners were decided; though that, of course, has happened before,—an ailing woman transformed by having a child, as one might say, released from witchcraft.

Ditte herself did not seem to miss a mother's tender care: she grew well in spite of the artificial food, and soon became so big that she could keep wooden shoes on her small feet, and, with the help of old Sören's hand, walk on the downs. And then she was well looked after.

However, at times things would go badly. For Maren had quite enough of her own work to do, which could not be neglected, and the little one was everywhere. And difficult it was suddenly to throw up what one had in hand—letting the milk boil over and the porridge burn—for the sake of running after the little one. Maren took a pride in her housework and found it hard at times to choose between the two. Then, God preserve her: the little one had to take her chance.

Ditte took it as it came and could be thankful that she was with her grandparents. She was an inquisitive little being, eager to meddle with everything; and a miracle it was that the firewood did not fall down. Hundreds of times in the day did she get into scrapes, heedless and thoughtless as she was. She would rush out, and lucky it was if there was anything to step on, otherwise she would have fallen down. Her little head was full of bruises, and she could never learn to look after herself in spite of all the knocks she got. It was too bad to be whipped into the bargain! When the hurt was very bad, Grandfather had to blow it, or Granny put the cold blade of the bread-knife on the bruise to make it well again.

"Better now," said she, turning a smiling face towards her granny; the tears still hanging on the long lashes, and her cheeks gradually becoming roughened by them.

"Yes, dear," answered Maren. "But, Girlie must take care."

This was her name in those days, and a real little girlie she was, square and funny. It was impossible to be angry with her, although at times she could make it somewhat difficult for the old ones. Her little head would not accept the fact that there were things one was not allowed to do; immediately she got an idea, her small hands acted upon it. "She's no forethought," said Sören significantly, "she's a woman. Wonder if a little rap over the fingers after all wouldn't——"

But Maren ignored this. Took the child inside with her and explained, perhaps for the hundredth time, that Girlie must not do so. And one day she had a narrow escape. Ditte had been up to mischief as usual in her careless way. But when she had finished, she offered her little pouting mouth to the two old ones: "Kiss me then—and say 'beg pardon'," said she.

And who could resist her?

"Now, perhaps, you'll say that she can't be taught what's right and wrong?" said Maren.

Sören laughed: "Ay, she first does the thing, and waits till after to think if it's right or wrong. She'll be a true woman, right enough."

At one time Ditte got into the habit of pulling down and breaking things. She always had her little snub nose into everything, and being too small to see what [Pg 29] was on the table, she pulled it down instead. Sören had to get a drill and learn to mend earthenware to make up for the worst of her depredations. A great many things fell over Ditte without alarming her in the least.

"She'll neither break nor bend—she's a woman all over," said Sören, inwardly rather proud of her power of endurance. But Maren had to be ever on the watch, and was in daily fear for the things and the child herself.

One day Ditte spilled a basin of hot milk over herself and was badly scalded; that cured her of inquisitiveness. Maren put her to bed and treated her burns with egg-oil and slices of new potato; and it was some time before Ditte was herself again. But when she was again about, there was not so much as a scar to be seen. This accident made Maren famous as a curer of burns and people sought her help for their injuries. "You're a wise one," said they, and gave her bacon or fish by way of thanks. "But 'tis not to be wondered at, after all."

The allusion to the fact that her mother had been a "wise woman" did not please Maren at all. But the bacon and the herrings came to an empty cupboard, and—as Sören said: "Beggars cannot be choosers and must swallow their pride with their food."

Ditte shot up like a young plant, day by day putting forth new leaves. She was no sooner in the midst of one difficult situation, and her troubled grandparents, [Pg 30] putting their heads together, had decided to take strong measures, than she was out of it again and into something else. It was just like sailing over a flat bottom—thought Sören—passing away under one and making room for something new. The old ones could not help wondering if they themselves and their children had ever been like this. They had never thought of it before, having had little time to spend on their offspring beyond what was strictly necessary; the one had quite enough to do in procuring food and the other in keeping the home together. But now they could not *help* thinking; however much they had to do, and they marveled much over many things.

"'Tis strange how a bit of a child can open a body's eyes, for all one's old. Ay, there's a lot to learn," said Maren.

"Stupid," said Sören. From his tone it could be gathered that he himself had been thinking the same.

Ditte was indeed full of character. Little as she had had to inherit, she nevertheless was richly endowed; her first smile brought joy; her feeble tears, sorrow. A gift she was, born out of emptiness, thrown up on the beach for the wornout old couple. No one had done anything to deserve her,—on the contrary, all had done their utmost to put her out of existence. Notwithstanding, there she lay one day with blinking eyes, blue and innocent as the skies of heaven. Anxiety she brought from the very beginning, many footsteps had trodden round her cradle, and questioning thoughts [Pg 31] surrounded her sleep. It was even more exciting when she began to take notice; when only a week old she knew their faces, and at three she laughed to Sören. He was quite foolish that day and in the evening had to go down to the tap-room to tell them all about it. Had any one ever known such a child? She could laugh already! And when she first began to understand play, it was difficult to tear oneself away—particularly for Sören. Every other moment he had to go in and caress her with his crooked fingers. Nothing was so delightful as to have the room filled with her gurgling, and Maren had to chase him away from the cradle, at least twenty times a day. And when she took her first toddling steps!—that little helpless, illegitimate child who had come defiantly into existence, and who, in return for life brightened the days of the two old wornout people. It had become pleasant once more to wake in the morning to a new day: life was worth living again.

Her stumbling, slow walk was in itself a pleasure; and the contemplative gravity with which she crossed the doorstep, both hands full, trotted down the road—straight on as if there was nothing behind her, and with drooping head—was altogether irresistible. Then Maren would slink out round the corner and beckon to Sören to make haste and come, and Sören would throw down his ax and come racing over the grass of the downs with his tongue between his lips. "Heaven only knows what she is up to now," said he, and the two crept after her down the road. When she had wandered a little distance, in deep thought, she would suddenly realize her loneliness, and begin to howl, a picture of misery, left alone and forsaken. Then the two old people would appear on the scene, and she would throw herself into their arms overjoyed at finding them again.

Then quite suddenly she got over it—the idea that things were gone forever if she lost sight of them for a moment. She began to look out and up into people's faces: hitherto, she had only seen the feet of those who came within her horizon. One day she actually went off by herself, having caught sight of the houses down in the hamlet. They had to look after her more seriously now that the outside world had tempted her.

"We're not enough for her, seems like," said Sören despondently, "got a fancy for the unknown already."

It was the first time she had turned away from them, and Sören recognized in that something of what he had experienced before, and for a moment a feeling of loneliness came over him. But Maren, wise as she had grown since the coming of the little one, again found a way. She threw her kerchief over her head and went down to the hamlet with Ditte, to let her play with other children.

CHAPTER V
GRANDFATHER STRIKES OUT AFRESH

All that Sören possessed—with the exception of the house—was a third share in a boat and gear. He had already, before Ditte came into the world, let out his part of the boat to a young fisher boy from the hamlet, who having no money to buy a share in a boat repaid Sören with half of his catch. It was not much, but he and Maren had frugal habits, and as to Sören, she occasionally went out to work and helped to make ends meet. They just managed to scrape along with their sixth share of the catch, and such odd jobs as Sören could do at home.

Once again there was a little one to feed and clothe. For the present, of course, Ditte's requirements were small, but her advent had opened out new prospects. It was no good now to be content with toiling the time away, until one's last resting-place was reached, patiently thinking the hut would pay for the burial. It was not sufficient to wear out old clothes, eat dried fish, and keep out of the workhouse until they were well under the ground. Sören and Maren were now no longer at the end of things, there was one in the cradle who demanded everything from the beginning, and spurred them on to new efforts. It would never do to let their infirmity grow upon them or allow themselves to become pensioners on what a sixth share of a boat might happen to bring home. Duty called for a new start.

The old days had left their mark on them both. They came into line with the little one, even her childish cries under the low ceiling carried the old couple a quarter of a century back, to the days when the weight of years was not yet felt, and they could do their work with ease. And once there, the way to still earlier days was not so far—to that beautiful time when tiredness was unknown, and Sören after a hard day's work would walk miles over the common, to where Maren was in service, stay with her until dawn, and then walk miles back home again, to be the first man at work.

Inevitably they were young again! Had they not a little one in the house? A little pouting mouth was screaming and grunting for milk. Sören came out of his old man's habit, and turned his gaze once more towards the sea and sky. He took back his share in the boat and went to sea again.

Things went tolerably well to begin with. It was summer time when Ditte had pushed him back to his old occupation again; it was as if she had really given the old people a second youth. But it was hard to keep up with the others, in taking an oar and pulling up nets by the hour. Moreover in the autumn when the herrings were deeper in the sea, the nets went right down, and were often caught by the heavy undertow, Sören had not strength to draw them up like the other men, and had to put up with the offer of lighter work. This was humiliating; and even more humiliating was it to break down from night watches in the cold, when he knew how strong he had been in days gone by.

Sören turned to the memories of old days for support, that he might assert himself over the others. Far and wide he told tales of his youth, to all who would listen.

In those days implements were poor, and clothes were thin, and the winter was harder than now. There was ice everywhere, and in order to obtain food they had to trail over the ice with their gear on a wooden sledge right out to the great channel, and chop holes to fish through. Woollen underclothing was unknown, and oilskins were things none could afford; a pair of thick leather trousers were worn—with stockings and wooden shoes. Often one fell in—and worked on in wet clothes, which were frozen so stiff that it was impossible to draw them off.

To Sören it was a consolation to dwell upon all this, when he had to give up such strenuous work as the rowing over to the Swedish coast, before he could get a good catch. There he would sit in the stern feeling small and useless, talking away and fidgeting with the sails in spite of the lack of wind. His partners, toiling with the heavy oars, hardly listened to him. It was all true enough, they knew that from their fathers, but it gained nothing in being repeated by Sören's toothless mouth. His boasting did not make the boat any lighter to pull; old Sören was like a stone in the net.

Maren was probably the only one, who at her own expense could afford to give a helping hand. She saw how easily he became tired, try as he would to hide it from her—and she made up her mind to trust in Providence for food. It was hard for him to turn out in the middle of the night, his old limbs were as heavy as lead, and Maren had to help him up in bed.

"'Tis rough tonight!" said she, "stay at home and rest." And the next night she would persuade him again, with another excuse. She took care not to suggest that he should give up the sea entirely; Sören was stubborn and proud. Could she only keep him at home from time to time, the question would soon be decided by his partners.

So Sören remained at home first one day and then another; Maren said that he was ill. He fell easily into the trap, and when this had gone on for some little time, his partners got tired of it, and forced him to sell his part of the boat and implements. Now that he was driven to remain at home, he grumbled and scolded, but settled down to it after a while. He busied himself with odd jobs, patched oilskins and mended wooden shoes for the fishermen and became quite brisk again. Maren could feel the improvement, when he good-naturedly began to chaff her again as before.

He was happiest out on the downs, with Ditte holding his hand, looking after the sheep. Sören could hardly do without the little one; when she was not holding his hand, he felt like a cripple without his staff. Was it not he whom she had chosen for her first smile, when but three weeks old! And when only four or five months old dropped her comforter and turned her head on hearing his tottering steps.

"'Tis all very well for you," said Maren half annoyed. "'Tis you she plays with, while I've the looking after and feeding of her; and that's another thing." But in her heart she did not grudge him first place with the little one; after all he was the man—and needed a little happiness.

There was no one who understood Ditte as did her grandfather. They two could entertain each other by the hour. They spoke about sheep and ships and trees, which Ditte did not like, because they stood and made the wind blow. Sören explained to her that it was God who made the wind blow—so that the fishermen need not toil with their oars so much. Trees on the contrary did no work at all and as a punishment God had chained them to the spot.

"What does God look like?" asked Ditte. The question staggered Sören. There he had lived a long life and always professed the religion taught him in childhood; at times when things looked dark, he had even called upon God; nevertheless, it had never occurred to him to consider what the good God really looked like. And here he was confounded by the words of a little child, exactly as in the Bible.

"God?" began Sören hesitating on the word, to gain time. "Well, He's both His hands full, He has. And even so it seems to us others, that at times He's taken more upon Himself than He can do—and that's what He looks like!"

And so Ditte was satisfied.

To begin with Sören talked most, and the child listened. But soon it was she who led the conversation, and the old man who listened entranced. Everything his girlie said was simply wonderful, and all of it worth repetition, if only he could remember it. Sören remembered a good deal, but was annoyed with himself when some of it escaped his memory.

"Never knew such a child," said he to Maren, when they came in from their walk. "She's different from our girls somehow."

"Well, you see she's the child of a farmer's son," answered Maren, who had never got over the greatest disappointment of her life, and eagerly caught at anything that might soften it.

But Sören laughed scornfully and said: "You're a fool, Maren, and that's all about it."

CHAPTER VI
THE DEATH OF SÖREN MAN

One day Sören came crawling on all fours over the doorstep. Once inside, he stumbled to his feet and moved with great difficulty towards the fireplace, where he clung with both hands to the mantelpiece, swaying to and fro and groaning pitifully the while. He collapsed just as Maren came in from the kitchen, she ran to him, got off his clothes and put him to bed.

"Seems like I'm done for now," said Sören, when he had rested a little.

"What's wrong with you, Sören?" asked Maren anxiously.

"'Tis naught but something's given inside," said Sören sullenly.

He refused to say more, but Maren got out of him afterwards that it had happened when drawing the tethering-peg out of the ground. Usually it was loose enough. But today it was firm as a rock, as if some one was holding it down in the earth. Sören put the tethering-rope round his neck and pulled with all his might, it did give way; but at the same time something seemed to break inside him. Everything went dark, and a big black hole appeared in the earth.

Maren gazed at him with terror. "Was 't square?" asked she.

Sören thought it was square.

"And what of Girlie?" asked Maren suddenly.

She had disappeared when Sören fainted.

Maren ran out on the hills with anxious eyes. She found Ditte playing in the midst of a patch of wild pansies, fortunately Maren could find no hole in the ground. But the old rotten rope had parted. Sören, unsteady on his feet, had probably fallen backwards and hurt himself. Maren knotted the rope together again and went towards the little one. "Come along, dearie," said she, "we'll go home and make a nice cup of coffee for Grandad." But suddenly she stood transfixed. Was it not a cross the child had plaited of grass, and set among the pansies? Quietly Maren took the child by the hand and went in. Now she knew.

Sören stayed in bed. There was no outward hurt to be seen, but he showed no inclination to get up. He hardly slept at all, but lay all day long gazing at the ceiling, and fumbling with the bedclothes.

Now and then he groaned, and Maren would hurry to his side. "What ails you, Sören, can't you tell me?" said she earnestly.

"Ails me? Nothing ails me, Maren, but death," answered Sören. Maren would have liked to try her own remedies on him, but might just as well spare her arts for a better occasion; Sören had seen a black hole in the ground; there was no cure for that.

So matters stood. Maren knew as well as he, that this was the end; but she was a sturdy nature, and never liked to give in. She would have wrestled with God himself for Sören, had there been anything definite to fight about. But he was fading away, and for this there was no cure; though if only the poison could be got out of his blood, he might even yet be strong again.

"Maybe 'tis bleeding you want."

But Sören refused to be bled. "Folks die quickly enough without," said he, incredulous as he had always been. Maren was silent and went back to her work with a sigh. Sören never did believe in anything, he was just as unbelieving as he had been in his young days—if only God would not be too hard on him.

At first Sören longed to have the child with him always, and every other minute Maren had to bring her to the bedside. The little one did not like to sit quietly on a chair beside Grandad's bed, and as soon as she saw a chance of escape, off she would run. This was hardest of all to Sören, he felt alone and forsaken, all was blackness and despair.

Before long, however, he lost all interest in the child, as he did in everything else. His mind began to wander from the present back to bygone days; Maren knew well what it meant. He went further and still further back to his youth and childhood. Strange it was how much he could remember things which otherwise had been forgotten. And it was not rambling nonsense that he talked, but all true enough; people older than he who came from the hamlet to visit him confirmed it, and wondered at hearing him speak of events that must have happened when he was but two or three years old. Sören forgot the latter years of his life, indeed he might never have lived them so completely had they faded from his mind.

This saddened Maren. They had lived a long life, and gone through so much together, and how much more pleasant it would have been, if they could have talked of the past together once more before they parted. But Sören would not listen, when it came to their mutual memories. No, the garden on the old farm—where Sören lived when five years old—that he could remember! Where this tree stood, and that—and what kind of fruit it bore.

And when he had gone as far back as he could remember, his mind would wander forward again, and in his delirium he would rave of his days as a shepherd boy or sailor boy and heaven knows what.

In his uneasy dreams he mixed up all his experiences, the travels of his youth, his work and difficulties. At one minute he would be on the sea furling sail in the storm, the next he would struggle with the ground. Maren who stood over him listened with terror to all that he toiled with; he seemed to be taking his life in one long stride. Many were the tribulations he had been through, and of which she now heard for the first time. When his mind cleared once more, he would be worn out with beads of perspiration standing on his forehead.

His old partners came to see him, and then they went through it again—Sören *had* to talk of old times. He could only say a few words, weak as he was; but then the others would continue. Maren begged them not to speak too much, as it made him restless, and he would struggle with it in his dreams.

It was worst when he imagined himself on the old farm; pitiful to see how he fought against the sea's greedy advance, clutching the bedclothes with his wasted fingers. It was a wearisome leave-taking with existence, as wearisome as existence itself had been to him.

One day when Maren had been to the village shop, Ditte ran out screaming, as she came back. "Grandad's dead!" she burst out sobbing. Sören lay bruised and senseless across the doorstep to the kitchen. He had been up on the big chest, meddling with the hands of the clock. Maren dragged him to bed and bathed his wounds, and when it was done he lay quietly following her movements with his eyes. Now and then he would ask in a low voice what the time was, and from this Maren knew that he was nearing his end.

On the morning of the day he died he was altogether changed again. It was as if he had come home to take a last farewell of everybody and everything; he was weak but quite in his senses. There was so much he wanted to touch upon once again. His talk jumped [Pg 44] from one thing to another and he seemed quite happy. For the first time for many months he could sit on the edge of the bed drinking his morning coffee, chatting to Maren whenever she came near. He was exactly like a big child, and Maren could not but put his old head to hers and caress it. "You've worn well, Sören," said she, stroking his hair—"your hair's as soft as when we were young."

Sören fell back, and lay with her hand in his, gazing silently at her with worship in his faded eyes. "Maren, would you let down your hair for me?" he whispered bashfully at last. The words came with some difficulty.

"Nay, but what nonsense!" said Maren, hiding her face against his chest; "we're old now, you know, dear."

"Let down your hair for me!" whispered he, persisting, and tried with shaking fingers to loosen it himself. Maren remembered an evening long ago, an evening behind a drawn-up boat on the beach, and with sobs she loosened her gray hair and let it fall down over Sören's head, so that it hid their faces. "It's long and thick," he whispered softly, "enough to hide us both." The words came as an echo from their bygone youth.

"Nay, nay," said Maren, crying, "it's gray and thin and rough. But how fond you were of it once."

With closed eyes Sören lay holding Maren's hand. There was much to do in the kitchen, and she tried again and again to draw her hand away, but he opened [Pg 45] his eyes each time, so she sat down, letting the things look after themselves, and there she was with the tears running down her furrowed face, while her thoughts ran on. She and Sören had lived happily together; they had had their quarrels, but if anything serious happened, they always faced it together; neither of them had lived and worked for themselves only. It was so strange that they were now to be separated, Maren could not understand it. Why could they not be taken together? Where Sören went, Maren felt she too should be. Perhaps in the place where he was going he needed no one to mend his clothes and to see that he kept his feet dry, but at least they might have walked hand in hand in the Garden of Eden. They had often talked about going into the country to see what was hidden behind the big forest. But it never came to anything, as one thing or another always kept Maren at home. How beautiful it would have been to go with Sören now; Maren would willingly have made the journey with him, to see what was on the other side—had it not been for Ditte. A child had always kept her back, and thus it was now. Maren's own time was not yet; she must wait, letting Sören go alone.

Sören now slept more quietly, and she drew her hand gently out of his. But as soon as she rose, he opened his eyes, gazing at Maren's loosened hair and tear-stained face.

"Don't cry, Maren," said he, "you and Ditte'll get [Pg 46] on all right. But do this for me, put up your hair as you did at our wedding, will you, Maren?"

"But I can't do it myself, Sören," answered the old woman, overwhelmed and beginning to cry again. But Sören held to his point.

Then Maren gave in, and as she could not leave Sören alone for long, she ran as fast as she could to the hamlet, where one of the women dressed her thin gray hair in bridal fashion. On her return she found Sören restless, but he soon calmed down; he looked at her a long time, as she sat crying by the bed with his hand in hers. He was breathing with much difficulty.

Then suddenly he spoke in a stronger voice than he had done for many days.

"We've shared good and bad together, Maren—and now it's over. Will you be true to me for the time you have left?" He rose on his elbow, looking earnestly into her face.

Maren dried her bleared eyes, and looked faithfully into his. "Ay," she said slowly and firmly—"no one else has ever been in my thought nor ever shall be. 'Tis Christ Himself I take as a witness, you can trust me, Sören."

Sören then fell back with closed eyes, and after a while his hand slipped out of hers.

[Pg 47]

CHAPTER VII
THE WIDOW AND THE FATHERLESS

After Sören's death there were hard days in store for the two in the hut on the Naze. Feeble as he had been, yet he had always earned something, and had indeed been their sheet anchor. They were now alone, with no man to work for them. Not only had Maren to make things go as far as possible, but she had to find the money as well. This was a task she had never done before.

All they had once received for their share in the boat and its fittings had gone too; and the funeral took what was left. Their affairs could be settled by every one, and at the time of Sören's death there was much multiplying and subtracting in the homes round about on Maren's behalf. But to one question there was no answer; what had become of the two hundred crowns paid for Ditte for once and for all? Ay, where had they gone? The two old people had bought nothing new at that time, and Sören had firmly refused to invest in a new kind of fishing-net—an invention tried in other places and said to be a great success. Indeed, there were cases where the net had paid for itself in a single night. However, Sören would not, and as so much [Pg 48]money never came twice to the hamlet in one generation, they carried on with their old implements as usual.

The money had certainly not been used, nor had it been eaten up, that was understood. The two old folk had lived exactly as before, and it would have been known if the money had gone up through the chimney. There was no other explanation, than that Maren had put it by; probably as something for Ditte to fall back upon, when the two old ones had gone.

There was a great deal of talking in the homes, mostly of how Maren and Ditte were to live. But with that, their interest stopped. She had grown-up children of her own, who were her nearest, and ought to look after her affairs. One or two of them turned up at the funeral, more to see if there was anything to be had, and as soon as Sören was well underground they left, practically vanishing without leaving a trace, and with no invitation to Maren, who indeed hardly found out where they lived. Well, Maren was not sorry to see the last of them. She knew, in some measure, the object of her children's homecoming; and for all she cared they might never tread that way again—if only she might keep Ditte. Henceforth they were the only two in the world.

"They might at least have given you a helping hand," said the women of the hamlet—"after all, you're their mother."

"Nay, why so," said Maren. They had used her as a pathway to existence—and it had not always been [Pg 49]easy; perhaps they did not thank her for their being here on earth, since they thought they owed her nothing. One mother can care for eight children if necessary, but has any one ever heard of eight children caring for one mother? No, Maren was thankful they kept away, and did not come poking round their old home.

She tried to sell the hut and the allotment in order to provide means, but as no buyers offered for either, she let the hut to a workman and his family, only keeping one room and an end of the kitchen for herself. After settling this she studded her own and the child's wooden shoes with heavy nails. She brought forth Sören's old stick, wrapped herself and the little one well up—and wandered out into the country.

Day after day, in all weathers, they would set out in the early morning, visiting huts and farms. Maren knew fairly well for whom Sören had worked, and it was quite time they paid their debts. She never asked directly for the money, but would stand just inside the door with the child in front of her, rattling a big leather purse such as fisher folk used, and drone:

"God bless your work and your food—one and all for sure! Times is hard—ay, money's scarce—ay, 'tis dear to live, and folks get old! And all's to be bought—fat and meat and bread, ay, every scrap!—faith, an old wife needs the money!"

Although Maren only asked for what was her due, it was called begging, when she went on this errand, and she and the child were treated accordingly. They often [Pg 50]stood waiting in the scullery or just inside the living room, while every one ran to and fro to their work without appearing to notice them. People must be taught their proper place, and nothing is so good as letting them stand waiting, and that without any reason. If they are not crushed by this, something must be wrong.

Maren felt the slight, and the smart went deep; but in no way shook her purpose—inwardly she was furious, though too wise to show it, and, old as she was, quietly added experience to experience. Perhaps after all it was the child who made it easier for her to submit to circumstances. So that was how she was treated when she needed help! But when they themselves needed help, it was a different matter; they were not too proud to ask *her* advice. Then they would hurry down to her, often in the middle of the night, knocking at the window with the handle of a whip; she *must* come, and that at once.

Maren was not stupid, and could perfectly well put two and two together, only neglecting what she had no use for. As long as Sören was by her side and held the reins, she had kept in the background, knowing that one master in the house was quite enough; and only on special occasions—when something of importance was at stake—would she lend a guiding hand, preferably so unostentatiously that Sören never noticed it.

Blockhead, he used to call her—right up to his illness. About a week before his death they had spoken [Pg 51]of the future, and Sören had comforted Maren by saying: "'Twill all be right for you, Maren—if but you weren't such a blockhead."

For the first time Maren had protested against this, and Sören, as was his wont, referred to the case of Sörine: "Ay, and did you see what was wrong with the girl, what all saw who set eyes on her? And was it not yourself that fed her with soft soap and paraffin?"

"Maybe 'twas," answered Maren, unmoved.

Sören looked at her with surprise: well to be sure—but behind her look of innocence gleamed something which staggered him for once. "Ay, ay," said he. "Ay, ay! 'twas nigh jail that time."

Maren good-naturedly blinked her heavy eyelids. "'Tis too good some folks are to be put there," answered she.

Sören felt as if cold water were running down his back; here had he lived with Maren by his side for forty-five years, and never taken her for anything else but a good-natured blockhead—and he had nearly gone to his grave with that opinion. And perhaps after all it was she who had mastered him, and that by seeming a fool herself.

CHAPTER VIII
WISE MAREN

The heavy waves crashed on the shore. Large wet flakes of snow hurled themselves on bushes and grass; what was not caught by the high cliffs was frozen to ice in the air and chased before the storm.

The sea was foaming. The skies were all one great dark gray whirl, with the roaring breakers beneath. It was as if the abyss itself threw out its inexhaustible flood of cold and wickedness. Endlessly it mounted from the great deep; dense to battle against, and as fire of hell to breathe.

Two clumsy figures worked their way forward over the sandhills, an old grandmother holding a little girl by the hand. They were so muffled up, that they could hardly be distinguished in the thick haze.

Their movements were followed by watchful eyes, in the huts on the hills women stood with faces pressed flat against the window-panes! "'Tis wise Maren battling against the storm," they told the old and the sick within. And all who could, crawled to the window. They must see for themselves.

"'Tis proper weather for witches to be out," said youth, and laughed. "But where is her broomstick?"

The old ones shook their heads. Maren ought not to be made fun of; she had the *Gift* and did much good. Maybe that once or twice she had misused her talents—but who would not have done the same in her place? On a day like this she would be full of power; it would have been wise to consult her.

The two outside kept to the path that ran along the edge of the steep cliff, hollowed out in many places by the sea. Beneath them thundered the surf, water and air and sand in one yellow ferment, and over it seagulls and other sea birds, shrieking and whipping the air with their wings. When a wave broke they would swoop down and come up again with food in their beaks—some fish left stunned by the waves to roll about in the foam.

It seemed foolish of the two keeping just inside the edge of the cliff, against which the storm was throwing itself with all its might, to fall down well inland. The old woman and the child clung to each other, gasping for breath.

At one place the path went through a thicket of thorns, bent inland by the strong sea wind, and here they took shelter from the storm to regain their breath. Ditte whimpered, she was tired and hungry.

"Be a big girl," said the old one, "we'll soon be home now." She drew the child towards her under the shawl, with shaking hands brushing the snow from her hair, and blowing her frozen fingers. "Ay, just big," she said encouragingly, "and you'll get cakes and nice hot coffee when we get home. I've the coffee beans in the bag—ah, just smell!"

Granny opened the bag, which she had fastened round her waist underneath her shawl. Into it went all that she was given, food and other odds and ends.

The little one poked her nose down into the bag, but was not comforted at once.

"We've nothing to warm it with," said she sulkily.

"And haven't we then? Granny was on the beach last night, and saw the old boat, she did. But Ditte was in the land of Nod, and never knew."

"Is there more firewood?"

"Hush, child, the coastguard might hear us. He's long ears—and the Magistrate pays him for keeping poor folks from getting warm. That's why he himself takes all that's washed ashore."

"But you're not frightened of him, Granny, you're a witch and can send him away."

"Ay, ay, of course Granny can—and more too, if he doesn't behave. She'll strike him down with rheumatism, so that he can't move, and have to send for wise Maren to rub his back. Ah me, old Granny's legs are full of water, and aches and pains in every limb; a horrid witch they call her, ay—and a thieving woman too! But there must be some of both when an old worn woman has to feed two mouths; and you may be glad that Granny's the witch she is. None but she cares for you—and lazy, no folks shall ever call her that. She's two-and-seventy years now, and 'tis for others her hands have toiled all along. But never a hand that's lifted to help old Maren."

They sat well sheltered, and soon Ditte became sleepy, and they started out again. "We'll fall asleep if we don't, and then the black man'll come and take us," said Granny as she tied her shawl round the little one.

"Who's the black man?" Ditte stopped, clinging to her grandmother from very excitement.

"The black man lives in the churchyard under the ground. 'Tis he who lets out the graves to the dead folks, and he likes to have a full house."

Ditte had no wish to go down and live with a black man, and tripped briskly along hand in hand with the old one. The path now ran straight inland, and the wind was at their back—the storm had abated somewhat.

When they came to the Sand farm, she refused to go further. "Let's go in there and ask for something," said she, dragging her grandmother. "I'm so hungry."

"Lord—are you mad, child! We daren't set foot inside there."

"Then I'll go alone," declared Ditte firmly. She let go her granny's hand and ran towards the entrance. When there, however, she hesitated. "And why daren't we go in there?" she shouted back.

Maren came and took her hand again: "Because [Pg 56] your own father might come and drive us away with a whip," said she slowly. "Come now and be a good girl."

"Are you afraid of him?" asked the little one persistently. She was not accustomed to seeing her granny turned aside for anything.

Afraid, indeed no—the times were too bad for that! Poor people must be prepared to face all evils and accept them too. And why should they go out of their way to avoid the Sand farm as if it were holy ground. If he did not care to take the chance of seeing his own offspring occasionally, he could move his farm elsewhere. They two had done nothing to be shamed into running away, that was true enough. Perhaps there was some ulterior motive behind the child's obstinacy? Maren was not the one to oppose Providence—still less if it lent her a helping hand.

"Well, come then!" said she, pushing the gate open. "They can but eat us."

They went through the deep porch which served as wood and tool house as well. At one side turf was piled neatly up right to the beams. Apparently they had no thought of being cold throughout the winter. Maren looked at the familiar surroundings as they crossed the yard towards the scullery. Once in her young days she had been in service here—for the sake of being nearer the home of her childhood and Sören. It was some years ago, that! The grandfather of the present young farmer reigned then—a real Tartar who [Pg 57] begrudged his servant both food and sleep. But he made money! The old farmer, who died about the same time as Sören, was young then, and went with stocking feet under the servants' windows! He and Sören cared nought for each other! Maren had not been here since—Sören would not allow it. And he himself never set foot inside, since that dreary visit about Sörine. A promise was a promise.

But now it was so long ago, and two hundred crowns could not last forever. Sören was dead, and Maren saw things differently in her old days. Cold and hardship raised her passion, as never before, against those sitting sheltered inside, who had no need to go hunting about like a dog in all weathers, and against those who for a short-lived joy threw years of heavy burden on poor old shoulders. Why had she waited so long in presenting his offspring to the farmer? Perhaps they were longing for it. And why should not the little one have her own way? Perhaps it was the will of Providence, speaking through her, in her obstinate desire to enter her father's house.

All the same, Maren's conscience was not quite clear while standing with Ditte beside her, waiting for some one to come. The farmer apparently was out, and for that she was thankful. She could hear the servant milking in the shed, they would hardly have a man at this time of the year.

The cracked millstone still lay in front of the door, [Pg 58] and in the middle of the floor was a large flat tombstone with ornaments in the corners, the inscription quite worn away.

A young woman came from the inner rooms. Maren had not seen her before. She was better dressed than the young wives of the neighborhood, and had a kind face and gentle manners. She asked them into the living room, took off their shawls, which she hung by the fire to dry. She then made them sit down and gave them food and drink, speaking kindly to them all the while; to Ditte in particular, which softened Maren's heart.

"And where do you come from?" asked she, seating herself beside them.

"Ay, where do folk come from?" answered Maren mumblingly. "Where's there room for poor people like us? Some have plenty—and for all that go where they have no right to be; others the Lord's given naught but a corner in the churchyard. But you don't belong to these parts, since you ask."

No, the young woman came from Falster; her voice grew tender as she spoke of her birthplace.

"Is't far from here?" said Maren, glancing at her.

"Yes, it takes a whole day by train and by coach, and from the town too!"

"Has it come to that, that the men of the Sand farm must travel by train to find wives for themselves? But the hamlet is good enough for sweethearts." [Pg 59]

The young woman looked uncertainly at her. "We met each other at the Continuation School," said she.

"Well, well, has he been to Continuation School too? Ay, 'tis fine all must be nowadays. Anyway, 'twas time he got settled."

The young woman flushed. "You speak so strangely," said she.

"Belike you'll tell me how an old wife should speak? 'Tis strange indeed that a father sits sheltered at home while his little one runs barefoot and begs."

"What do you mean?" whispered the young woman anxiously!

"What the Lord and every one knows, but no-one's told you. Look you at the child *there*—faces don't tell lies, she's the image of her father. If all was fair, 'twould be my daughter sitting here in your stead—ay, and no hunger and cold for me."

As she spoke, Maren sucked a ham bone. She had no teeth, and the fat ran down over her chin and hands.

The young woman took out her handkerchief. "Let me help you, mother," said she, gently drying her face. She was white to the lips, and her hands shook.

Maren allowed herself to be cared for. Her sunken mouth was set and hard. Suddenly she grasped the young woman by the hips with her earth-stained hands. "'Tis light and pure!" she mumbled, making signs over her. "In childbirth 'twill go badly with you." [Pg 60] The woman swayed in her hands and fell to the ground without a sound; little Ditte began to scream.

Maren was so terrified by the consequence of her act, that she never thought of offering help. She tore down the shawls from the fire and ran out, dragging the child after her. It was not until they reached the last house in the hamlet, the lifeboat shed, that she stopped to wrap themselves up.

Ditte still shook. "Did you kill her?" asked she.

The old woman started, alarmed at the word. "Nay, but of course not. 'Tis nothing to prate about: come along home," said she harshly, pushing the child. Ditte was unaccustomed to be spoken to in this manner, and she hurried along.

The house was cold as they entered it, and Maren put the little one straight to bed. Then having gathered sticks for the fire, she put on water for the coffee, talking to herself all the while. "Ugh, just so; but who's to blame? The innocent must suffer, to make the guilty speak."

"What did you say, Granny?" asked Ditte from the alcove.

"'Twas only I'm thinking your father'll soon find his way down here after this."

A trap came hurrying through the dark and stopped outside. In burst the owner of the Sand farm. There was no good in store for them; his face was red with anger and he started abusing them almost before he got inside the door. Maren had her head well wrapped [Pg 61] up against the cold, and pretended to hear nothing. "Well, well, you're a sight for sore eyes," said she, smilingly inviting him in.

"Don't suppose that I've come to make a fuss of you, you crafty old hag!" stormed Anders Olsen in his thin cracked voice. "No, I've come to fetch you, I have, and that at once. So you'd better come!" seizing her by the arm.

Maren wrenched herself out of his grasp. "What's wrong with you?" asked she, staring at him in amazement.

"Wrong with me?—you dare to ask that, you old witch, you. Haven't you been up to the farm this afternoon—dragging the brat with you? though you were bought and paid to keep off the premises. Made trouble you have, you old hag, and bewitched my wife, so she's dazed with pain. But I'll drag you to justice and have you burned at the stake, you old devil!" He foamed at the mouth and shook his clenched fist in her face.

"So you order folks to be burnt, do you?" said Maren scornfully. "Then you'd best light up and stoke up for yourself as well. Seemingly you've taken more on your back than you can carry."

"What do you mean by that?" hissed the farmer, gesticulating, as if prepared at any moment to pounce upon Maren and drag her to the trap. "Maybe it's a lie, that you've been to the farm and scared my wife?" He went threateningly round her, but without touching [Pg 62] her. "What have you to do with my back?" shouted he loudly, with fear in his eyes. "D'you want to bewitch me too, what?"

"'Tis nothing with your back I've to do, or yourself either. But all can see that the miser's cake'll be eaten, ay, even by crow and raven if need be. Keep your strength for your young wife—you might overstrain yourself on an old witch like me. And where'd she be then, eh?"

Anders Olsen had come with the intention of throwing the old witch into the trap and taking her home with him—by fair means or foul—so that she could undo her magic on the spot. And there he sat on the woodbox, his cap between his hands, a pitiful sight. Maren had judged him aright, there was nothing manly about him, he fought with words instead of fists. The men of the Sand farm were a poor breed, petty and grasping. This one was already bald, the muscles of his neck stood sharply out, and his mouth was like a tightly shut purse. It was no enviable position to be his wife; the miser was already uppermost in him! Already he was shivering with cold down his back—having forgotten his fear for his wife in his thought for himself.

Maren put a cup of coffee on the kitchen table, then sat down herself on the steps leading to the attic with a cracked cup between her fingers. "Just you drink it up," said she, as he hesitated—"there's no-one here that'll harm you and yours."

"But you've been home and made mischief," he [Pg 63] mumbled, stretching out his hand for the cup; he seemed equally afraid of drinking or leaving the coffee.

"We've been at the farm we two, 'tis true enough. The bad storm drove us in, 'twas sore against our will." Maren spoke placidly and with forbearance. "And as to your wife, belike it made her ill, and couldn't bear to hear what a man she's got. A kind and good woman she is—miles too good for you. She gave us nought but the best, while you're just longing to burn us. Ay, ay, 'twould be plenty warm enough then! For here 'tis cold, and there's no-one to bring a load of peat to the house."

"Maybe you'd like *me* to bring you a load?" snapped the farmer, closing his mouth like a trap.

"The child's yours for all that; she's cold and hungry, work as I may."

"Well, she was paid for once and for all."

"Ay, 'twas easy enough for you! Let your own offspring want; 'tis the only child, we'll hope, the Lord'll trust you with."

The farmer started, as if awakened to his senses. "Cast off your spell from my wife!" he shouted, striking the table with his hands.

"I've nought against your wife. But just you see, if the Lord'll put a child in your care. 'Tis not likely to me."

"You leave the Lord alone—and cast off the spell," he whispered hoarsely, making for the old woman, "or I'll throttle you, old witch that you are." He was gray in the face, and his thin, crooked fingers clutched the air.

"Have a care, your own child lies abed and can hear you." Maren pushed open the door to the inner room. "D'you hear that, Ditte, your father's going to throttle me."

Anders Olsen turned away from her and went towards the door. He stood a moment fumbling with the door handle, as if not knowing what he did; then came back, and sank down on the woodbox, gazing at the clay floor. He looked uncommonly old and had always done so ever since his childhood, it was said people of the Sand farm were always born toothless.

Maren came and placed herself in front of him. "Maybe you're thinking of the son your wife should bear? And maybe seeing him already running by your side in the fields, just like a little foal, and learning to hold the plow. Ay! many a one's no son to save for, but enjoys putting by for all that. And often 'tis a close-fisted father has a spendthrift son; belike 'tis the Lord punishing them for their greedy ways. You may fight on till you break up—like many another one. Or sell the farm to strangers, when there's no more work in you—and shift in to the town to a fine little house! For folks with money there's many a way!"

The farmer lifted his head. "Cast off your spell from my wife," he said beseechingly, "and I'll make it worth your while."

"On the Sand farm we'll never set foot again, neither me nor the child. But you can send your wife down here—'tis no harm she'll come to, but don't forget if good's to come of it, on a load of peat she must ride!"

Early next morning the pretty young wife from the Sand farm, could be seen driving through the hamlet seated on top of a swinging cartload of peat. Apparently the farmer did not care to be seen with his wife like this, for he himself was not there; a lad drove the cart. Many wondered where they were going, and with their faces against the window-panes watched them pass. From one or another hut, with no outlook, a woman would come throwing a shawl over her head as she hurried towards the Naze. As the lad carried the peat into Maren's woodshed, and the farmer's wife unpacked eggs, ham, cakes, butter and many other good things on the table in the little sitting room, they came streaming past, staring through the window—visiting the people in the other part of the house with one or other foolish excuse. Maren knew quite well why they came, but it did not worry her any longer. She was accustomed to people keeping an eye on her and using her neighbors as a spying ground.

A few days afterwards the news ran round the neighborhood that the farmer had begun to take notice of his illegitimate child—not altogether with a good will perhaps. Maren was supposed to have had a hand in the arrangement. No-one understood her long patience with him; especially as she had right on her side. But now it would seem she had tired of it and had begun casting spells over the farmer's young wife—first charmed a child into her, and then away again, according to her will. Some declared Ditte was used for this purpose—by conjuring her backwards, right back to her unborn days, so that the child was obliged to seek a mother, and it was because of this she never grew properly. Ditte was extraordinarily small for her age, for all she was never really ill. Probably she was not allowed to grow as she should do, or she would be too big to will away to nothing.

There was much to be said both for and against having such as wise Maren in the district. That she was a witch was well known; but as they went she was in the main a good woman. She never used her talents in the service of the Devil, that is as far as any one knew—and she was kind to the poor; curing many a one without taking payment for it. And as to the farmer of the Sand farm, he only got what he deserved.

Maren's fame was established after this. People have short memories, when it is to their own advantage, and Anders Olsen was seldom generous to them. There would be long intervals in between his visits, then suddenly he would take to coming often. The men of the Sand farm had always been plagued by witchcraft. They might be working in the fields, and bending down to pick up a stone or a weed, when all of a sudden some unseen deviltry would strike them with such excruciating pains in the back, that they could not straighten themselves, and had to crawl home on all fours. There they would lie groaning for weeks, suffering greatly from doing nothing, and treated by cupping, leeches and good advice, till one day the pain would disappear as quickly as it had come. They themselves put it down to the evil eye of women, who perhaps felt themselves ignored and took their revenge in this mean fashion; others thought it was a punishment from Heaven for having too fat a back. At all events this was their weak spot, and whenever the farmer felt a twinge of pain in his back he would hurry to propitiate wise Maren.

This was not sufficient to live on, but her fame increased, and with it her circle of patients.

Maren herself never understood why she had become so famous; but she accepted the fact as it was, and turned it to the best account she could. She took up one thing or another of what she remembered from her childhood of her mother's good advice—and left the rest to look after itself; generally she was guided by circumstances as to what to say and do.

Maren had heard so often that she was a witch, and occasionally believed it herself. Other times she would marvel at people's stupidity. But she always thought with a sigh of the days when Sören still lived and she was nothing more than his "blockhead"—those were happy days.

Now she was lonely. Sören lay under the ground, [Pg 68] and every one else avoided her like the plague, when they did not require her services. Others met and enjoyed a gossip, but no one thought of running in to Maren for a cup of coffee. Even her neighbors kept themselves carefully away, though they often required a helping hand and got it too. She had but one living friend, who looked to her with confidence and who was not afraid of her—Ditte.

It was a sad and sorry task to be a wise woman—only more so as it was not her own choice; but it gave her a livelihood.

[Pg 69]

CHAPTER IX
DITTE VISITS FAIRYLAND

Ditte was now big enough to venture out alone, and would often run away from home, without making Maren uneasy. She needed some one to play with, and sought for playmates in the hamlet and the huts at the edge of the forest. But the parents would call their children in when they saw her coming. Eventually the children themselves learned to beware of her; they would throw stones at her when she came near, and shout nicknames: bastard and witch's brat. Then she tried children in other places and met the same fate; at last it dawned upon her that she stood apart. She was not even sure of the children at home; just as she was playing with them on the sandhills, making necklaces and rings of small blue scabious, the mother would run out and tear the children away.

She had to learn to play alone and be content with the society of the things around her; which she did. Ditte quickly invested her playthings with life; sticks and stones were all given a part and they were wonderfully easy to manage. Almost too well behaved, and Ditte herself sometimes had to put a little naughtiness [Pg 70] into them; or they would be too dull. There was an old wornout wooden shoe of Sören's; Maren had painted a face on it and given it an old shawl as a dress. In Ditte's world it took the part of a boy—a rascal of a boy—always up to mischief and in some scrape or other. It was constantly breaking things, and every minute Ditte had to punish it and give it a good whipping.

One day she was sitting outside in the sun busily engaged in scolding this naughty boy of a doll, in a voice deep with motherly sorrow and annoyance. Maren, who stood inside the kitchen door cleaning herrings, listened with amusement. "If you do it once more," said the child, "we'll take you up to the old witch, and she'll eat you all up."

Maren came quickly out. "Who says that?" asked she, her furrowed face quivering.

"The Bogie-man says it," said Ditte cheerfully.

"Rubbish, child, be serious. Who's taught you that? Tell me at once."

Ditte tried hard to be solemn. "Bogie-doggie said it—tomorrow!" bubbling over with mirth.

No-one could get the better of her; she was bored, and just invented any nonsense that came into her head. Maren gave it up and returned to her work quietly and in deep thought.

She stood crying over her herrings, with the salt tears dropping down into the pickle. She often cried of late, over herself and over the world in general; the [Pg 71] people treated her as if she were infected with the plague, poisoning the air round her with their meanness and hate, while as far as she knew she had always helped them to the best of her ability. They did not hesitate in asking her advice when in trouble, though at the same time they would blame *her* for having brought it upon them—calling her every name they could think of when she had gone. Even the child's *innocent* lips called her a witch.

Since Sören's death sorrow and tears had reddened Maren's eyes with inflammation and turned her eyelids, but her neighbors only took it as another sign of her hardened witchcraft. Her sight was failing too, and she often had to depend upon Ditte's young eyes; and then it would happen that the child took advantage of the opportunity and played pranks.

Ditte was not bad—she was neither bad nor good. She was simply a little creature, whose temperament required change. And so little happened in her world, that she seized on whatever offered to prevent herself from being bored to death.

One day something did happen! From one of the big farms, lying at the other side of the common, with woods bounding the sandhills, Maren had received permission to gather sticks in the wood every Tuesday. There was not much heat in them, but they were good enough for making a cup of coffee.

These Tuesdays were made into picnics. They took their meals with them, which they enjoyed in some [Pg 72]pleasant spot, preferably by the edge of the lake, and Ditte would sit on the wheelbarrow on both journeys. When they had got their load, they would pick berries or—in the autumn—crab-apples and sloes, which were afterwards cooked in the oven.

Now Granny was ill, having cried so much that she could no longer see—which Ditte quite understood—but the extraordinary part of it was that the water seemed to have gone to her legs, so that she could not stand on them. The little one had to trudge all alone to the forest for the sticks. It was a long way, but to make up for it, the forest was full of interest. Now she could go right in, where otherwise she was not allowed to go, because Granny was afraid of getting lost, and always kept to the outskirts. There were singing birds in there, their twittering sounded wonderful under the green trees, the air was like green water with rays of light in it, and it hummed and seethed in the darkness under the bushes.

Ditte was not afraid, though it must be admitted she occasionally shivered. Every other minute she stopped to listen, and when a dry stick snapped, she started, thrilled with excitement. She was not bored here, her little body was brimming over with the wonder of it; each step brought her fresh experiences full of unknown solemnity. Suddenly it would jump out at her with a frightful: pshaw!—exactly as the fire did when Granny poured paraffin over it—and she would hurry away, [Pg 73]as quickly as her small feet would carry her, until she came to an opening in the wood.

On one of these flights she came to a wide river, with trees bending over it. It was like a wide stream of greenness flowing down, and Ditte stood transfixed, in breathless wonder. The green of the river she quickly grasped, for this was the color poured down on all trees—and the river here was the end of the world. Over on the other side the Lord lived; if she looked very hard she could just catch a glimpse of his gray bearded face in a thicket of thorns. But how was all this greenness made?

She ran for some distance along the edge of the river, watching it, until she was stopped by two ladies, so beautiful that she had never seen anything like them before. Though there was no rain, and they were walking under the trees in the shadow, they held parasols, on which the sun gleamed through the green leaves, looking like glowing coins raining down on to their parasols. They knelt in front of Ditte as if she were a little princess, lifting her bare feet and peeping under the soles, as they questioned her.

Well, her name was Ditte. Ditte Mischief and Ditte Goodgirl—and Ditte child o' Man!

The ladies looked at each other and laughed, and asked her where she lived.

In Granny's house, of course.

"What Granny?" asked the stupid ladies again.

Ditte stamped her little bare foot on the grass:[Pg 74]

"Oh, Granny! that's blind sometimes 'cos she cries so much. Ditte's own Granny."

Then they pretended to be much wiser, and asked her to go home with them for a little while. Ditte gave her little hand trustingly to one of them and trotted along; she did not mind seeing if they lived on the other side of the river—with the Lord. Then it would be angels she had met.

They went along the river; Ditte, impatient with excitement, thought it would never end. At last they came to a footbridge, arched across the river. At the end of the bridge was a barred gate with railings on each side, which it was impossible to climb over or under. The ladies opened the gate with a key and carefully locked it again, and Ditte found herself in a most beautiful garden. By the path stood lovely flowers in clusters, red and blue, swaying their pretty heads; and on low bushes were delicious large red berries such as she had never tasted before.

Ditte knew at once that this was Paradise. She threw herself against one of the ladies, her mouth red with the juice of the berries, looking up at her with an unfathomable expression in her dark blue eyes and said: "Am I dead now?"

The ladies laughed and took her into the house, through beautiful rooms where one walked on thick soft shawls with one's boots on. In the innermost room a little lady was sitting in an armchair. She was white-haired [Pg 75]and wrinkled and had spectacles on her nose; and wore a white nightcap in spite of it being the middle of the day. "This is our Granny!" said one of the ladies.

"Grandmother, look, we have caught a little wood goblin," they shouted into the old lady's ear. Just think, this Granny was deaf—her own was only blind.

Ditte went round peeping inquisitively into the different rooms. "Where's the Lord?" asked she suddenly.

"What is the child saying?" exclaimed one of the ladies. But the one who had taken Ditte by the hand, drew the little one towards her and said: "The Lord does not live here, he lives up in Heaven. She thinks this is Paradise," she added, turning to her sister.

It worried them to see her running about barefooted, and they carefully examined her feet, fearing she might have been bitten by some creeping thing in the wood. "Why does not the child wear boots?"

said the old lady. Her head shook so funnily when she spoke, all the white curls bobbed—just like bluebells.

Ditte had no boots.

"Good Heavens! do you hear that, Grandmother, the child has no boots. Have you nothing at all to put on your feet?"

"Bogie-man," burst out Ditte, laughing roguishly.

She was tired now of answering all their questions. However, they dragged out of her that she had a pair of wooden shoes, which were being kept for winter.

"Then with the help of God she shall have a pair of my cloth ones," said the old lady. "Give her a pair, Asta; and take a fairly good pair."

"Certainly, Grandmother," answered one of the young women—the one Ditte liked best.

So Ditte was put into the cloth boots. Then she was given different kinds of food, such as she had never tasted before, and did not care for either; she kept to the bread, being most familiar with that—greatly to the astonishment of the three women.

"She is fastidious," said one of the young ladies.

"It can hardly be called that, when she prefers bread to anything else," answered Miss Asta eagerly. "But she is evidently accustomed to very plain food, and yet see how healthy she is." She drew the little one to her and kissed her.

"Let her take it home with her," said the old lady, "such children of nature never eat in captivity. My husband once captured a little wild monkey down on the Gold Coast, but was obliged to let it go again because it refused to eat."

Then Ditte was given the food packed into a pretty little basket of red and white straw; a Leghorn hat was put upon her head, and a large red bow adorned her breast. She enjoyed all this very much—but suddenly, remembering her Granny, wanted to go home. She stood pulling the door handle, and they had to let this amusing little wood goblin out again. Hurriedly a few strawberries were put into the basket, and off she disappeared into the wood.

"I hope she can find her way back again," said Miss Asta looking after her with dreaming eyes.

Ditte certainly found her way home. It was fortunate that in her longing to be there, she entirely forgot what was in the basket. Otherwise old Maren would have gone to her grave without ever having tasted strawberries.

After that Ditte often ran deep into the forest, in the hope that the adventure would repeat itself. It had been a wonderful experience, the most wonderful in her life. Old Maren encouraged her too. "You just go right into the thicket," she said. "Naught can harm you, for you're a Sunday child. And when you get to the charmed house, you must ask for a pair of cloth boots for me too. Say that old Granny has water in her legs and can hardly bear shoes on her feet."

The river was easily found, but she did not meet the beautiful ladies again, and the footbridge with the gate had disappeared. There were woods on the other side of the river just as on this, the Lord's face she could no longer find either, look as she might; Fairyland was no more.

"You'll see, 'twas naught but a dream," said old Maren.

"But, Granny, the strawberries," answered Ditte.

Ay, the strawberries—that was true enough! Maren had eaten some of them herself, and she had never tasted anything so delicious either. Twenty times bigger than wild strawberries, and satisfying too—so unlike other berries, which only upset one.

"The dream goblin, who took you to Fairyland, gave you those so that other folks might taste them too," said the old one at last.

And with this explanation they were satisfied.

CHAPTER X
DITTE GETS A FATHER

On getting up one morning, Maren found her tenants had gone, they had moved in the middle of the night. "The Devil has been and fetched them," she said cheerfully. She was not at all sorry that they had vanished; they were a sour and quarrelsome family! But the worst of it was that they owed her twelve weeks' rent—twelve crowns—which was all she had to meet the winter with.

Maren put up a notice and waited for new tenants, but none offered themselves; the old ones had spread the rumor that the house was haunted.

Maren felt the loss of the rent so much more as she had given up her profession. She would no longer be a wise woman, it was impossible to bear the curse. "Go to those who are wiser, and leave me in peace," she answered, when they came for advice or to fetch her, and they had to go away with their object unaccomplished, and soon it was said that Maren had lost her witchcraft.

Yes, her strength diminished, her sight was almost gone, and her legs refused to carry her. She spun and knitted for people and took to begging again, Ditte leading her from farm to farm. They were weary journeys; the old woman always complaining and leaning heavily on the child's shoulder. Ditte could not understand it at all, the flowers in the ditches and a hundred other things called her, she longed to shake off the leaden arm and run about alone, Granny's everlasting wailing filled her with a hopeless loathing. Then a mischievous thought would seize her. "I can't find the way, Granny," she would suddenly declare, refusing to go a step further, or she would slip away, hiding herself nearby. Maren scolded and threatened for a while, but as it had no effect, she would sit down on the edge of the ditch crying; this softened Ditte and she would hurry back, putting her arms around her grandmother's neck. Thus they cried together, in sorrow over the miserable world and joy at having found each other again.

A little way inland lived a baker, who gave them a loaf of bread every week. The child was sent for it when Maren was ill in bed. Ditte was hungry, and this was a great temptation, so she always ran the whole way home to keep the tempter at bay; when she succeeded in bringing the bread back untouched, she and her Granny were equally proud. But it sometimes happened that the pangs of hunger were too strong, and she would tear out the crump from the side of the warm bread as she ran. It was not meant to be seen, and for that reason she took it from the side of the bread—just [Pg 81] a little, but before she knew what had happened the whole loaf was hollowed out. Then she would be furious, at herself and Granny and everything.

"Here's the bread, Granny," she would say in an offhand voice, throwing the bread on the table.

"Thank you, dear, is it new?"

"Yes, Granny," and Ditte disappeared.

Thereupon the old woman would sit gnawing the crust with her sore gums, all the while grumbling at the child. Wicked girl—she should be whipped. She should be turned out, to the workhouse.

To their minds there was nothing worse than the workhouse; in all their existence, it had been as a sword over their heads, and when brought forth by Maren, Ditte would come out from her hiding-place, crying and begging for pardon. The old woman would cry too, and the one would soothe the other, until both were comforted.

"Ay, ay, 'tis hard to live," old Maren would say. "If you'd but had a father—one worth having. Maybe you'd have got the thrashings all folks need, and poor old Granny'd have lived with you instead of begging her food!"

Maren had barely finished speaking, when a cart with a bony old nag in the shafts stopped outside on the road. A big stooping man with tousled hair and beard sprang down from the cart, threw the reins over the back of the nag, and came towards the house. He looked like a coalheaver. [Pg 82]

"He's selling herrings," said Ditte, who was kneeling on a stool by the window. "Shall I let him in?"

"Ay, just open the door."

Ditte unbolted the door, and the man came staggering in. He wore heavy wooden boots, into which his trousers were pushed; and each step he took rang through the room, which was too low for him to stand upright in. He stood looking round just inside the door; Ditte had taken refuge behind Granny's spinning wheel. He came towards the living room, holding out his hand.

Ditte burst into laughter at his confusion when the old woman did not accept it. "Why, Granny's blind!" she said, bubbling over with mirth.

"Oh, that's it? Then it's hardly to be expected that you could see," he said, taking the old woman's hand. "Well, I'm your son-in-law, there's news for you." His voice rang with good-humor.

Maren quickly raised her head. "Which of the girls is it?" asked she.

"The mother of this young one," answered he, aiming at Ditte with his big battered hat. "It's not what you might call legal yet; we've done without the parson till he's needed—so much comes afore that. But a house and a home we've got, though poor it may be. We live a good seven miles inland on the other side of the common—on the *sand*—folks call it the 'Crow's Nest'!"

"And what's your name?" asked Maren again. [Pg 83]

"Lars Peter Hansen, I was christened."

The old woman considered for a while, then shook her head. "I've never heard of you."

"My father was called the hangman. Maybe you know me now?"

"Ay, 'tis a known name—if not of the best."

"Folks can't always choose their own names, or character either, and must just be satisfied with a clear conscience. But as I was passing I thought I'd just look in and see you. When we're having the parson to give us his blessing, Sörine and me, I'll come with the trap and fetch the two of you to church. That's if you don't care to move down to us at once—seems like that would be best."

"Did Sörine send the message?" asked Maren suspiciously.

Lars Peter Hansen mumbled something, which might be taken for either yes or no.

"Ay, I thought so, you hit on it yourself, and thanks to you for your kindness; but we'd better stay where we are. Though we'd like to go to the wedding. 'Tis eight children I've brought into the world, and nigh all married now, but I've never been asked to a wedding afore." Maren became thoughtful. "And what's your trade?" she asked soon after.

"I hawk herrings—and anything else to be got. Buy rags and bones too when folks have any."

"You can hardly make much at that—for folks wear their rags as long as there's a thread left—and there's few better off than that. Or maybe they're more well-to-do in other places?"

"Nay, 'tis the same there as here, clothes worn out to the last thread, and bones used until they crumble," answered the man with a laugh. "But a living's to be made."

"Ay, that's so, food's to be got from somewhere! But you must be hungry? 'Tisn't much we've got to offer you, though we can manage a cup of coffee, if that's good enough—Ditte, run along to the baker and tell him what you've done to the bread, and that we've got company. Maybe he'll scold you and give you another—if he doesn't, we'll have to go without next week. But tell the truth. Hurry up now—and don't pull out the crump."

With lingering feet Ditte went out of the door. It was a hard punishment, and she hung back in the hope that Granny would relent and let her off fetching the bread. Pull out the crump—no, never again, today or as long as she lived. Her ears burned with shame at the thought that her new father should know her misdeeds, the baker too would know what a wicked girl she was to Granny. She would not tell an untruth, for Granny always said to clear oneself with a lie was like cutting thistles: cut off the head of one and half a dozen will spring up in its place. Ditte knew from experience that lies always came back on one with redoubled trouble; consequently she had made up her little mind, that it did not pay to avoid the truth.

Lars Peter Hansen sat by the window gazing after the child, who loitered along the road, and as she suddenly began to run, he turned to the old woman, asking: "Can you manage her?"

"Ay, she's good enough," said Maren from the kitchen, fumbling with the sticks in trying to light the fire. "I've no one better to lean on—and don't want it either. But she's a child, and I'm old and troublesome—so the one makes up for the other. The foal will kick backwards, and the old horse will stand. But 'tis dull to spend one's childhood with one that's old and weak and all."

Ditte was breathless when she reached the baker's, so quickly had she run in order to get back as soon as possible to the big stooping man with the good-natured growl.

"Now I've got a father, just like other children," she shouted breathlessly. "He's at home with Granny—and he's got a horse and cart."

"Nay, is that so?" said they, opening their eyes, "and what's his name?"

"He's called the rag and bone man!" answered Ditte proudly.

And they knew him here! Ditte saw them exchange glances.

"Then you belong to a grand family," said the baker's wife, laying the loaf of bread on the counter—without realizing that the child had already had her weekly loaf, so taken up was she with the news.

And Ditte, who was even more so, seized the bread and ran. Not until she was halfway home did she remember what she ought to have confessed; it was too late then.

Before Lars Peter Hansen left, he presented them with a dozen herrings, and repeated his promise of coming to fetch them to the wedding.

CHAPTER XI
THE NEW FATHER

When Ditte was six months old, she had the bad habit of putting things into her mouth—everything went that way. This was the proof whether they could be eaten or not.

Ditte laughed when Granny told about it, because she was so much wiser now. There were things one could not eat and yet get pleasure from, and other things which could be eaten, but gave more enjoyment if one left them alone, content in the thought of how they would taste if——Then one hugged oneself with delight at keeping it so much longer. "You're foolish," said Granny, "eat it up before it goes bad!" But Ditte understood how to put by. She would dream over one or other thing she had got: a red apple, for instance, she would press to her cheek and mouth and kiss. Or she would hide it and go about thinking of it with silent devotion. Should she return and find it spoiled, well, in imagination she had eaten it over and over again. This was beyond Granny; her helplessness had made her greedy, and she could never get enough to eat; now it was she who put everything into her mouth.

But then they had watched the child, for fear she should eat something which might harm her. More so Sören. "Not into your mouth!" he often said. Whereupon the child would gaze at him, take the thing out of her own mouth and try to put it into his. Was it an attempt to get an accomplice, or did the little one think it was because he himself wanted to suck the thing, that he forbade her? Sören was never quite clear on this point.

At all events, Ditte had learned at an early age to reckon with other people's selfishness. If they gave good advice or corrected her, it was not so much out of consideration for her as for their own ends. Should she meet the bigger girls on the road, and happen to have an apple in her hand, they would say to her: "Fling that horrible apple away, or you'll get worms!" But Ditte no longer threw the apple away; she had found out that they only picked it up as soon as she had gone, to eat it themselves. Things were not what they appeared to be, more often than not there was something behind what one saw and heard.

Some people declared, that things really meant for one were put behind a back—a stick, for instance; it was always wise to be on the watch.

With Granny naturally it was not like this. She was simply Granny through all their ups and downs, and one need never beware of her. She was only more whining than she used to be, and could no longer earn their living. Ditte had to bear the greatest share of the burden, and was already capable of getting necessities for the house; she knew when the farmers were killing or churning, and would stand barefooted begging for a little for Granny. "Why don't you get poor relief?" said some, but gave all the same; the needy must not be turned away from one's door, if one's food were to be blessed. But under these new conditions it was impossible to have any respect for Granny, who was treated more as a spoiled child, and often corrected and then comforted.

"Ay, 'tis all very well for you," said the old woman—"you've got sight and good legs, the whole world's afore you. But I've only the grave to look forward to."

"Do you want to die?" asked Ditte, "and go to old Grandfather Sören?"

Indeed, no, Granny did not wish to die. But she could not help thinking of the grave; it drew her and yet frightened her. Her tired limbs were never really rested, and a long, long sleep under the green by Sören's side was a tempting thought, if only one could be sure of not feeling the cold. Yes, and that the child was looked after, of course.

"Then I'll go over to my new father," declared Ditte whenever it was spoken of. Granny need have no fear for her. "But do you think Grandfather Sören's still there?"

Yes, that was what old Maren was not quite sure of herself. She could so well imagine the grave as the end of everything, and rest peacefully with that thought; oh! the blissfulness of laying one's tired head where no carts could be heard, and to be free for all eternity from aches and pains and troubles, and only rest. Perhaps this would not be allowed—there was so much talking: the parson said one thing and the lay preacher another. Sören might not be there any longer, and she would have to search for him till she found him, which would be difficult enough if after death he had been transformed to youth again. Sören had been wild and dissipated. Where he was, Maren must also be, there was no doubt about that. But she preferred to have it arranged so that she could have a long rest by Sören's side, as a reward for all those weary years.

"Then I'll go to my new father!" repeated Ditte. This had become her refrain.

"Ay, just as ye like!" answered Maren harshly. She did not like the child taking the subject so calmly.

But Ditte needed some one who could secure her future. Granny was no good, she was too old and helpless, and she was a woman. There ought to be a man! And now she had found him. She lay down to sleep behind Granny with a new feeling now; she had a real father, just like other children, one who was married to her mother, and in addition possessed a horse and cart. The bald young owner of the Sand farm, who was so thin and mean that he froze everybody near him, she never took to, he was too cold for that. But the rag and bone man had taken her on his knee and shouted in her ear with his big blustering voice. They might shout "brat" after her as much as they liked, for all she cared. She had a father taller than any of theirs, he had to bend his head when he stood under the beams in Granny's sitting room.

The outlook was so much better now, one fell asleep feeling richer and woke again—not disappointed as when one had dreamt—but with a feeling of security. Such a father was much better to depend upon, than an old blind Granny, who was nothing but a bundle of rags. Every night when Granny undressed, Ditte was equally astonished at seeing her take off skirt after skirt, getting thinner and thinner until, as if by witchcraft, nothing was left of the fat grandmother but a skeleton, a withered little crone, who wheezed like the leaky bellows by the fireplace.

They looked forward to the day when the new father would come and fetch them to the wedding. Then of course it would be in a grand carriage—the other one was only a cart. It would happen when they were most wearied with life, not knowing where to turn for food or coffee. Suddenly they would hear the cheerful crack of a whip outside, and there he would stand, saluting with his whip, the rascal; and as they got into the carriage, he would sit at attention with his whip—like the coachman on the estate.

Maren, poor soul, had never seen a carriage at her door; she was almost more excited than the child, and described it all to her. "And little I thought any carriage would ever come for me, but the one that took me to the churchyard," she would say each time. "But your mother, she always had a weakness for what is grand."

There had come excitement into their poor lives. Ditte was no longer bored, and did not have to invent mischief to keep her little mind occupied. She had also developed a certain feeling of responsibility towards her grandmother, now that she was dependent on her—they got on much better together. "You're very good to your old Granny, child," Maren would often say, and then they would cry over each other without knowing why.

The little wide-awake girl now had to be eyes for Granny as well, and old Maren had to learn to see things through Ditte. And as soon as she got used to it and put implicit faith in the child, all went well.

Whenever Ditte was tempted to make fun, Maren had only to say: "You're not playing tricks, are you, child?" and she would immediately stop. She was intelligent and quick, and Maren could wish for no better eyes than hers, failing the use of her own. There she would sit fumbling and turning her sightless eyes towards every sound without discovering what it could be. But thanks to Ditte she was able by degrees to take up part of her old life again.

Perhaps after all she missed the skies more than anything else. The weather had always played a great part in Maren's life; not so much the weather that was, as that to come. This was the fishergirl in her; she took after her mother—and her mother again—from the time she began to take notice she would peer at the skies early and late. Everything was governed by them, even their food from day to day, and when they were dark—it cleared the table once and for all by taking the bread-winner. The sky was the first thing her eyes sought for in the morning, and the last to dwell upon at night. "There'll be a storm in the night," she would say, as she came in, or: "It'll be a good day for fishing tomorrow!" Ditte never understood how she knew this.

Maren seldom went out now, so it did not matter to her what the weather was, but she was still as much interested in it. "What's the sky like?" she would often ask. Ditte would run out and peer anxiously at the skies, very much taken up with her commission.

"'Tis red," she announced on her return, "and there's a man riding over it on a wet, wet horse. Is it going to rain then?"

"Is the sun going down into a sack?" asked Granny. Ditte ran out again to see.

"There's no sun at all," she came in and announced with excitement.

But Granny shook her head, there was nothing to be made of the child's explanation; she was too imaginative.

"Have you seen the cat eat grass today?" asked Maren after a short silence.

No, Ditte had not seen it do that. But it had jumped after flies.

Maren considered for a while. Well, well, it probably meant nothing good. "Go and see if there are stars under the coffee kettle," said she.

Ditte lifted the heavy copper kettle from the fire—yes, there were stars of fire in the soot, they swarmed over the bottom of the kettle in a glittering mass.

"Then it'll be stormy," said Granny relieved. "I've felt it for days in my bones." Should there be a storm, Maren always remembered to say: "Now, you see, I was right." And Ditte wondered over her Granny's wisdom.

"Is that why folks call you 'wise Maren'?" asked she.

"Ay, that's it. But it doesn't need much to be wiser than the others—if only one has sight. For folks are stupid—most of them."

Lars Peter Hansen they neither saw nor heard of for nearly a year. When people drove past, who they thought might come from his locality, they would make inquiries; but were never much wiser for all they heard. At last they began to wonder whether he really did exist; it was surely not a dream like the fairy-house in the wood?

And then one day he actually stood at the door. He did not exactly crack his whip—a long hazel-stick with a piece of string at the end—but he tried to do it, and the old nag answered by throwing back its head and whinnying. It was the same cart as before, but a seat with a green upholstered back, from which the stuffing protruded, had been put on. His big battered hat was the same too, it was shiny from age and full of dust, and with bits of straw and spiders' webs in the dents. From underneath it his tousled hair showed, so covered with dust and burrs and other things that the birds of the air might be tempted to build their nests in it.

"Now, what do you say to a little drive today?" he shouted gaily, as he tramped in. "I've brought fine weather with me, what?"

He might easily do that, for even yesterday Granny had seen to it that the weather should be fine, although she knew nothing of this. Last evening she touched the dew on the window-pane with her hand and had said: "There's dew for the morning sun to sparkle on."

Lars Peter Hansen had to wait, while Ditte lit the fire and made coffee for him. "What a clever girl you are," he burst out, as she put it in front of him, "you must have a kiss." He took her in his arms and kissed her; Ditte put her face against his rough cheek and did not speak a word. Suddenly he realized his cheek was wet, and turned her face toward his. "Have I hurt you?" he asked alarmed, and put her down.

"Nay, never a bit," said the old woman. "The child has been looking forward to a kiss from her father, and now it has come to pass—little as it is. You let her have her cry out; childish tears only wet the cheeks."

But Lars Peter Hansen went into the peat shed, where he found Ditte sobbing. Gently raising her, he dried her cheeks with his checked handkerchief, which looked as if it had been out many times before today.

"We'll be friends sure enough, we two—we'll be friends sure enough," he repeated soothingly. His deep voice comforted the child, she took his hand and followed him back again.

Granny, who was very fond of coffee, though she would never say so, had seized the opportunity to take an extra cup while they were out. In her haste to pour it out, some had been spilt on the table, and now she was trying to wipe it up in the hope it might not be seen. Ditte helped her to take off her apron, and washed her skirt with a wet cloth, so that it should not leave a mark; she looked quite motherly. She herself would have no coffee, she was so overwhelmed with happiness, that she could not eat.

Then the old woman was well wrapped up, and Lars Peter lifted them into the cart. Granny was put on the seat by his side, while Ditte, who was to have sat on the fodder-bag at the back, placed herself at their feet, for company. Lars took up the reins, pulled them tightly, and loosened them again; having done this several times, the old nag started with a jerk, which [Pg 97] almost upset their balance, and off they went into the country.

It was glorious sunshine. Straight ahead the rolling downs lay bathed in it—and beyond, the country with forest and hill. It all looked so different from the cart, than when walking with bare feet along the road; all seemed to curtsey to Ditte, hills and forests and everything. She was not used to driving, and this was the first time she had driven in state and looked down on things. All those dreary hills that on other days stretched so heavily and monotonously in front of her, and had often been too much for her small feet, today lay down and said: "Yes, Ditte, you may drive over us with pleasure!" Granny did not share in all this, but she could feel the sun on her old back and was quite in holiday mood.

The old nag took its own time, and Lars Peter Hansen had no objection. He sat the whole time lightly touching it with his whip, a habit of his, and one without which the horse could not proceed. Should he stop for one moment, while pointing with his whip at the landscape, it would toss its head with impatience and look back—greatly to Ditte's enjoyment.

"Can't it gallop at all?" asked she, propping herself up between his knees.

"Rather, just you wait and see!" answered Lars Peter Hansen proudly. He pulled in the reins, but the nag only stopped, turned round, and looked at him with astonishment. For each lash of the whip, it threw up [Pg 98] its tail and sawed the air with its head. Ditte's little body tingled with enjoyment.

"'Tisn't in the mood today," said Lars Peter Hansen, when he had at last got it into its old trot again. "It thinks it's a fraud to expect it to gallop, when it's been taking such long paces all the time."

"Did it say that?" asked Ditte, her eyes traveling from the one to the other.

"That's what it's supposed to mean. It's not far wrong."

Long paces it certainly did take—about that there was no mistake—but never two of equal length, and the cart was rolling in a zigzag all the time. What a funny horse it was. It looked as if it was made of odd parts, so bony and misshapen was it. No two parts matched, and its limbs groaned and creaked with every movement.

They drove past the big estate, where the squire lived, over the common, and still further out into the country which Granny had never seen before.

"But you can't see it now either," corrected Ditte pedantically.

"Oh, you always want to split hairs, 'course I can see it! When I hear you two speak, I see everything quite plainly. 'Tis a gift of God, to live through all this in my old days. But I smell something sweet, what is it?"

"Maybe 'tis the fresh water, Granny," said Lars Peter. "Two or three miles down to the left is the [Pg 99] big lake. Granny has a sharp nose for anything that's wet." He chuckled over his little joke.

"'Tis water folks can drink without harm," said Maren thoughtfully; "Sören's told me about it. We were going to take a trip down there fishing for eels, but we never did. Ay, they say 'tis a pretty sight over the water to see the glare of the fires on the summer nights."

In between Lars Peter told them about conditions in his home. It was not exactly the wedding they were going to, for they had married about nine months ago—secretly. "'Twas done in a hurry," he apologetically explained, "or you two would have been there."

Maren became silent; she had looked forward to being present at the wedding of one of her girls at least, and nothing had come of it. Otherwise, it was a lovely trip.

"Have you any little ones then?" she asked shortly after.

"A boy," answered Lars Peter, "a proper little monkey—the image of his mother!" He was quite enthusiastic at the thought of the child. "Sörine's expecting another one soon," he added quietly.

"You're getting on," said Maren. "How is she?"

"Not quite so well this time. 'Tis the heartburn, she says."

"Then 'twill be a long-haired girl," Maren declared definitely. "And well on the way she must be, for the hair to stick in the mother's throat." [Pg 100]

It was a beautiful September day. Everything smelt of mold, and the air was full of moisture, which could be seen as crystal drops over the sunlit land; a blue haze hung between the trees sinking to rest in the undergrowth, so that meadow and moor looked like a glimmering white sea.

Ditte marveled at the endlessness of the world. Constantly something new could be seen: forests, villages, churches; only the end of the world, which she expected every moment to see and put an end to everything, failed to appear. To the south some towers shone in the sun; it was a king's palace, said her father—her little heart mounted to her throat when he said that. And still further ahead——

"What's that I smell now?" Granny suddenly said, sniffing the air. "'Tis salt! We must be near the sea."

"Not just what one would call near, 'tis over seven miles away. Can you really smell the sea?"

Ay, ay, no-one need tell Maren that they neared the sea; she had spent all her life near it and ought to know. "And what sea is that?" asked she.

"The same as yours," answered Lars Peter.

"That's little enough to drive through the country for," said Maren laughingly.

And then they were at the end of their journey. It was quite a shock to them, when the nag suddenly stopped and Lars Peter sprang down from the cart. "Now, then," said he, lifting them down. Sörine came out with the boy in her arms; she was big and strong and had rough manners.

Ditte was afraid of this big red woman, and took refuge behind Granny. "She doesn't know you, that's why," said Maren, "she'll soon be all right."

But Sörine was angry. "Now, no more nonsense, child," said she, dragging her forward. "Kiss your mother at once."

Ditte began to howl, and tore herself away from her. Sörine looked as if she would have liked to use a parent's privilege and punish the child then and there. Her husband came between by snatching the child from her and placing her on the back of the horse. "Pat the kind horse and say thank you for the nice drive," said he. Thus he quieted Ditte, and carried her to Sörine. "Kiss mother," he said, and Ditte put forth her little mouth invitingly. But now Sörine refused. She looked at the child angrily, and went to get water for the horse.

Sörine had killed a couple of chickens in their honor, and on the whole made them comfortable, as far as their food and drink went; but there was a lack of friendliness which made itself felt. She had always been cold and selfish, and had not improved with years. By the next morning old Maren saw it was quite time for them to return home, and against this Sörine did not demur. After dinner Lars Peter harnessed the old nag, lifted them into the cart, and off they set homewards, relieved that it was over. Even Lars Peter was different out in the open to what he was at home. He sang and cracked jokes, while home he was quiet and said little.

They were thankful to be home again in the hut on the Naze. "Thank the Lord, 'tis not your mother we've to look to for our daily bread," said Granny, when Lars Peter Hansen had taken leave; and Ditte threw her arms round the old woman's neck and kissed her. Today she realized fully Granny's true worth.

It had been somewhat of a disappointment. Sörine was not what they had expected her to be, and her home was not up to much. As far as Granny found out from Ditte's description, it was more like a mud-hut, which had been given the name of dwelling-house, barn, etc. In no way could it be compared with the hut on the Naze.

But the drive had been beautiful.

CHAPTER XII
THE RAG AND BONE MAN

All who knew Lars Peter Hansen agreed that he was a comical fellow. He was always in a good temper, and really there was no reason why he should be—especially where he was concerned. He belonged to a race of rag and bone men, who as far back as any one could remember, had traded in what others would not touch, and had therefore been given the name of rag and bone folk. His father drove with dogs and bought up rags and bones and other unclean refuse; when a sick or tainted animal had to be done away with he was always sent for. He was a fellow who never minded what he did, and would bury his arms up to the elbows in the worst kind of carrion, and then go straight to his dinner without even rinsing his fingers in water; people declared that in the middle of the night he would go and dig up the dead animals and strip them of their skin. His father, it was said, had gone as a boy to give his uncle a helping hand. As an example of the boy's depravity, it was said that when the rope would not tighten round the neck of a man who was being hung, he would climb up the gallows, drop down on to the unfortunate man's shoulder, and sit there.

There was not much to inherit, and there was absolutely nothing to be proud of. Lars Peter had probably felt this, for when quite young he had turned his back on the home of his childhood. He crossed the water and tried for work in North Sea land—his ambition was to be a farmer. He was a steady and respectable fellow, and as strong as a horse, any farmer would willingly employ him.

But if he thought he could run away from things, he was mistaken. Rumors of his origin followed faithfully at his heels, and harmed him at every turn. He might just as well have tried to fly from his own shadow.

Fortunately it did not affect him much. He was good-natured—wherever he had got it from—there was not a bad thought in his mind. His strength and trustworthiness made up for his low origin, so that he was able to hold his own with other young men; it even happened, that a well-to-do girl fell in love with his strength and black hair, and wanted him for a husband. In spite of her family's opposition they became engaged; but very soon she died, so he did not get hold of her money.

So unlucky was he in everything, that it seemed as if the sins of his fathers were visited upon him. But Lars Peter took it as the way of the world. He toiled and saved, till he had scraped together sufficient money to [Pg 105] clear a small piece of land on the Sand—and once again looked for a wife. He met a girl from one of the fishing-hamlets; they took to each other, and he married her.

There are people, upon whose roof the bird of misfortune always sits flapping its black wings. It is generally invisible to all but the inmates of the house; but it may happen, that all others see it, except those whom it visits.

Lars Peter was one of those whom people always watched for something to happen. To his race stuck the two biggest mysteries of all—the blood and the curse; that he himself was good and happy made it no less exciting. Something surely was in store for him; every one could see the bird of misfortune on his roof.

He himself saw nothing, and with confidence took his bride home. No one told him that she had been engaged to a sailor, who was drowned; and anyway, what good would it have done? Lars Peter was not the man to be frightened away by the dead, he was at odds with no man. And no one can escape his fate.

They were as happy together as any two human beings can be; Lars Peter was good to her, and when he had finished his own work, would help her with the milking, and carry water in for her. Hansine was happy and satisfied; every one could see she had got a good husband. The bird that lived on their roof could [Pg 106] be none other than the stork, for before long Hansine confided in Lars Peter that she was with child.

It was the most glorious news he had ever had in his life, and if he had worked hard before he did even more so now. His evenings were spent in the woodshed; there was a cradle to be made, and a rocking-chair, and small wooden shoes to be carved. As he worked he would hum, something slightly resembling a melody, but always the same tune; then suddenly Hansine would come running out throwing herself into his arms. She had become so strange under her pregnancy, she could find no rest, and would sit for hours with her thoughts far away—as if listening to distant voices—and could not be roused up again. Lars Peter put it down to her condition, and took it all good-humoredly. His even temperament had a soothing effect upon her, and she was soon happy again. But at times she was full of anxiety, and would run out to him in the fields, almost beside herself. It was almost impossible to persuade her to return to the house, he only succeeded after promising to keep within sight. She was afraid of one thing or another at home, but when he urged her to tell him the reason, she would look dumbly at him.

After the child's birth, she was her old self again. Their delight was great in the little one, and they were happier even than before.

But this strange phase returned when she again became pregnant, only in a stronger degree. There [Pg 107] were times, when her fear forced her out of the house, and she would run into the fields, wring her hands in anguish. The distracted husband would fetch the screaming child to her, thus tempting her home again. This time she gave in and confided in him, that she had been engaged to a sailor, who had made her promise that she would remain faithful, if anything happened to him at sea.

"Did he never come back then?" asked Lars Peter slowly.

Hansine shook her head. And he had threatened to return and claim her, if she broke her word. He had said, he would tap on the trap-door in the ceiling.

"Did you promise of your own free will?" Lars Peter said ponderously.

No, Hansine thought he had pressed her.

"Then you're not bound by it," said he. "My family, maybe, are not much to go by, scum of the earth as we are. But my father and my grandfather always used to say, there's no need to fear the dead; they were easier to get away from than the living." She sat bending over the babe, which had cried itself to sleep on her knees, and Lars Peter stood with his arms round her shoulder, softly rocking her backwards and forwards, as he tried to talk her to reason. "You must think of the little one here—and the other little one to come! The only thing which can't be forgiven, is unkindness to those given to us."

Hansine took his hand and pressed it against her [Pg 108] tearful eyes. Then rising herself she put the child to bed; she was calm now.

The rag and bone man had no superstition of any kind, or fear either, it was the only bright touch in the darkness of his race that they possessed; this property caused them to be outcasts—and decided their trade. Those who are not haunted, haunt others.

The only curse he knew, was the curse of being an outcast and feared; and this, thank the Lord, had been removed where he was concerned. He did not believe in persecution from a dead man. But he understood the serious effect it had upon Hansine, and was much troubled on her account. Before going to bed, he took down the trap-door and hid it under the roof.

Thus they had children one after the other, and with it trouble and depression. Instead of becoming better it grew worse with each one; and as much as Lars Peter loved his children, he hoped each one would be the last. The children themselves bore no mark of having been carried under a heart full of fear. They were like small shining suns, who encircled him all day long from the moment they could move. They added enjoyment to his work, and as each new one made its appearance, he received it as a gift of God. His huge fists entirely covered the newly born babe, when handed to him by the midwife—looking in its swaddling clothes like the leg of a boot—as he lifted it to the ceiling. His voice in its joy was like the deep chime of a bell, and the babe's head rolled from side to side, while blinking [Pg 109] its eyes at the light. Never had any one been so grateful for children, wife and everything else as Lars Peter. He was filled with admiration for them all, it was a glorious world.

He did not exactly make headway on his little farm. It was poor land, and Lars Peter was said to be unlucky. Either he lost an animal or the crop was spoiled by hail. Other people kept an account of these accidents, Lars Peter himself had no feeling of being treated badly. On the contrary he was thankful for his farm, and toiled patiently on it. Nothing affected him.

When Hansine was to have her fifth child, she was worse than ever. She had made him put up the trap-door again, on the pretense that she could not stay in the kitchen for the draught, and she would be nowhere else but there—she was waiting for the tap. She complained no longer nor on the whole was she anxious either. It was as if she had learned to endure what could not be evaded; she was absent-minded, and Lars Peter had the sad feeling that she no longer belonged to him. In the night he would suddenly realize that she was missing from his side—and would find her in the kitchen stiff with cold. He carried her back to bed, soothing her like a little child, and she would fall asleep on his breast.

Her condition was such, that he never dared go from home, and leave her alone with the children; he had to engage a woman to keep an eye on her, and look after [Pg 110] the house. She now neglected everything and looked at the children as if they were the cause of her trouble.

One day when he was taking a load of peat to town, an awful thing happened. What Hansine had been waiting for so long, now actually took place. She sent the woman, who was supposed to be with her, away on some excuse or other; and when Lars Peter returned, the animals were bellowing and every door open. There was no sign of wife or children. The poultry slipped past him, as he went round calling. He found them all in the well. It was a fearful sight to see the mother and four children lying in a row, first on the cobble-stoned yard, wet and pitiful, and afterwards on the sitting-room table dressed for burial. Without a doubt the sailor had claimed his right! The mother had jumped down last, with the youngest in her arms; they found her like this, tightly clasping the child, though she had not deserved it.

Every one was deeply shocked by this dreadful occurrence. They would willingly have given him a comforting and helping hand now; but it seemed that nothing could be done to help him in his trouble. He did not easily accept favors.

He busied himself round and about the dead, until the day of the funeral. No one saw him shed a single tear, not even when the earth was thrown on to the coffins, and people wondered at his composure; he had clung so closely to them. He was probably one of those [Pg 111] who were cursed with inability to cry, thought the women.

After the funeral, he asked a neighbor to look after his animals; he had to go to town, said he. With that he disappeared, and for two years he was not seen; it was understood that he had gone to sea. The farm was taken over by the creditors; there was no more than would pay what he owed, so that at all events, he did not lose anything by it.

One day he suddenly cropped up again, the same old Lars Peter, prepared, like Job, to start again from the beginning. He had saved a little money in the last two years, and bought a partly ruined hut, a short distance north of his former farm. With the hut went a bit of marsh, and a few acres of poor land, which had never been under the plow. He bought a few sheep and poultry, put up an outhouse of peat and reeds taken from the marsh—and settled himself in. He dug peat and sold it, and when there was a good catch of herrings, would go down to the nearest fishing hamlet with his wheelbarrow and buy a load, taking them from hut to hut. He preferred to barter them, taking in exchange old metal, rags and bones, etc. It was the trade of his race he took up again, and although he had never practised it before, he fell into it quite easily. One day he took home a big bony horse, which he had got cheap, because no-one else had any use for it; another day he brought Sörine home. Everything went well for him. [Pg 112]

He had met Sörine at some gathering down in one of the fishing huts, and they quickly made a match of it. She was tired of her place and he of being alone; so they threw in their lot together.

He was out the whole day long, and often at night too. When the fishing season was in full swing, he would leave home at one or two o'clock in the night, to be at the hamlet when the first boats came in. On these occasions Sörine stayed up to see that he did not oversleep himself. This irregular life came as naturally to her as to him, and she was a great help to him. So now once more he had a wife, and one who could work too. He possessed a horse, which had no equal in all the land—and a farm! It was not what could be called an estate, the house was built of hay, mud and sticks; people would point laughingly at it as they passed. Lars Peter alone was thankful for it.

He was a satisfied being—rather too much so, thought Sörine. She was of a different nature, always straining forward, and pushing him along so that her position might be bettered. She was an ambitious woman. When he was away, she managed everything; and the first summer helped him to build a proper outhouse, of old beams and bricks, which she made herself by drying clay in the sun. "Now we've a place for the animals just like other people," said she, when it was finished. But her voice showed that she was not satisfied.

At times Lars Peter Hansen would suggest that they ought to take Granny and Ditte to live with them. "They're so lonely and dull," said he, "and the Lord only knows where they get food from."

But this Sörine would not hear of. "We've enough to do without them," answered she sharply, "and Mother's not in want, I'm sure. She was always clever at helping herself. If they come here, I'll have the money paid for Ditte. 'Tis mine by right."

"They'll have eaten that up long ago," said Lars Peter.

But Sörine did not think so; it would not be like her father or her mother. She was convinced that her mother had hidden it somewhere or other. "If she would only sell the hut, and give the money to us," said she. "Then we could build a new house."

"Much wants more!" answered Lars Peter smilingly. In his opinion the house they lived in was quite good enough. But he was a man who thought anything good enough for him, and nothing too good for others. If he were allowed to rule they would soon end in the workhouse!

So Lars Peter avoided the question, and after Granny's visit, and having seen her and Sörine together, he understood they would be best apart. They did not come to his home again, but when he was buying up in their part of the country, he would call in at the hut on the Naze and take a cup of coffee with them. He would then bring a paper of coffee and some cakes with him, so as not to take them unawares, and had other small gifts too. These were days of rejoicing in the little hut. They longed for him, from one visit to another, and could talk of very little else. Whenever there were sounds of wheels, Ditte would fly to the window, and Granny would open wide her sightless eyes. Ditte gathered old iron from the shore as a surprise for her father; and when he drove home, she would go with him as far as the big hill, behind which the sun went down.

Lars Peter said nothing of these visits when he got home.

CHAPTER XIII
DITTE HAS A VISION

Before losing her sight Maren had taught Ditte to read, which came in very useful now. They never went to church; their clothes were too shabby, and the way too long. Maren was not particularly zealous in her attendance, a life-long experience had taught her to take what the parson said with a grain of salt. But on Sundays, when people streamed past on their way to church, they were both neatly dressed, Ditte with a clean pinafore and polished wooden shoes, and Granny with a stringed cap. Then Granny would be sitting in the armchair at the table, spectacles on her nose and the Bible in front of her, and Ditte standing beside her reading the scriptures for the day. In spite of her blindness, Maren insisted upon wearing her spectacles and having the holy book in front of her, according to custom, otherwise it was not right.

Ditte was nearly of school age, but Maren took no notice of it, and kept her home. She was afraid of the child not getting on with the other children—and could not imagine how she herself could spare her the whole day long. But at the end of six months they were found out, and Maren was threatened, that unless the child was sent to school, she would be taken from her altogether.

Having fitted out Ditte as well as she could, she sent her off with a heavy heart. The birth certificate she purposely omitted giving her; as it bore in the corner the fateful: born out of wedlock. Maren could not understand why an innocent child should be stamped as unclean; the child had enough to fight against without that. But Ditte returned with strict injunctions to bring the certificate the next day, and Maren was obliged to give it to her. It was hopeless to fight against injustice.

Maren knew well that magistrates were no institution of God's making—she had been born with this knowledge! They only oppressed her and her kind; and with this end in view used their own hard method, which was none of God's doing at all. He, on the contrary, was a friend of the poor; at least His only son, who was sitting on His right hand, whispered good things of the poor, and it was reasonable to expect that He would willingly help. But what did it help when the mighty ones would have it otherwise? It was the squire and his like, who had the power! It was towards them the parson turned when preaching, letting the poor folks look after themselves, and towards them the deacon glanced when singing. It was all very fine for them, with the magistrate carrying their trains, and opening their carriage door, with a peasant woman always ready to lay herself on all fours to prevent them wetting their feet as they stepped in. No "born out of wedlock" on *their* birth certificate; although one often might question their genuineness!

"But why does the Lord let it be like that?" asked Ditte wonderingly.

"He has to, or there'd be no churches built nor no fuss made of Him," answered Maren. "Grandfather Sören always said, that the Lord lived in the pockets of the mighty, and it seems as if he's right."

Ditte now went three times a week to school, which lay an hour's journey away, over the common. She went together with the other children from the hamlet, and got on well with them.

Children are thoughtless, but not wicked; this they learn from their elders. They had only called after her what they had heard at home; it was their parents' gossip and judgment they had repeated. They meant nothing by it; Ditte, who was observant in this respect, soon found out that they treated each other just in the same way. They would shout witch's brat, at her one minute and the next be quite friendly; they did not mean to look down upon her. This discovery took the sting from the abusive word—fortunately she was not sensitive. And the parents no longer, in superstition, warned their children against her; the time when Maren rode about as a witch was entirely forgotten. Now she was only a poor old woman left alone with an illegitimate child.

To the school came children just as far in the opposite direction, from the neighborhood of Sand. And it happened, that from them Maren and Ditte could make inquiries about Sörine and Lars Peter. They had not seen Ditte's father for some time, and he might easily have met with an accident, being on the roads night and day in all sorts of weather. It was fortunate that Ditte met children from those parts, who could assure her that all was well. Sörine had never been any good to her mother, although she was her own flesh and blood.

One day Ditte came home with the news that she was to go to her parents; one of the children had brought the message.

Old Maren began to shake, so that her knitting needles clinked.

"But they said they didn't want you!" she broke out, her face quivering.

"Yes, but now they want me—you see, I've to help with the little ones," answered Ditte proudly, gathering her possessions together and putting them on the table. Each time she put a thing down was like a stab to the old woman; then she would comfort and stroke Granny's shaking hand, which was nothing but blue veins. Maren sat dumbly knitting; her face was strangely set and dead-looking.

"Of course I'll come home and see you; but then you must take it sensibly. Can't you understand that I couldn't stay with you always? I'll bring some coffee when I come, and we'll have a lovely time. But you must promise not to cry, 'cause your eyes can't stand it."

Ditte stood talking in a would-be wise voice, as she tied up her things.

"And now I must go, or I shan't get there till night, and then mother will be angry." She said the word "mother" with a certain reverence as if it swept away all objections. "Good-by, dear, *dear* Granny!" She kissed the old woman's cheek and hurried off with her bundle.

As soon as the door had closed on her Maren began crying, and calling for her; in a monotonous undertone she poured out all her troubles, sorrow and want and longing for death. She had had so many heavy burdens and had barely finished with one when another appeared. Her hardships had cut deeply—most of them; and it did her good to live through them again and again. She went on for some time, and would have gone on still longer had she not suddenly felt two arms round her neck and a wet cheek against her own. It was the mischievous child, who had returned, saying that after all she was not leaving her.

Ditte had gone some distance, as far as the baker's, who wondered where she was going with the big parcel and stopped her. Her explanation, that she was going home to her parents, they refused to believe; her father had said nothing about it when the baker had met him at the market the day before, indeed he had sent his love to them. Ditte stood perplexed on hearing all this. A sudden doubt flashed through her mind; she turned round with a jerk—quick as she was in all her movements—and set off home for the hut on the Naze. How it had all happened she did not bother to think, such was her relief at being allowed to return to Granny.

Granny laughed and cried at the same time, asked questions and could make no sense of it.

"Aren't you going at all, then?" she broke out, thanking God, and hardly able to believe it.

"Of course I'm not going. Haven't I just told you, the baker said I wasn't to."

"Ay, the baker—what's he got to do with it? You'd got the message to go."

Ditte was busily poking her nose into Granny's cheek.

Maren lifted her head: "Hadn't you, child? Answer me!"

"I don't know, Granny," said Ditte, hiding her face against her.

Granny held her at an arm's length: "Then you've been playing tricks, you bad girl! Shame on you, to treat my poor old heart like this." Maren began sobbing again and could not stop; it had all come so unexpectedly. If only one could get to the bottom of it; but the child had declared that she had not told a lie. She was quite certain of having had the message, and was grieved at Granny not believing her. She never told an untruth when it came to the point, so after all must have had the message. On the other side the child herself said that she was not going—although the baker's counter orders carried no authority. They had simply stopped her, because her expedition seemed so extraordinary. It was beyond Maren—unless the child had imagined it all.

Ditte kept close to the old woman, constantly taking hold of her chin. "Now I know how sorry you'll be to lose me altogether," she said quietly.

Maren raised her face: "Do you think you'll soon be called away?"

Ditte shook her head so vehemently that Granny felt it.

Old Maren was deep in thought; she had known before that the child understood, that it was bound to come.

"Whatever it may be," said she after a few moments, "you've behaved like the great man I once read about, who rehearsed his own funeral—with four black horses, hearse and everything. All his servants had to pretend they were the procession, dressed in black, they had even to cry. He himself was watching from an attic window, and when he saw the servants laughing behind their handkerchiefs instead of crying, he took it so to heart that he died. 'Tis dangerous for folks to make fun of their own passing away—wherever they may be going!"[Pg 122]

"I wasn't making fun, Granny," Ditte assured her again.

From that day Maren went in daily dread of the child being claimed by her parents. "My ears are burning," she often said, "maybe 'tis your mother talking of us."

Sörine certainly did talk of them in those days. Ditte was now old enough to make herself useful; her mother would not mind having her home to look after the little ones. "She's nearly nine years old now and we'll have to take her sooner or later," she explained.

Lars Peter demurred; he thought it was a shame to take her from Granny. "Let's take them both then," said he.

Sörine refused to listen, and nagged for so long that she overcame his opposition.

"We've been expecting you," said Maren when at last he came to fetch the child. "We've known for long that you'd come on this errand."

"'Tisn't exactly with my good will. But in a way a mother has a right to her own child, and Sörine thinks she'd like to have her," answered Lars Peter. He wanted to smooth it down for both sides.

"I know you've done your best. Well, it can't be helped. And how's every one at home? There's another mouth to feed, I've heard."

"Ay, he's nearly six months old now." Lars Peter brightened up, as he always did when speaking of his children.[Pg 123]

They got into the cart. "We shan't forget you, either of us," said Lars Peter huskily, while trying to get the old nag off.

Then the old woman stumbled in, they saw her feeling her way over the doorstep with her foot and closing the door behind her.

"'Tis lonely to be old and blind," said Lars Peter, lashing his whip as usual.

Ditte heard nothing; she was sitting with her face in one big smile. She was driving towards something new; she had no thought for Granny just then.

[Pg 124]

CHAPTER XIV
AT HOME WITH MOTHER

The rag and bone man's property—the Crow's Nest—stood a little way back from the road, and the piece up towards the road he had planted with willows, partly to hide the half-ruined abode, and partly to have material for making baskets during the winter, when there was little business to be done. The willows grew quickly, and already made a beautiful place for playing hide and seek. He made the house look as well as it could, with tar and whitewash, but miserable looking it ever would be, leaking and falling to pieces; it was the dream of Sörine's life, that they should build a new dwelling-house up by the road, using this as outhouse. The surroundings were desolate and barren, and a long way from neighbors. The view towards the northwest was shut off by a big forest, and on the opposite side was the big lake, which reflected all kinds of weather. On the dark nights could be heard the quacking of the ducks in the rushes on its banks, and on rainy days, boats would glide like shadows over it, with a dark motionless figure in the bow, the eel-fisher. He held his eel-fork slantingly [Pg 125]in front of him, prodded the water sleepily now and then, and slid past. It was like a dream picture, and the whole lake was in keeping. When Ditte felt dull she would pretend that she ran down to the banks, hid herself in the rushes, and dream herself home to Granny. Or perhaps away to something still better; something unknown, which was in store for her somewhere or other. Ditte never doubted but that there was something special in reserve for her, so glorious that it was impossible even to imagine it.

In her play too, her thoughts would go seawards, and when her longing for Granny was too strong, she would run round the corner of the house and gaze over the wide expanse of water. Now she knew Granny's true worth.

She had not yet been down to the sea; as a matter of fact there was no time to play. At six o'clock in the morning, the youngest babe made himself heard, as regularly as clockwork, and she had to get up in a hurry, take him from his mother and dress him. Lars Peter would be at his morning jobs, if he had not already gone to the beach for fish. When he was at home, Sörine would get up with the children; but otherwise she would take a longer nap, letting Ditte do the heaviest part of the work for the day. Then her morning duties would be left undone, the two animals bellowed from the barn, the pigs squealed over their empty trough, and the hens flocked together at the hen-house door waiting to be let out. Ditte soon found out that her mother was more industrious when the father was at home than when he was out; then she would trail about the whole morning, her hair undone and an old skirt over her nightdress, and a pair of down-trodden shoes on her bare feet, while everything was allowed to slide.

Ditte thought this was a topsy-turvy world. She herself took her duties seriously, and had not yet been sufficiently with grown-up people to learn to shirk work. She washed and dressed the little ones. They were full of life, mischievous and unmanageable, and she had as much as she could do in looking after the three of them. As soon as they saw an opportunity, the two eldest would slip away from her, naked as they were; then she had to tie up the youngest while she went after them.

The days she went to school she felt as a relief. She had just time to get the children ready, and eat her porridge, before leaving. At the last moment her mother would find something or other, which had to be done, and she had to run the whole way.

She was often late, and was scolded for it, yet she loved going to school. She enjoyed sitting quietly in the warm schoolroom for hours at a stretch, resting body and mind; the lessons were easy, and the schoolmaster kind. He often let them run out for hours, when he would work in his field, and it constantly happened that the whole school helped him to gather in his corn or dig up his potatoes. This was a treat indeed. The children were like a flock of screaming birds, chattering, making fun and racing each other at the work. And when they returned, the schoolmaster's wife would give them coffee.

More than anything else Ditte loved the singing-class. She had never heard any one but Granny sing, and she only did it when she was spinning—to prevent the thread from being uneven, and the wheel from swinging, said she. It was always the same monotonous, gliding melody; Ditte thought she had composed it herself, because it was short or long according to her mood.

The schoolmaster always closed the school with a song, and the first time Ditte heard the full chorus, she burst into tears with emotion. She put her head on the desk, and howled. The schoolmaster stopped the singing and came down to her.

"She must have been frightened," said the girls nearest to her.

He comforted her, and she stopped crying. "Have you never heard singing before, child?" he asked wonderingly, when she had calmed down.

"Yes, the spinning-song," sniffed Ditte.

"Who sang it to you then?"

"Granny——" Ditte suddenly stopped and began to choke again, the thought of Granny was too much for her. "Granny used to sing it when she was spinning," she managed at last to say.

"That must be a good old Granny, you have. Do you love her?"

Ditte did not answer, but the face she turned to him was like sunshine after the storm.

"Will you sing us the spinning-song?"

Ditte looked from the one to the other; the whole class gazed breathlessly at her; she felt something was expected of her. She threw a hasty glance at the schoolmaster's face; then fixed her eyes on her desk and began singing in a delicate little voice, which vibrated with conflicting feelings; shyness, the solemnity of the occasion, and sorrow at the thought of Granny, who might now sit longing for her. Unconsciously she moved one foot up and down as she sang, as one who spins. One or two attempted to giggle, but one look from the master silenced them.

Now we spin for Ditte for stockings and for vest,Spin, spin away, Oh, and spin, spin away!Some shall be of silver and golden all the rest,Fal-de-ray, fal-de-ray, de-ray, ray, ray!

Ditte went awalking, so soft and round and red,Spin, spin away, Oh, and spin, spin away,Met a little princeling who doff'd his cap and said,Fal-de-ray, fal-de-ray, de-ray, ray, ray!

Oh, come with me, fair maiden, to father's castle fine,Spin, spin away, Oh, and spin, spin away!We'll play the livelong day and have a lovely time,Fal-de-ray, fal-de-ray, de-ray, ray, ray!

Alas, dear little prince, your question makes me grieve,Spin, spin away, Oh, and spin, spin away!There's Granny waits at home for me, and her I cannot leave,Fal-de-ray, fal-de-ray, de-ray, ray, ray!

She's blind, poor old dear, 'tis sad to see, alack!Spin, spin away, Oh, and spin, spin away!She's water in her legs and pains all down her back,Fal-de-ray, fal-de-ray, de-ray, ray, ray!

—If 'tis but for a child, she's cried her poor eyes out,Spin, spin away, Oh, and spin, spin away!Then she shall never want of that there is no doubt,Fal-de-ray, fal-de-ray, de-ray, ray, ray!

When toil and troubles tell and legs begin to ache,Spin, spin away, Oh, and spin, spin away!We'll dress her up in furs and drive her out in state,Fal-de-ray, fal-de-ray, de-ray, ray, ray!

Now Granny spins once more for sheet and bolster long,Spin, spin away, Oh, and spin away!For Ditte and the prince to lie and rest upon,Fal-de-ray, fal-de-ray, de-ray, ray, ray!

When she had finished her song, there was stillness for a few moments in the schoolroom.

"She thinks she's going to marry a prince," said one of the girls.

"And that she probably will!" answered the schoolmaster. "And then Granny can have all she wants," he added, stroking her hair.

Without knowing it, Ditte at one stroke had won both the master's and the other children's liking. She had sung to the whole class, quite alone, which none of the others dared do. The schoolmaster liked her for her fearlessness, and for some time shut his eyes whenever she was late. But one day it was too much for him, and he ordered her to stay in. Ditte began to cry.

"'Tis a shame," said the other girls, "she runs the whole way, and she's whipped if she's late home. Her mother stands every day at the corner of the house waiting for her—she's so strict."

"Then we'll have to get hold of your mother," said the schoolmaster. "This can't go on!" Ditte escaped staying in, but was given a note to take home.

This having no effect, the schoolmaster went with her home to speak to her mother. But Sörine refused to take any responsibility. If the child arrived late at school, it was simply because she loitered on the way. Ditte listened to her in amazement; she could not make out how her mother could look so undisturbed when telling such untruths.

Ditte, to help herself, now began acting a lie too. Each morning she seized the opportunity of putting the little Swiss clock a quarter of an hour forward. It worked quite well in the morning, so that she was in time for school; but she would be late in arriving home.

"You're taking a quarter of an hour longer on the road now," scolded her mother.

"We got out late today," lied Ditte, trying to copy her mother's unconcerned face, as she had seen it when *she* lied. Her heart was in her mouth, but all went well—wonderful to relate! How much wiser she was now! During the day she quietly put the clock back again.

One day, in the dusk, as she stood on the chair putting the clock back, her mother came behind her. Ditte threw herself down from the chair, quickly picking up little Povl from the floor, where he was crawling; in her fear, she tried to hide behind the little one. But her mother tore him from her, and began thrashing her.

Ditte had had a rap now and then, when she was naughty, but this was the first time she had been really whipped. She was like an animal, kicking and biting, and shrieking, so that it was all her mother could do to manage her. The three little ones' howls equaled hers.

When Sörine thought she had had enough, she dragged her to the woodshed and locked her in. "Lie there and howl, maybe it'll teach you not to try those tricks again!" she shouted, and went in. She was so out of breath that she had to sit down; that wicked child had almost got the better of her.

Ditte, quite beyond herself, went on screaming and kicking for some time. Her cries gradually quietened down to a despairing wail of: "Granny, Granny!" It was quite dark in the woodshed, and whenever she called for Granny, she heard a comforting rustling sound from the darkness at the back of the shed. She gazed confidently towards it, and saw two green fire-balls shining in the darkness, which came and went by turns. Ditte was not afraid of the dark. "Puss, puss," she whispered. The fire-balls disappeared, and the next moment she felt something soft touching her. And now she broke down again, this caress was too much for her, and she pitied herself intensely. Puss, little puss! There was after all one who cared for her! Now she would go home to Granny.

She got up, dazed and bruised, and felt her way to the shutter. When Sörine thought that she had been locked in long enough, and came to release her, she had vanished.

Ditte ran into the darkness, sobbing; it was cold and windy, and the rain was beating on her face. She wore no knickers under her dress—these her mother had taken for the little ones, together with the thick woollen vest Granny had knitted for her—the wet edge of her skirt cut her bare legs, which were swollen from the lash of the cane. But the silent rain did her good. Suddenly something flew up from beside her; she heard the sound of rushes standing rustling in the water—and knew that she had got away from the road. She collapsed, and crawled into the undergrowth, and lay shivering in a heap, like a sick puppy.

There she lay groaning without really having any more pain; the cold had numbed her limbs and deadened the smart. It was distress of soul which made her wince now and then; it was wrung by the emptiness and meaninglessness of her existence. She needed soothing hands, a mother first of all, who would fondle her—but she got only hard words and blows from that quarter. Yet it was expected that she should give what she herself missed most of all—a mother's long-suffering patience and tender care to the three tiresome little ones, who were scarcely more helpless than she was.

Her black despair little by little gave place to numbness. Hate and anger, feebleness and want, had all fought in her mind and worn her out. The cold did the rest, and she fell into a doze.

A peculiar, grinding, creaking and jolting noise came from the road. Only one cart in all the world could produce that sound. Ditte opened her eyes, and a feeling of joy went through her—her father! She tried to call, but no sound came, and each time she tried to rise her legs gave way under her. She crawled up with difficulty over the edge of the ditch, out into the middle of the road, and there collapsed.

As the nag neared that spot, it stopped, threw up its head, snorted, and refused to go on. Lars Peter jumped down and ran to the horse's head to see what was wrong; there he found Ditte, stiff with cold and senseless.

Under his warm driving cape she came to herself again, and life returned to the cold limbs. Lars Peter thawed them one by one in his huge fists. Ditte lay perfectly quiet in his arms; she could hear the beat of [Pg 134] his great heart underneath his clothes, throb, throb! Each beat was like the soft nosing of some animal, and his deep voice sounded to her like an organ. His big hands, which took hold of so much that was hard and ugly, were the warmest she had ever known. Just like Granny's cheek—the softest thing in all the world—were they.

"Now we must get out and run a little," said the father suddenly. Ditte was unwilling to move, she was so warm and comfortable. There was no help for it however. "We must get the blood to run again," said he, lifting her out of the cart. Then they ran for some time by the side of the nag, which threw out its big hoofs in a jog-trot, so as not to be outdone.

"Shall we soon be home?" asked Ditte, when she was in the cart again, well wrapped up.

"Oh-h, there's a bit left—you've run seven miles, child! Now tell me what's the meaning of your running about like this."

Then Ditte told him about the school, the injustice she had had to bear, the whipping and everything. In between there were growls from Lars Peter, as he stamped his feet on the bottom of the cart—he could hardly tolerate to listen to this tale. "But you won't tell Sörine, will you?" she added with fear. "Mother, I mean," she hastily corrected herself.

"You needn't be afraid," was all he said.

He was silent for the rest of the journey, and was very slow in unharnessing; Ditte kept beside him. [Pg 135] Sörine came out with a lantern and spoke to him, but he did not answer. She cast a look of fear at him and the child, hung up the lantern, and hurried in.

Soon after he came in, holding Ditte by the hand, her little hand shaking in his. His face was gray; in his right hand was a thick stick. Sörine fled from his glance; right under the clock; pressing herself into the corner, gazing at them with perplexity.

"Ay, you may well gaze at us," said he, coming forward—"'tis a child accusing you. What's to be done about it?" He had seated himself under the lamp, and lifting Ditte's frock, he carefully pressed his palm against the blue swollen weals, which smarted with the slightest touch. "It still hurts—you're good at thrashing! let's see if you're equally good at healing. Come and kiss the child, where you've struck her, a kiss for each stroke!"

He sat waiting. "Well——"

Sörine's face was full of disgust.

"Oh, you think your mouth's too good to kiss what your hand's struck." He reached out for the stick.

Sörine had sunk down on the ground, she put out her hands beseechingly. But he looked inexorably at her, not at all like himself. "Well——"

Sörine lingered a few moments longer, then on her knees went and kissed the child's bruised limbs. Ditte threw her arms violently round her mother's neck. "Mother," said she. [Pg 136]

But Sörine got up and went out to get the supper. She never looked at them the whole evening.

Lars Peter was his old self the next morning. He woke Sörine with a kiss as usual, humming as he dressed. Sörine still looked at him with malice, but he pretended not to notice it. It was quite dark, and as he sat eating his breakfast, with the lantern in front of him on the table, he kept looking at the three little ones, in bed. They were all in a heap—like young birds. "When Povl has to join them, we'll have to put two at each end," he said thoughtfully. "Better still, if we could afford another bed."

There was no answer from Sörine.

When ready to leave, he bent over Ditte, who lay like a little mother with the children in her arms. "That's a good little girl, you've given us," said he, straightening himself.

"She tells lies," answered Sörine from beside the fireplace.

"Then it's because she's had to. My family's not thought much of, Sörine—and maybe they don't deserve it either. But never a hand was laid on us children, I'll tell you. I remember plainly my father's death-bed, how he looked at his hands, and said: 'These have dealt with much, but never has the rag and bone man's hands been turned against the helpless!' I'd like to say that when my time comes, and I'd advise you to think of it too."

Then he drove away. Sörine put the lantern in the [Pg 137] window, to act as a guide to him, and crept back to bed, but could not sleep. For the first time Lars Peter had given her something to think of. She had found that in him which she had never expected, something strange which warned her to be careful. A decent soul, she had always taken him for—just as the others. And how awful he could be in his rage—it made her flesh creep, when thinking of it. She certainly would be careful not to come up against him again.

CHAPTER XV
RAIN AND SUNSHINE

On the days when Ditte did not go to school, there were thousands of things for her to do. She had to look after the little ones, care for the sheep and hens too, and gather nettles in a sack for the pigs. At times Lars Peter came home early, having been unlucky in selling his fish. Then she would sit up with her parents until one or two o'clock in the night, cleaning the fish, to prevent it spoiling. Sörine was one of those people who fuss about without doing much. She could not bear the child resting for a moment, and drove her from one task to another. Often when Ditte went to bed, she was so tired that she could not sleep. Sörine had the miserable habit of making the day unhappy for the children. She was rough with them should they get in her way; and always left children's tears like streams of water behind her. When Ditte went to gather sticks, or pick berries, she always dragged the little ones with her, so as not to leave them to their mother's tender mercy. There were days when Sörine was not quite so bad—she was never quite happy and kind, but at other times she was almost mad with anger, and the only thing to do was to keep out of her way. Then they would all hide, and only appear when their father came home.

Sörine was careful not to strike Ditte, and sent her off to school in good time—she had no wish to see Lars Peter again as he was that evening. But she had no love for the child, she wanted to get on in life; it was her ambition to build a new dwelling-house, get more land and animals—and be on the same footing with the other women on the small farms round about. The child was a blot on her. Whenever she looked at Ditte, she would think: Because of that brat, all the other women look down on me!

The child certainly was a good worker, even Sörine grudgingly admitted it to Lars Peter. It was Ditte who made butter, first in a bottle, which had to be shaken, often by the hour, before the butter would come—and now in the new churn. Sörine herself could not stand the hard work of churning. Ditte gathered berries and sold them in the market, ran errands, fetched water and sticks, and looked after the sheep, carrying fat little Povl wherever she went. He cried if she left him behind, and she was quite crooked with carrying him.

Autumn was the worst time for the children. It was the herring season, and their father would stay down at the fishing hamlet—often for a month at a time—helping with the catch. Sörine was then difficult to get on with; the only thing which kept her within bounds was Ditte's threat of running away. There were not many men left in the neighborhood in the autumn, and Sörine went in daily dread of tramps. Should they knock at the door in the evening, she would let Ditte answer it.

Ditte was not afraid. This and her cleverness gave her moral power over her mother; she had no fear of answering her back now. She was quicker with her fingers than her mother, both in making baskets and brooms, and did better work too.

What money they made in this way, Sörine had permission to keep for herself. She never spent a penny of it, but put it by, shilling by shilling, towards building the new house. They must try hard to make enough, so that Lars Peter could work at home instead of hawking his goods on the road. As long as the people had the right to call him rag and bone man, it was natural they should show no respect. Land they must have, and for this, money was necessary.

Money! money! That word was always in Sörine's mind and humming in her ears. She scraped together shilling after shilling, and yet the end was far from being in sight, unless something unexpected happened. And what could happen to shorten the wearisome way to her goal, only one thing—that her mother should die. She had really lived long enough and been a burden to others. Sörine thought it was quite time she departed, but no such luck.

It happened that Lars Peter returned one day in the middle of the afternoon. The shabby turn-out could be seen from afar. The cart rocked with every turn of the wheels, creaking and groaning as it was dragged along. It was as if all the parts of the cart spoke and sang at once, and when the children heard the well-known noise along the road, they would rush out, full of excitement. The old nag, which grew more and more like a wandering bag of bones, snorted and puffed, and rumbled, as if all the winds from the four corners of the earth were locked in its belly. And Lars Peter's deep hum joined the happy chorus.

When the horse saw the little ones, it whinnied; Lars Peter raised himself from his stooping position and stopped singing, and the cart came to a standstill. He lifted them up in the air, all three or four together in a bunch, held them up to the sky for a moment, and put them into the cart as carefully as if they were made of glass. The one who had seen him first was allowed to hold the reins.

When Lars Peter came home and found Sörine in a temper and the house upside down, he was not disturbed at all, but soon cheered them all up. He always brought something home with him, peppermints for the children, a new shawl for mother—and perhaps love from Granny to Ditte, whispering it to her so that Sörine could not hear. His good humor was infectious; the children forgot their grievances, and even Sörine had to laugh whether she wanted to or not. And if the children were fond of him, so too were the animals. They would welcome him with their different cries and run to meet him; he could let the pig out and make it follow him in the funniest gallop round the field.

However late he was in returning, and however tired, he never went to bed without having first been the round to see that the animals wanted for nothing. Sörine easily forgot them and they were often hungry. Then the hens flew down from their perch on hearing his step, the pigs came out and grunted over their trough, and a soft back rubbed itself up against his legs—the cat.

Lars Peter brought joy with him home, and a happier man than he could hardly be found for miles. He loved his wife for what she was, more sharp than really clever. He admired her for her firmness, and thought her an exceedingly capable woman, and was truly thankful for the children she gave him, for those he was father to—and for Ditte. Perhaps if anything he cared most for her.

Such was Lars Peter's nature that he began where others ended. All his troubles had softened instead of hardening him; his mind involuntarily turned to what was neglected, perhaps it was because of this that people thought nothing throve for him.

His ground was sour and sandy, none but he would think of plowing it. No-one grudged him his wife, and most of the animals he had saved from being killed, on his trips round the farms. He could afford to be happy with his possessions, thinking they were better than what others had. He was jealous of no-one, and no exchange would tempt him.

On Sundays the horse had to rest, and it would not do either to go on his rounds that day. Therefore Lars Peter would creep up to the hayloft to have a sleep. He would sleep on until late in the afternoon, having had very little during the week, and Ditte had her work cut out to keep the little ones from him; they made as much noise as they possibly could, hoping to waken him so that he might play with them, but Ditte watched carefully, that he had his sleep in peace.

Twice a year they all drove to the market at Hillerød, on top of the loaded cart. The children were put into the baskets which were stacked in the back of the cart, the brooms hung over the sides, under the seat were baskets of butter and eggs, and in front—under Lars' and Sörine's feet, were a couple of sheep tied up. These were the great events of the year, from which everything was dated.

CHAPTER XVI
POOR GRANNY

On rare occasions Ditte was permitted to go and stay with Granny for a few days. It was the father who managed this, and he arranged his round so that he could either bring or fetch her home.

Granny was always in bed when she arrived—she never got up now. "Why should I trudge on, when you're not here? If I stay in bed, then sometimes kind folks remember me and bring me a little food and clean up for me. Oh, dear! 'twould be much better to die; nobody wants me," she complained. But she got up all the same, and put on water for the coffee; Ditte cleaned the room, which was in a deplorable condition, and they enjoyed themselves together.

When the time was up and Ditte had to go, the old woman cried. Ditte stood outside listening to her wailings; she held on to the doorpost trying to pull herself together. She *had* to go home, and began running with closed eyes the first part of the way, until she could hear Granny's cries no longer, then—— But she got more and more sick at heart, and knew no more, until she found herself with her arms round Granny's neck. "I'm allowed to stay until tomorrow," said she.

"You're not playing tricks, child?" said the old woman anxiously. "For then Sörine'll be angry. Ay, ay," said she shortly afterwards, "stay until tomorrow then. The Lord'll make it all right for you—for the sake of your good heart. We don't have much chance of seeing each other, we two."

The next day it was no better; Maren had not the strength to send the child away. There was so much to tell her, and what was one day after the accumulation of months of sorrow and longing? And Ditte listened seriously to all her woes; she understood now what sorrow and longing meant. "You've quite changed," said Granny. "I notice it from the way you listen to me. If only the time would pass quickly so that you might go out to service."

And one day it was all over; Lars Peter had come to fetch her. "You'd better come home now," said he, wrapping her up, "the little ones are crying for you."

"Ay, you're not to be feared," said old Maren. "But it seems like Sörine might be kinder to her."

"I think it's better now—and the little ones are fond of her. She's quite a little mother to them."

Yes, there were the children! Ditte's heart warmed at the thought of them. They had gained her affection in their own peculiar way; by adding burdens to her little life they had wound themselves round her heart.

"How's Povl?" asked she, when they had driven over the big hill, and Granny's hut was out of sight.

"Well, you know, he's always crying when you're not at home," said the father quietly.

Ditte knew this. He was cutting his teeth just now, and needed nursing, his cheeks were red with fever, and his mouth hot and swollen. He would hang on to his mother's skirt, only to be brushed impatiently aside, and would fall and hurt himself. Who then was there to take him on their knee and comfort him? It was like an accusation to Ditte's big heart; she was sorry she had deserted him, and longed to have him in her arms again. It hurt her back to carry him—yes, and the schoolmaster scolded her for stooping. "It's your own fault," the mother would say; "stop dragging that big child about! He can walk if he likes, he can." But when he was in pain and cried, Ditte knew all too well from her own experience the child's need of being held against a beating heart. She still had that longing herself, though a mother's care had never been offered her.

Sörine was cross when Lars Peter returned with Ditte, and ignored her for several days. But at last curiosity got the upper hand. "How's the old woman—is she worse?" asked she.

Ditte, who thought her mother asked out of sympathy, gave full details of the miserable condition that Granny was in. "She's always in bed, and only gets food when any one takes it to her." [Pg 147]

"Then she can't last much longer," thought the mother.

At this Ditte began to cry. Then her mother scolded her:

"Stupid girl, there's nothing to cry for. Old folks can't live on forever, being a burden to others. And when Granny dies we'll get a new dwelling-house."

"No, 'cause Granny says, what comes from the house is to be divided equally. And the rest——" Ditte broke off suddenly.

"What rest?" Sörine bent forward with distended nostrils.

But Ditte closed her lips firmly. Granny had strictly forbidden her to mention the subject—and here she had almost let it out.

"Stupid girl! don't you suppose I know you're thinking of the two hundred crowns that was paid for you? What's to be done with it?"

Ditte looked with suspicion at her mother. "I'm to have it," she whispered.

"Then the old woman should let us keep it for you, instead of hanging on to it herself," said Sörine.

Ditte was terrified. That was exactly what Granny was afraid of, that Sörine should get hold of it. "Granny has hidden it safely," said she.

"Oh, has she, and where?—in the eiderdown of course!"

"No!" Ditte assured her, shaking her head vehemently. [Pg 148] But any one could see that was where it was hidden.

"Oh, that's lucky, for that eiderdown I'm going to fetch some day. That you can tell Granny, with my love, next time you see her. Each of my sisters when they married was given an eiderdown, and I claim mine too."

"Granny only has one eiderdown!" Ditte protested—perhaps for the twentieth time.

"Then she'll just have to take one of her many under-quilts. She lies propped up nearly to the ceiling, with all those bedclothes."

Yes, Granny's bed was soft, Ditte knew that better than any one else. Granny's bedclothes were heavy, and yet warmer than anything else in the whole world, and there was a straw mat against the wall. It had been so cosy and comfortable sleeping with Granny.

Ditte was small for her age, all the hardships she had endured had stunted her growth. But her mind was above the average; she was thoughtful by nature, and her life had taught her not to shirk, but to take up her burden. She had none of the carelessness of childhood, but was full of forethought and troubles. She *had* to worry—for her little sisters and brothers the few days she was with Granny, and for Granny all the time she was not with her.

As a punishment, for having prolonged her visit to Granny without permission, Sörine for a long time refused to let her go again. Then Ditte went about [Pg 149] thinking of the old woman, worrying herself into a morbid self-reproach; most of all at night, when she could not sleep for cold, would her sorrows overwhelm her, and she would bury her head in the eiderdown, so that her mother should not hear her sobs.

She would remember all the sweet ways of the old woman, and bitterly repent the tricks and mischief she had played upon her. This was her punishment; she had repaid Granny badly for all her care, and now she was alone and forsaken. She had never been really good to the old woman; she would willingly be so now—but it was too late! There were hundreds of ways of making Granny happy, and Ditte knew them all, but she had been a horrid, lazy girl. If she could only go back now, she certainly would see that Granny always had a lump of sugar for her second cup of coffee—instead of stealing it herself. And she would remember every evening to heat the stone, and put it at the foot of the bed, so Granny's feet should not be cold. "You've forgotten the stone again," said Granny almost every night, "my feet are like ice. And what are yours like? Why, they're quite cold, child." Then Granny would rub the child's feet until they were warm; but nothing was done to her own—it was all so hopeless to think of it now.

She thought, if she only promised to be better in the future, something must happen to take her back to Granny again. But nothing did happen! And one day she could stand it no longer, and set off running [Pg 150] over the fields. Sörine wanted her brought home at once; but Lars Peter took it more calmly.

"Just wait a few days," said he, "'tis a long time since she's seen the old woman." And he arranged his round so that Ditte could spend a few days with her grandmother.

"Bring back the eiderdown with you," said Sörine. "It's cold now, and it'll be useful for the children."

"We'll see about it," answered Lars Peter. When she got a thing into her head, she would nag on and on about it, so that she would have driven most people mad. But Lars Peter did not belong to the family of Man; all her haggling had no effect on his good-natured stubbornness.

[Pg 151]

CHAPTER XVII
WHEN THE CAT'S AWAY

Ditte was awakened by the sound of iron being struck, and opened her eyes. The smoking lamp stood on the table, and in front of the fire was her mother hammering a ring off the kettle with a poker. She was not yet dressed; the flames from the fire flickered over her untidy red hair and naked throat. Ditte hastily closed her eyes again, so that her mother should not discover that she was awake. The room was cold, and through the window-panes could be seen the darkness of the night.

Then her father came tramping in with the lantern, which he put out and hung it up behind the door. He was already dressed, and had been out doing his morning jobs. There was a smell of coffee in the room. "Ah!" said he, seating himself by the table. Ditte peeped out at him; when he was there, there was no fear of being turned out of bed.

"Oh, there you are, little wagtail," said he. "Go to sleep again, it's only five o'clock—but maybe you're thinking of a cup of coffee in bed?"

Ditte glanced at her mother, who stood with her back to her. Then she nodded her head eagerly. [Pg 152]

Lars Peter drank half of his coffee, put some more sugar in the cup, and handed it to the child.

Sörine was dressing by the fireplace. "Now keep quiet," said she, "while I tell you what to do. There's flour and milk for you to make pancakes for dinner; but don't dare to put an egg in."

"Good Lord, what's an egg or two," Lars Peter tried to say.

"You leave the housekeeping to me," answered Sörine, "and you'd better get up at once before we leave, and begin work."

"What's the good of that?" said Lars Peter again. "Leave the children in bed till it's daylight. I've fed the animals, and it's no good wasting oil."

This last appealed to Sörine. "Very well, then, but be careful with the fire—and don't use too much sugar."

Then they drove away. Lars Peter was going to the shore to fetch fish as usual, but would first drive Sörine into town, where she would dispose of the month's collection of butter and eggs, and buy in what could not be got from the grocer in the hamlet. Ditte listened to the cart until she dropped asleep again.

When it was daylight, she got up and lit the fire again. The others wanted to get up too, but by promising them coffee instead of their usual porridge and milk she kept them in bed until she had tidied up the room. They got permission to crawl over to their parents' bed, and thoroughly enjoyed themselves there, while Ditte put wet sand on the floor, and swept it. Kristian, [Pg 153] who was now five years old, told stories in a deep voice of a dreadful cat that went about the fields eating up all the moo-cows; the two little ones lay across him, their eyes fixed on his lips, and breathless with excitement. They could see it quite plainly—the pussy-cat, the moo-cow and everything—and little Povl, out of sheer eagerness to hurry up the events, put his fat little hand right down Kristian's throat. Ditte went about her duties smiling in her old-fashioned way at their childish talk. She looked very mysterious as she gave them their coffee; and when the time came for them to be dressed, the surprise came out. "Oh, we're going to have our best clothes on—hip, hip, hooray!" shouted Kristian, beginning to jump up and down on the bed. Ditte smacked him, he was spoiling the bedclothes!

"If you'll be really good and not tell any one, I'll take you out for a drive," said Ditte, dressing them in their best clothes. These were of many colors, their mother having made them from odd scraps of material, taken from the rag and bone man's cart.

"Oh—to the market?" shouted Kristian, beginning to jump again.

"No, to the forest," said the little sister, stroking Ditte's cheeks beseechingly with her dirty little hands, which were blue with cold. She had seen it from afar, and longed to go there.

"Yes, to the forest. But you must be good; it's a long way." [Pg 154]

"May we tell pussy?" Söster looked at Ditte with her big expressive eyes.

"Yes, and papa," Kristian joined in with.

"Yes, but not any one else," Ditte impressed upon them. "Now remember that!"

The two little ones were put into the wheelbarrow, and Kristian held on to the side, and thus they set off. There was snow everywhere, the bushes were weighted down with it, and on the cart track the ice cracked under the wheel. It was all so jolly, the black crows, the magpies which screamed at them from the thorn-bushes, and the rime which suddenly dropped from the trees, right on to their heads.

It was three miles to the forest, but Ditte was used to much longer distances, and counted this as nothing. Kristian and Söster took turns in walking, Povl wanted to walk in the snow too, but was told to stay where he was and be good.

All went well until they had got halfway. Then the little ones began to tire of it, asking impatiently for the forest. They were cold, and Ditte had to stop every other moment to rub their fingers. The sun had melted the snow, making it dirty and heavy under foot, and she herself was getting tired. She tried to cheer them up, and trailed on a little further; but outside the bailiff's farm they all came to a hopeless standstill. A big fierce dog thought their hesitation suspicious and barred their way.

Per Nielsen came out on the porch to see why the dog barked so furiously; he at once saw what had happened, and took the children indoors. It was dinner-time, the wife was in the kitchen frying bacon and apples together. It smelt delicious. She thawed their frozen fingers in cold water; when they were all right again, all three stood round the fire. Ditte tried to get them away, but they were hungry.

"You shall have some too," said the bailiff's wife, "but sit down on that bench and be good; you're in my way." They were each given a piece of cake, and then seated at the scoured table. They had never been out before, their eyes went greedily from one thing to another, as they were eating; on the walls hung copperware, which shone like the sun, and on the fire was a big bright copper kettle with a cover to the spout. It was like a huge hen sitting on eggs.

When they had finished their meal, Per Nielsen took them out and showed them the little pigs, lying like rolls of sausages round the mother. Then they went into the house again, and the wife gave them apples and cakes, but the best of all came last, when Per Nielsen harnessed the beautiful spring-cart to drive them home. The wheelbarrow was put in the back, so that too got a drive. The little ones laughed so much that it caught in their throats.

"Stupid children, coming out like that all alone," said the bailiff's wife, as she stood wrapping them up. "Fortunately 'twas more good luck than management that you came here." And they all agreed that the return to the Crow's Nest was much grander than the set-off.

The trip had been glorious, but now there was work to be done. The mother had not taken picnics into account, and had put a large bundle of rags out on the threshing-floor to be sorted, all the wool to be separated from the cotton. Kristian and Söster could give a helping hand if they liked; but they would not be serious today. They were excited by the trip, and threw the rags at each other's heads. "Now, you mustn't fight," repeated Ditte every minute, but it did no good.

When darkness fell, they had only half finished. Ditte fetched the little lamp, in which they used half oil and half petroleum, and went on working; she cried despairingly when she found that they could not finish by the time her parents would return. At the sight of her tears the children became serious, and for a while the work went on briskly. But soon they were on the floor again chasing each other; and by accident Kristian kicked the lamp, which fell down and broke. This put an end to their wildness; the darkness fixed them to the spot; they dared not move. "Ditte take me," came wailingly from each corner.

Ditte opened the trap-door. "Find your own way out!" said she harshly, fumbling about for Povl, who was sleeping on a bundle of rags; she was angry. "Now you shall go to bed for punishment," said she.

Kristian was sobbing all the time. "Don't let mother whip me, don't let her!" he said over and over again. He put his arms round Ditte's neck as if seeking refuge there. And this put an end to her anger.

When she had lit the lantern she helped them to undress. "Now if you'll be good and go straight to sleep, then Ditte will run to the store and buy a lamp." She dared not leave the children with the light burning, and put it out before she left. As a rule they were afraid of being left alone in the dark; but under the present conditions it was no good making a fuss.

Ditte had a sixpence! Granny had given it to her once in their well-to-do-days, and she had kept it faithfully through all temptations up to now. It was to have bought her so many beautiful things, and now it had to go—to save little Kristian from a whipping. Slowly she kneeled down in front of the hole at the foot of the wall where it was hidden, and took the stone away; it really hurt her to do it. Then she got up and ran off to the store as quickly as she could—before she could repent.

On her return the little ones were asleep. She lit the lantern and began to peel off the withered leaves from the birches which were to be made into brooms; she was tired after the long eventful day, but could not idle. The strong fragrance from the birches was penetrating, and she fell asleep over her work. Thus her parents found her.

Sörine's sharp eyes soon saw that everything was not as it should be. "Why've you got the lantern lit?" asked she, as she unbuttoned her coat.

Ditte had to own up, "but I've bought another!" she hastened to add.

"Oh—and where is it?" said the mother, looking round the room.

The next moment Sörine stood in the doorway. "Who gave you permission to get things on credit?" asked she.

"I bought it with my own money," Ditte whispered.

Own money—then began a cross-examination, which looked as if it would never end. Lars Peter had to interfere.

There was no fire in the room, so they went early to bed; Ditte had forgotten the fire. "She's had enough to do," said Lars Peter excusingly. And Sörine had nothing to say—she had no objection when it meant saving.

There was a hard frost. Ditte was cold and could not sleep, she lay gazing at her breath, which showed white, and listening to the crackling of the frost on the walls. Outside it was moonlight, and the beams shone coldly over the floor and the chair with the children's clothes. If she lifted her head, she could peep out through the cracks in the wall, catching glimpses of the white landscape; the cold blew in her face.

The room got colder and colder. She had to lie with one arm outstretched, holding the eiderdown over the others, and the cold nipped her shoulders. Söster began to be restless, she was the most thin-blooded of the three and felt the cold. It was an eiderdown which was little else than a thick cover, the feathers having disappeared, and those they got when killing poultry were too good to be used—the mother wanted them turned into money.

Now Povl began to whimper. Ditte took the children's clothes from the chair and spread them over the bed. From their parents' bed came the mother's voice. "You're to be quiet," said she. The father got up, fetched his driving-cape, and spread it over them; it was heavy with dust and dirt, but it warmed them!

"'Tis dreadful the way the wind blows through these walls," said he when again in bed; "the air's like ice in the room! I must try to get some planks to patch up the walls."

"You'd better be thinking of building; this rotten old case isn't worth patching up."

Lars Peter laughed: "Ay, that's all very well; but where's the money to come from?"

"We've got a little. And then the old woman'll die soon—I can feel it in my bones."

Ditte's heart began to jump—was Granny going to die? Her mother had said it so decidedly. She listened breathlessly to the conversation.

"And what of that?" she heard her father say, "that won't alter matters."

"I believe the old woman's got more than we think," answered Sörine in a low voice. "Are you asleep, Ditte?" she called out, raising herself on her elbow listening. Ditte lay perfectly still.

"Do you know?" Sörine began again, "I'm sure the old woman has sewn the money up in the quilt. That's why she won't part with it."

Lars Peter yawned loudly; "What money?" It could be gathered from the sound of his voice, that he wanted to sleep now.

"The two hundred crowns, of course."

"What's that to do with us?"

"Isn't she my mother? But the money'll go to the child, and aren't we the proper ones to look after it for her. If the old woman dies and there's an auction—there'll be good bids for it, and whoever buys the quilt'll get the two hundred crowns as well. You'd better go over and have a talk with her, and make her leave everything to us."

"Why not you?" said Lars Peter, and turned round towards the wall.

Then everything was quiet. Ditte lay in a heap, with hands pressed against mouth, and her little heart throbbing with fear; she almost screamed with anxiety. Perhaps Granny would die in the night! It was some time since she had visited her, and she had an overpowering longing for Granny.

She crept out of bed and put on her shoes.

Her mother raised herself; "Where're you going?"

"Just going outside," answered Ditte faintly.

"Put a skirt on, it's very cold," said Lars Peter—"we might just as well have kept the new piece of furniture in here," he growled shortly afterwards.

What a long time the child took—Lars Peter got up and peeped out. He caught sight of her far down the moonlit road. Hastily throwing on some clothes, he rushed after her. He could see her ahead, tearing off for all she was worth. He ran and shouted, ran and shouted, his heavy wooden shoes echoing on the road. But the distance between them only increased; at last she disappeared altogether from view. He stood a little longer shouting; his voice resounded in the stillness of the night; and then turned round and went home.

Ditte tore on through the moonlit country. The road was as hard as stone, and the ice cut through her cloth shoes; from bog and ditch came the sound, crack, crack, crack; and the sea boomed on the shore. But Ditte did not feel the cold, her heart was beating wildly. Granny's dying, Granny's dying! went continuously through her mind.

By midnight she had reached the end of her journey, she was almost dropping with fatigue. She stopped at the corner of the house to gain breath; from inside could be heard Granny's hacking cough. "I'm coming, Granny!" she cried, tapping on the window, sobbing with joy.

"How cold you are, child!" said the old woman, when they were both under the eiderdown. "Your feet are like lumps of ice—warm them on me." Ditte nestled in to her, and lay there quietly.

"Granny! mother knows you've hidden the money in the eiderdown," she said suddenly.

"I guessed that, my child. Feel!" The old woman guided Ditte's hand to her breast, where a little packet was hidden. "Here 'tis, Maren can take care of what's trusted to her. Ay, ay, 'tissad to be like us two, no-one to care for us, and always in the way—to our own folks most of all. They can't make much use of you yet, and they're finished with me—I'm worn out. That's how it is."

Ditte listened to the old woman's talk. It hummed in her ears and gave her a feeling of security. She was now comfortable and warm, and soon fell asleep.

But old Maren for some time continued pouring out her grievances against existence.

CHAPTER XVIII
THE RAVEN FLIES BY NIGHT

It was a hard winter. All through December the snow swept the fields, drifting into the willows in front of the Crow's Nest, the only place in the neighborhood where a little shelter was to be found.

The lake was entirely frozen; one could walk across it from shore to shore. When there was a moon, the rag and bone man would go down and with his wooden shoe break the ice round the seagulls and wild ducks, which were frozen in the lake, and then carry them home under his snow-covered cape. He would put them on the peat beside the fireplace, where for days they stood on one leg gazing sickly into the embers, until Sörine at last took them into the kitchen and wrung their necks.

In spite of there being a fire day and night, the cold was felt intensely in the Crow's Nest; it was impossible to heat the room. Sörine, with the bread-knife, stuffed old rags into the cracks in the wall; but one day when doing this, a big piece of the wall collapsed. She filled up the hole with the eiderdown, and when Lars Peter came home at night, he patched it up and nailed planks across to keep it in place. The roof was not up too much either; the rats and house-martens had worked havoc in it, so that it was like a sieve, and the snow drifted into the loft. It was all bad.

Every day Sörine tried to rouse Lars Peter to do something.

But what could he do? "I can't work harder than I do, and steal I won't," said he.

"What do the others do, who live in a pretty and comfortable house?"

Yes, how did other people manage? Lars Peter could not imagine. He had never envied any one, nor drawn comparisons, so had never faced the question before.

"You toil and toil, but never get any further, that I can see," Sörine continued.

"Do you really mean that?" Lars Peter looked at her with surprise and sorrow.

"Yes, I do. What have you done? Aren't we just where we started?"

Lars Peter bent his head on hearing her hard words. But it was all quite true; except for strict necessities, they had never money to spare.

"There's so much wanted, and everything's so dear," said he excusingly. "There's no trade either! We must just have patience, till it comes round again."

"You with your patience and patience—maybe we can live on your being patient and content? D'you know why folk call this the Crow's Nest? Because nothing thrives for us, they say."

Lars Peter took his big hat from the nail behind the door and went out. He was depressed, and sought comfort with the animals; they and the children he understood, but grown-up people he could not. After all, there must be something lacking in him, since all thought him a peculiar fellow, just because he was happy and patient.

As soon as he had left the kitchen, the nag recognized his footstep, and welcomed him with a whinny. He went into the stall and stroked its back; it was like a wreck lying keel upwards. It certainly was a skeleton, and could not be called handsome. People smiled when they saw the two of them coming along the road—he knew it quite well! But they had shared bad and good together, and the nag was not particular; it took everything as it came, just as he did.

Lars Peter had never cared for other people's opinion; but now his existence was shaken, and it was necessary to defend himself and his own. In the stall beside the horse lay the cow. True enough, if taken to market now it would not fetch much; it was weak on its legs and preferred to lie down. But with spring, when it got out to grass, this would right itself. And it was a good cow for a small family like his; it did not give much milk at a time, but to make up for it gave milk all the year round. And rich milk too! When uncomplimentary remarks were made about it, Lars Peter would chaffingly declare that he could skim the milk three times, and then there was nothing but cream left. He was very fond of it, and more so for the good milk it had given the little ones.

One corner of the outhouse was boarded off for the pig. It too had heard him, and stood waiting for him to come and scratch its neck. It suffered from intestinal hernia; it had been given to Lars Peter by a farmer who wanted to get rid of it. It was not a pretty sight, but under the circumstances had thriven well, he thought, and would taste all right when salted. Perhaps it was this Sörine wanted?

The snow lay deep on the fields, but he recognized every landmark through the white covering. It was sandy soil, and yielded poor crops, yet for all that Lars Peter was fond of it. To him it was like a face with dear living features, and he would no more criticize it than he would his own mother. He stood at the door of the barn gazing lingeringly at his land. He was not happy—as he usually was on Sundays when he went about looking at his possessions. Today he could understand nothing!

Every day Sörine would return to the same subject, with some new proposal. They would buy her mother's house and move over there; the beams were of oak, and the hut would last for many years. Or they would take her as a pensioner, while there was time—in return for getting all she owned. Her thoughts were ever with her mother and her possessions. "Suppose she goes to some one else as a pensioner, and leaves everything to them! or fritters away Ditte's two hundred crowns!" said she. "She's in her second childhood!"

She was mad on the subject, but Lars Peter let her talk on.

"Isn't it true, Ditte, that Granny would be much better with us?" Sörine would continue. She quite expected the child to agree with her, crazy as she was over her grandmother.

"I don't know," answered Ditte sullenly. Her mother lately had done her best to get her over to her side, but Ditte was suspicious of her. She would love to be with Granny again, but not in that way. She would only be treated badly. Ditte had no faith in her mother's care. It was more for her own wicked ends than for daughterly love, Granny herself had said.

Sörine was beyond comprehension. One morning she would declare that before long they would hear sad news about Granny, because she had heard the raven screaming in the willows during the night. "I'd better go over and see her," said she.

"Ay, that's right, you go," answered Lars Peter. "I'll drive you over. After all, the nag and I have nothing to do."

But Sörine wouldn't hear of it. "You've your own work to do at home," said she. However, she did not get off that day—something or other prevented her. She had grown very restless.

The next morning she was unusually friendly to the children. "I'll tell you something, Granny will soon be coming here—I dreamed it last night," said she, as she helped Ditte to dress them. "She can have the alcove, and father and I'll move into the little room. And then you won't be cold any longer."

"But yesterday you said that Granny was going to die soon," objected Ditte.

"Ay, but that was only nonsense. Hurry up home from school. I've some shopping to do, and likely won't be home till late." She put sugar on the bread Ditte took to school, and sent her off in good time.

Ditte set out, with satchel hanging from her arm, and her hands rolled up in the ends of her muffler. The father had driven away early, and she followed the wheel-tracks for some distance, and amused herself by stepping in the old nag's footprints. Then the trail turned towards the sea.

She could not follow the lessons today, she was perplexed in mind. Her mother's friendliness had roused her suspicions. It was so contrary to the conviction which the child from long experience had formed as to her mother's disposition. Perhaps she was not such a bad mother when it came to the point. The sugar on the bread almost melted Ditte's heart.

But at the end of the school hour, a fearful anxiety overwhelmed her; her heart began to flutter like a captured bird, and she pressed her hand against her mouth, to keep herself from screaming aloud. When leaving the school, she started running towards the Naze. "That's the wrong way, Ditte!" shouted the girls she used to go home with. But she only ran on.

It was thick with snow, and the air was still and heavy-laden. It had been like twilight all day long. As she neared the hill above the hut on the Naze, darkness began to fall. She had run all the way and only stopped at the corner of the house, to get her breath. There was a humming in her ears, and through the hum she heard angry voices: Granny's crying, and her mother's hard and merciless.

She was about to tap on the window-pane, but hesitated, her mother's voice made her creep with fear. She shivered as she crept round the house towards the woodshed, opened the door, and stood in the kitchen, listening breathlessly. Her mother's voice drowned Granny's; it had often forced Ditte to her knees, but so frightful she had never heard it before. She was stiff with fear, and she had to squat on the ground, shivering with cold.

Through the keyhole she caught a glimpse of her mother's big body standing beside the alcove. She was bent over it, and from the movement of her back, it could be seen that she had got hold of the old woman. Granny was defending herself.

"Come out with it at once," Sörine shouted hoarsely. "Or I'll pull you out of bed."

"I'll call for some one," groaned Granny, hammering on the wall.

"Call for help if you like," ridiculed Sörine, [Pg 170]"there's no-one to hear you. Maybe you've got it in the eiderdown, since you hold it so tightly."

"Oh, hold your mouth, you thief," moaned Granny. Suddenly there was a scream, Sörine must have got hold of the packet on the old woman's breast.

Ditte jumped in and lifted the latch. "Granny," she shrieked, but she was not heard in the fearful noise. They fought, Granny's screams were like those of a dying animal. "I'll make you shut up, you witch!" shouted Sörine, and the old woman's scream died away to an uncanny rattle; Ditte wanted to assist her grandmother, but could not move, and suddenly fell unconscious to the ground. When she came to herself again, she was lying face downwards on the floor; her forehead hurt. She stumbled to her feet. The door stood open, and her mother had gone. Large white flakes of snow came floating in, showing white in the darkness.

Ditte's first thought was that it would be cold for Granny. She closed the door and went towards the bed. Old Maren lay crouched together among the untidy bedclothes. "Granny," called Ditte and crying groped for the sunken face. "It's only me, dear little Granny."

She took the old woman's face entreatingly between her thin toil-worn hands, crying over it for a while; then undressed herself and crept into bed beside her. She had once heard Granny say about some one she had been called to: "There is nothing to be done for him, he's quite cold!" And she was obsessed with that [Pg 171]thought, Granny must not be allowed to get cold, or she would have no Granny left. She crept close to the body, and worn out by tears and exhaustion soon fell asleep.

Towards morning she woke feeling cold; Granny was dead and cold. Suddenly she understood the awfulness of it all, and hurrying into her clothes, she fled.

She ran across the fields in the direction of home, but when she reached the road leading to the sea, she went along it to Per Nielsen's farm. There they picked her up, benumbed with misery. "Granny's dead!" she broke out over and over again, looking from one to the other with terror in her eyes. That was all they could get out of her. When they proposed taking her home to the Crow's Nest, she began to scream, so they put her to bed, to rest.

When she woke later in the day, Per Nielsen came in to her. "Well, I suppose you'd better be thinking of getting home," said he. "I'll go with you."

Ditte gazed at him with fear in her eyes.

"Are you afraid of your stepfather?" asked he. She did not answer. The wife came in.

"I don't know what we're to do," said he, "she's afraid to go home. The stepfather can't be very good to her."

Ditte turned sharply towards him. "I want to go home to Lars Peter," she said, sobbing.

[Pg 172]
CHAPTER XIX
ILL LUCK FOLLOWS THE RAVEN'S CALL

On receiving information of old Maren's death, four of her children assembled at the hut on the Naze, to look after their own interests, and watch that no-one ran off with anything. The other four on the other side of the globe, could of course not be there.

There was no money—not as much as a farthing was to be found, in spite of their searching, and the splitting up of the eiderdown—and the house was mortgaged up to the hilt. They then agreed to give Sörine and her husband what little there was, on condition that they provided the funeral. On this occasion, Sörine did not spare money, she wanted the funeral to be talked about. Old Maren was put into the ground with more grandeur than she had lived.

Ditte was at the funeral—naturally, as she was the only one who had ever cared for the dead woman. But in the churchyard she so lost control over herself, that Lars Peter had to take her aside, to prevent her disturbing the parson. She had such strong feelings, every one thought.[Pg 173]

But in this respect Ditte changed entirely. After Granny's death, she seemed to quieten. She went about doing her work, was not particularly lively, but not depressed either. Lars Peter observed that she and her mother quarreled no longer. This was a pleasant step in the right direction!

Ditte resigned herself to her lot. It cost her an effort to remain under the same roof as her mother; she would rather have left home. But this would have reflected on her stepfather, and her sense of justice rebelled against this. Then too the thought of her little brothers and sisters kept her back; what would become of them if she left?

She remained—and took up a definite position towards her mother. Sörine was kind and considerate to her, so much so that it was almost painful, but Ditte pretended not to notice it. All advances from her mother glanced off her. She was stubborn and determined, carrying through what she set her mind on—the mother was nothing to her.

Sörine's eyes constantly followed her when unobserved—she was afraid of her. Had the child been in the hut when it happened, or had she only arrived later? Sörine was not sure whether she herself had overturned the chair that evening in the darkness? How much did Ditte know? That she knew something her mother could tell from her face. She would have given much to find out, and often touched upon the question—with her uncertain glance at the girl.

"'Tis terrible to think that Granny should die alone," she would say, hoping the child would give herself away. But Ditte was obstinately silent.

One day Sörine gave Lars Peter a great surprise, by putting a large sum of money on the table in front of him. "Will that build the house, d'you think?" asked she.

Lars Peter looked at her; he was astounded.

"I've saved it by selling eggs and butter and wool," said she; "and by starving you," she added with an uncertain smile. "I know that I've been stingy and a miser; but in the end it pays you as well."

It was so seldom she smiled. "How pretty it made her!" thought Lars Peter, looking lovingly at her. She had lately been happier and more even tempered—no doubt the prospect of getting a better home.

He counted the money—over three hundred crowns! "That's a step forward," said he. The next evening when returning home he had bricks on the cart; and every evening he continued bringing home materials for building.

People who passed the Crow's Nest saw the erection of beams and bricks shoot up, and rumors began to float round the neighborhood. It began with a whisper that the old woman had left more than had been spoken of. Then it was said that perhaps, after all, old Maren had not died a natural death. And some remembered having seen Sörine on her way from the Crow's Nest towards the hamlet, on the same afternoon as her mother's death; little by little more was added to this, until it was declared that Sörine had strangled her own mother. Ditte was probably—with the exception of the mother—the only one who knew the real facts, and nothing could be got out of her when it affected her family—least of all on an occasion like this. But it was strange that she should happen to arrive just at the critical moment; and still more remarkable that she should run to Per Nielsen's and not home with the news of her grandmother's death.

Neither Sörine herself nor Lars Peter heard a word of these rumors. Ditte heard it at school through the other children, but did not repeat it. When her mother was more than usually considerate, her hate would seethe up in her—"Devil!" it whispered inside her, and suddenly she would feel an overwhelming desire to shout to her father: "Mother stifled Granny with the eiderdown!" It was worst of all when hearing her speak lovingly about the old woman. But the thought of his grief stopped her. He went about now like a great child, seeing nothing, and was more than ever in love with Sörine; he was overjoyed by the change for the better. Ditte and the others loved him as never before.

When Sörine was too hard on the children, they would hide from her outside the house, and only appear when their father returned at night. But since Granny's death there had been no need for this. The mother was entirely changed; when her temper was about to flare up, an unseen hand seemed to hold it back.

But it happened at times that Ditte could not bear to stay in the same room with her mother, and then she would go back to her old way and hide herself.

One evening she lay crouching in the willows. Sörine came time after time to the door, calling her in a friendly voice, and at each call a feeling of disgust went through the girl. "Ugh!" said she; it made her almost sick. After having searched for her round the house, Sörine went slowly up to the road and back again, peering about all the time: passing so close to Ditte that her dress brushed her face: then she went in.

Ditte was cold, and tired of hiding, but in she would not go—not till her father came home. He might not return until late, or not at all. Ditte had experienced this before, but then there had been a reason for it. It was no whipping she expected now!

No, but how lovely it had been to walk in holding her father's hand. He asked no question now, but only looked at the mother accusingly, and could not do enough for one. Perhaps he would make an excuse for a trip over to ... no ... this ... Ditte began to cry. It was terrible that however much she mourned for Granny—suddenly she would find she had forgotten Granny was dead. "Granny's dead, dear little Granny's dead," she would repeat to herself, so that it should not happen again, but the next minute it was just the same. It was so disloyal!

Now that it was too late, she was sorry she had not gone in when her mother called. She drew her feet up under her dress and began pulling up the grass to keep herself awake. Hearing a sound from the distance she jumped up—wheels approaching! but alas, it was not the well-known rumbling of her father's cart.

The cart turned from the road down in the direction of the Crow's Nest. Two men got out and went into the house; both wore caps with gold braid on. Ditte crept down to the house, behind the willows; her heart was beating loudly. The next moment they reappeared with her mother between them; she was struggling and shrieking wildly. "Lars Peter!" she cried heartrendingly in the darkness; they had to use force to get her into the cart. Inside the house the children could be heard crying in fear.

This sound made Ditte forget everything else, and she rushed forward. One of the men caught her by the arm, but let her go at a sign from the other man. "D'you belong to the house?" asked he.

Ditte nodded.

"Then go in to the little ones and tell them not to be afraid.... Drive on!"

Quick as lightning, Sörine put both legs over the side of the cart, but the policemen held her back. "Ditte, help me!" she screamed, as the cart swung up the road and disappeared.

Lars Peter was about three miles from the Crow's Nest, turning into the road beside the grocer's, when a cart drove past; in the light from the shop windows he caught sight of gold-braided caps. "The police are busy tonight!" said he, and shrugged his shoulders. He proceeded up the road and began humming again, mechanically flicking the nag with the whip as usual. He sat bent forward, thinking of them all at home, of what Sörine would have for him tonight—he was starving with hunger—and of the children. It was a shame that he was so late—it was pleasant when they all four rushed to meet him. Perhaps, after all, they might not be in bed.

The children stood out on the road, all four of them, waiting for him; the little ones dared not stay in the house. He stood as though turned to stone, holding on to the cart for support, while Ditte with tears told what had happened; it looked as if the big strong man would collapse altogether. Then he pulled himself together and went into the house with them, comforting them all the time; the nag of its own accord followed with the cart.

He helped Ditte put the children to bed. "Can you look after the little ones tonight?" he asked, when they had finished. "I must drive to town and fetch mother—it's all a misunderstanding."

His voice sounded hollow.

Ditte nodded and followed him out to the cart.

He turned and set the horse in motion, but suddenly he stopped.

"You know all about it, better than any one else, Ditte," said he. "You can clear your mother." He waited quietly, without looking at her, and listened. There was no answer.

Then he turned the cart slowly round and began to unharness.

PART II

CHAPTER I
MORNING AT THE CROW'S NEST

Klavs was munching busily in his stall, with a great deal of noise. He had his own peculiar way of feeding; always separating the corn from the straw, however well Lars Peter had mixed it. He would first half empty the manger—so as to lay a foundation. Then, having still plenty of room for further operations, he would push the whole together in the middle of the manger, blowing vigorously, so that the straw flew in all directions, and proceed to nuzzle all the corn. This once devoured, he would scrape his hoofs on the stone floor and whinny.

Ditte laughed. "He's asking for more sugar," said she. "Just like little Povl when he's eating porridge; he scrapes the top off too."

But Lars Peter growled. "Eat it all up, you old skeleton," said he. "These aren't times to pick and choose."

The nag would answer with a long affectionate whinny, and go on as before.

At last Lars Peter would get up and go to the manger, mixing the straw together in the middle. "Eat it up, you obstinate old thing!" said he, giving the horse a slap on the back. The horse, smelling the straw, turned its head towards Lars Peter; and looked reproachfully at him as though saying: "What's the matter with you today?" And nothing else would serve, but he must take a handful of corn and mix it with the straw. "But no tricks now," said he, letting his big hand rest on the creature's back. And this time everything was eaten up.

Lars Peter came back and sat under the lantern again.

"Old Klavs is wise," said Ditte, "he knows exactly how far to go. But he's very faddy all the same."

"I'll tell you, he knows that we're going on a long trip; and wants a big feed beforehand," answered Lars Peter as if in excuse. "Ay, he's a wise rascal!"

"But pussy's much sharper than that," said Ditte proudly, "for she can open the pantry door herself. I couldn't understand how she got in and drank the milk; I thought little Povl had left the door open, and was just going to smack him for it. But yesterday I came behind pussy, and can you imagine what she did? Jumped up on the sink, and flew against the pantry door, striking the latch with one paw so it came undone. Then she could just stand on the floor and push the door open."

They sat under the lantern, which hung from one of the beams, sorting rags, which lay round them in bundles; wool, linen and cotton—all carefully separated. Outside it was cold and dark, but here it was cosy. The old nag was working at his food like a threshing machine, the cow lay panting with well-being as it chewed the cud, and the hens were cackling sleepily from the hen-house. The new pig was probably dreaming of its mother—now and again a sucking could be heard. It had only left its mother a few days ago.

"Is this wool?" asked Ditte, holding out a big rag.

Lars Peter examined it, drew out a thread and put it in the flame of the lantern.

"It should be wool," said he at last, "for it melts and smells of horn. But Heaven knows," he felt the piece of cloth again meditatively. "Maybe 'tis some of those new-fashioned swindles; 'tis said they can make plant stuff, so folks can't see the difference between it and wool. And they make silk of glass too, I'm told."

Ditte jumped up and opened the shutter, listening, then disappeared across the yard. She returned shortly afterwards.

"Was anything wrong with the children?" asked Lars Peter.

"'Twas only little Povl crying; but how can they make silk of glass?" asked she suddenly, "glass is so brittle!"

"Ay, 'tis the new-fashioned silk though, and may be true enough. If you see a scrap of silk amongst the rags 'tis nearly always broken."

"And what queer thing's glass made of?"

"Ay, you may well ask that—if I could only tell you. It can't be any relation to ice, as it doesn't melt even when the sun shines on it. Maybe—no, I daren't try explaining it to you. 'Tis a pity not to have learned things properly; and think things out oneself."

"Can any folks do that?"

"Ay, there *must* be some, or how would everything begin—if no one hit on them. I used to think and ask about everything; but I've given it up now, I never got to the bottom of it. This with your mother doesn't make a fellow care much for life either." Lars Peter sighed.

Ditte bent over her work. When this topic came up, it was better to be silent.

For a few minutes neither spoke. Lars Peter's hands were working slowly, and at last stopped altogether. He sat staring straight ahead without perceiving anything; he was often like this of late. He rose abruptly, and went towards the shutter facing east, and opened it; it was still night, but the stars were beginning to pale. The nag was calling from the stall, quietly, almost unnoticeably. Lars Peter fastened the shutter, and stumbled out to the horse. Ditte followed him with her eyes.

"What d'you want now?" he asked in a dull voice, stroking the horse. The nag pushed its soft nose into his shoulder. It was the gentlest caress Lars Peter knew, and he gave it another supply of corn.

Ditte turned her head towards them—she felt anxious over her father's present condition. It was no good going about hanging one's head.

"Is it going to have another feed?" said she, trying to rouse him. "That animal'll eat us out of house and home!"

"Ay, but it's got something to do—and we've a long journey in front of us." Lars Peter came back and began sorting again.

"How many miles is it to Copenhagen then?"

"Six or seven hours' drive, I should say; we've got a load."

"Ugh, what a long way." Ditte shivered. "And it's so cold."

"Ay, if I'm to go alone. But you might go with me! 'Tisn't a pleasant errand, and the time'll go slowly all that long way. And one can't get away from sad thoughts!"

"I can't leave home," answered Ditte shortly.

For about the twentieth time Lars Peter tried to talk her over. "We can easily get Johansens to keep an eye on everything—and can send the children over to them for a few days," said he.

But Ditte was not to be shaken. Her mother was nothing to her, people could say what they liked; she *would* not go and see her in prison. And her father ought to stop talking like that or she would be angry; it reminded her of Granny. She hated her mother with all her heart, in a manner strange for her years. She never mentioned her, and when the others spoke of her, she would be dumb. Good and self-sacrificing as she was in all other respects, on this point she was hard as a stone.

To Lars Peter's good-natured mind this hatred was a mystery. However much he tried to reconcile her, in the end he had to give up.

"Look and see if there's anything you want for the house," said he.

"I want a packet of salt, the stuff they have at the grocer's is too coarse to put on the table. And I must have a little spice. I'm going to try making a cake myself, bought cakes get dry so quickly."

"D'you think you can?" said Lars Peter admiringly.

"There's more to be got," Ditte continued undisturbed, "but I'd better write it down; or you'll forget half the things like you did last time."

"Ay, that's best," answered Lars Peter meekly. "My memory's not as good as it used to be. I don't know—I used to do hundreds of errands without forgetting one. Maybe 'tis with your mother. And then belike—a man gets old. Grandfather, he could remember like a printed book, to the very last."

Ditte got up quickly and shook out her frock.

"There!" said she with a yawn. They put the rags in sacks and tied them up.

"This'll fetch a little money," said Lars Peter dragging the sacks to the door, where heaps of old iron and other metals lay in readiness to be taken to the town. "And what's the time now?—past six. Ought to be daylight soon."

As Ditte opened the door the frosty air poured in. In the east, over the lake, the skies were green, with a touch of gold—it was daybreak. In the openings in the ice the birds began to show signs of life. It was as if the noise from the Crow's Nest had ushered in the day for them, group after group began screaming and flew towards the sea.

"It'll be a fine day," said Lars Peter as he dragged out the cart. "There ought to be a thaw soon." He began loading the cart, while Ditte went in to light the fire for the coffee.

As Lars Peter came in, the flames from the open fireplace were flickering towards the ceiling, the room was full of a delicious fragrance, coffee and something or other being fried. Kristian was kneeling in front of the fire, feeding it with heather and dried sticks, and Ditte stood over a spluttering frying-pan, stirring with all her might. The two little ones sat on the end of the bench watching the operations with glee, the reflection of the fire gleaming in their eyes. The daylight peeped in hesitatingly through the frozen window-panes.

"Come along, father!" said Ditte, putting the frying-pan on the table on three little wooden supports. "'Tis only fried potatoes, with a few slices of bacon, but you're to eat it all yourself!"

Lars Peter laughed and sat down at the table. He soon, however, as was his wont, began giving some to the little ones; they got every alternate mouthful. They stood with their faces over the edge of the table, and wide open mouths—like two little birds. Kristian had his own fork, and stood between his father's knees and helped himself. Ditte stood against the table looking on, with a big kitchen knife in her hand.

"Aren't you going to have anything?" asked Lars Peter, pushing the frying-pan further on to the table.

"There's not a scrap more than you can eat yourself; we'll have something afterwards," answered Ditte, half annoyed. But Lars Peter calmly went on feeding them. He did not enjoy his food when there were no open mouths round him.

"'Tis worth while waking up for this, isn't it?" said he, laughing loudly; his voice was deep and warm again.

As he drank his coffee, Söster and Povl hurried into their clothes; they wanted to see him off. They ran in between his and the nag's legs as he was harnessing.

The sun was just rising. There was a red glitter over the ice-covered lake and the frosted landscape, the reeds crackled as if icicles were being crushed. From the horse's nostrils came puffs of air, showing white in the morning light, and the children's quick short breaths were like gusts of steam. They jumped round the cart in their cloth shoes like two frolicsome young puppies. "Love to Mother!" they shouted over and over again.

Lars Peter bent down from the top of the load, where he was half buried between the sacks. "Shan't I give her your love too?" asked he. Ditte turned away her head.

Then he took his whip and cracked it. And slowly Klavs set off on his journey.

CHAPTER II
THE HIGHROAD

"He's even more fond of the highroad than a human being," Lars Peter used to say of Klavs, and this was true; the horse was always in a good temper whenever preparations were being made for a long journey. For the short trips Klavs did not care at all; it was the real highroad trips with calls to right and left, and stopping at night in some stable, which appealed to him. What he found to enjoy in it would be difficult to say; hardly for the sake of a new experience—as with a man. Though God knows—'twas a wise enough rascal! At all events Klavs liked to feel himself on the highroad, and the longer the trip the happier he would be. He took it all with the same good temper—up hills where he had to strain in the shafts, and downhill where the full weight of the cart made itself felt. He would only stop when the hill was unusually steep—to give Lars Peter an opportunity of stretching his legs.

To Lars Peter the highroad was life itself. It gave daily bread to him and his, and satisfied his love of roaming. Such a piece of highroad between rows of trimmed poplars with endless by-ways off to farms and houses was full of possibilities. One could take this turning or that, according to one's mood at the moment, or leave the choice of the road to the nag. It always brought forth something.

And the highroad was only the outward sign of an endless chain. If one liked to wander straight on, instead of turning off, ay, then one would get far out in the world—as far as one cared. He did not do it of course; but the thought that it could be done was something in itself.

On the highroad he met people of his own blood: tramps who crawled up without permission on to his load, drawing a bottle from their pocket, offering it to him, and talking away. They were people who traveled far; yesterday they had come from Helsingör; in a week's time they would perhaps be over the borders in the south and down in Germany. They wore heavily nailed boots, and had a hollow instead of a stomach, a handkerchief round their throat and mittens on their red wrists—and were full of good humor. Klavs knew them quite well, and stopped of his own accord.

Klavs also stopped for poor women and school-children; Lars Peter and he agreed that all who cared to drive should have that pleasure. But respectable people they passed by; they of course would not condescend to drive with the rag and bone man.

They both knew the highroad with its by-ways equally well. When anything was doing, such as a thrashing-machine in the field, or a new house being built, one or other of them always stopped. Lars Peter pretended that it was the horse's inquisitiveness. "Well, have you seen enough?" he growled when they had stood for a short while, and gathered up the reins. Klavs did not mind the deception in the least, and in no way let it interfere with his own inclinations; Klavs liked his own way.

Things must be black indeed, if the highroad did not put the rag and bone man into a good temper. The calm rhythmic trot of the nag's hoofs against the firm road encouraged him to hum. The trees, the milestones with the crown above King Christian the Fifth's initials, the endless perspective ahead of him, with all its life and traffic—all had a cheering effect on him.

The snow had been trodden down, and only a thin layer covered with ice remained, which rang under the horse's big hoofs. The thin light air made breathing easy, and the sun shone redly over the snow. It was impossible to be anything but light-hearted. But then he remembered the object of the drive, and all was dark again.

Lars Peter had never done much thinking on his own account, or criticized existence. When something or other happened, it was because it could not be otherwise—and what was the good of speculating about it? When he was on the cart all these hours, he only hummed a kind of melody and had a sense of well-being. "I wonder what mother'll have for supper?" he would think, or "maybe the kiddies'll come to meet me today." That was all. He took bad and good trade as it came, and joy and sorrow just the same; he knew from experience that rain and sunshine come by turns. It had been thus in his parents' and grandparents' time, and his own had confirmed it. Then why speculate? If the bad weather lasted longer than usual, well, the good was so much better when it came.

And complaints were no good. Other people beside himself had to take things as they came. He had never had any strong feeling that there was a guiding hand behind it all.

But now he *had* to think, however useless he found it. Suddenly something would take him mercilessly by the neck, and always face him with the same hopeless: *Why?* A thousand times the thought of Sörine would crop up, making everything heavy and sad.

Lars Peter had been thoroughly out of luck before—and borne it as being part of his life's burden. He had a thick skull and a broad back—what good were they but for burdens; it was not his business to whimper or play the weakling. And fate had heaped troubles upon him: if he could bear that, then he can bear this!—till at last he would break down altogether under the burden. But his old stolidness was gone.

He had begun to think of his lot—and could fathom nothing: it was all so meaningless, now he compared himself with others. As soon as ever he got into the cart, and the nag into its old trot, these sad thoughts would reappear, and his mind would go round and round the subject until he was worn out. He could not unravel it. Why was he called the rag and bone man, and treated as if he were unclean? He earned his living as honestly as any one else. Why should his children be jeered at like outcasts—and his home called the Crow's Nest? And why did the bad luck follow him?—and fate? There was a great deal now that he did not understand, but which must be cleared up. Misfortune, which had so often knocked at his door without finding him at home, had now at last got its foot well inside the door.

However much Lars Peter puzzled over Sörine, he could find no way out of it. It was his nature to look on the bright side of things; and should it be otherwise they were no sooner over than forgotten. He had only seen her good points. She had been a clever wife, good at keeping the home together—and a hard worker. And she had given him fine children, that alone made up for everything. He had been fond of her, and proud of her firmness and ambition to get on in the world. And now as a reward for her pride she was in prison! For a long time he had clung to the hope that it must be a mistake. "Maybe they'll let her out one day," he thought. "Then she'll be standing in the doorway when you return, and it's all been a misunderstanding." It was some time now since the sentence had been pronounced, so it must be right. But it was equally difficult to understand!

There lay a horseshoe on the road. The nag stopped, according to custom, and turned its head. Lars Peter roused himself from his thoughts and peered in front of the horse, then drove on again. Klavs could not understand it, but left it at that: Lars Peter could no longer be bothered to get off the cart to pick up an old horseshoe.

He began whistling and looked out over the landscape to keep his thoughts at bay. Down in the marsh they were cutting ice for the dairies—it was high time too! And the farmer from Gadby was driving off in his best sledge, with his wife by his side. Others could enjoy themselves! If only he had his wife in the cart—driving in to the Capital. There now—he was beginning all over again! Lars Peter looked in the opposite direction, but what good was that. He could not get rid of his thoughts.

A woman came rushing up the highroad, from a little farm. "Lars Peter!" she cried. "Lars Peter!" The nag stopped.

"Are you going to town?" she asked breathlessly, leaning on the cart.

"Ay, that I am," Lars Peter answered quietly, as if afraid of her guessing his errand.

"Oh! would you mind buying us a chamber?"

"What! you're getting very grand!" Lars Peter's mouth twisted in some semblance of a smile.

"Ay, the child's got rheumatic fever, and the doctor won't let her go outside," the woman explained excusingly.

"I'll do that for you. How big d'you want it?"

"Well, as we must have it, it might as well be a big one. Here's sixpence, it can't be more than that." She gave him the money wrapped in a piece of paper, and the nag set off again.

When they had got halfway, Lars Peter turned off to an inn. The horse needed food, and something enlivening for himself would not come amiss. He felt downhearted. He drove into the yard, partly unharnessed, and put on its nosebag.

The fat inn-keeper came to the door, peering out with his small pig's eyes, which were deeply embedded in a huge expanse of flesh, like two raisins in rising dough. "Why, here comes the rag and bone man from Sand!" he shouted, shaking with laughter. "What brings such fine company today, I wonder?"

Lars Peter had heard this greeting before, and laughed at it, but today it affected him differently. He had come to the end of his patience. His blood began to rise. The long-suffering, thoughtful, slothful Lars Peter turned his head with a jerk—showing a gleam of teeth. But he checked himself, took off his cape, and spread it over the horse.

"'Tis he for sure," began the inn-keeper again. "His lordship of the Crow's Nest, doing us the honor."

But this time Lars Peter blazed out.

"Hold your mouth, you beer-swilling pig!" he thundered, stepping towards him with his heavy boots, "or I'll soon close it for you!"

The inn-keeper's open mouth closed with a snap. His small pig's eyes, which almost disappeared when he laughed, opened widely in terror. He turned round and rushed in. When Lars Peter, with a frown on his face, came tramping into the tap-room, he was bustling about, whistling softly with his fat tongue between his teeth and looking rather small.

"A dram and a beer," growled the rag and bone man, seating himself by the table and beginning to unpack his food.

The inn-keeper came towards him with a bottle and two glasses. He glanced uncertainly at Lars Peter, and poured out two brimming glassfuls. "Your health, old friend," said he ingratiatingly. The rag and bone man drank without answering his challenge; he had given the fat lump a fright, and now he was making up to him. It was odd to be able to make people shiver—quite a new feeling. But he rather liked it. And it did him good to give vent to his anger; he had a feeling of well-being after having let off steam. Here sat this insolent landlord trying to curry favor, just because one would not put up with everything. Lars Peter felt a sudden inclination to put his foot upon his neck, and give him a thorough shock. Or bend him over so that head and heels met. Why should he not use his superior strength once in a while? Then perhaps people would treat him with something like respect.

The inn-keeper sank down on a chair in front of him. "Well, Lars Peter Hansen, so you've become a socialist?" he began, blinking his eyes.

Lars Peter dropped his heavy fist on the table so that everything jumped—the inn-keeper included. "I'm done with being treated like dirt—do you understand! I'm just as good as you and all the rest of them. And if I hear any more nonsense, then to hell with you all."

"Of course, of course! 'twas only fun, Lars Peter Hansen. And how's every one at home? Wife and children well?" He still blinked whenever Lars Peter moved.

Lars Peter did not answer him, but helped himself to another dram. The rascal knew quite well all about Sörine.

"D'you know—you should have brought the wife with you. Womenfolk love a trip to town," the inn-keeper tried again. Lars Peter looked suspiciously at him.

"What d'you mean by this tomfoolery?" he said darkly. "You know quite well that she's in there."

"What—is she? Has she run away from you then?"

Lars Peter took another glass. "She's locked up, and you know it—curse you!" He put the glass down heavily on the table.

The landlord saw it was no good pretending ignorance. "I think I do remember hearing something about it," said he. "How was it—got into trouble with the law somehow?"

The rag and bone man gave a hollow laugh. "I should think so! She killed her own mother, 'tis said." The spirit was beginning to affect him.

"Dear, dear! was it so bad as that?" sighed the inn-keeper, turning and twisting as if he had a pain inside. "And now you're going to the King, I suppose?"

Lars Peter lifted his head. "To the King?" he asked. The thought struck him, perhaps this was the miracle he had been hoping for.

"Ay, the King decides whether it's to be life or death, you know. If there's any one he can't stand looking at, he only says: 'Take that fellow and chop off his head!' And he can let folk loose again too, if he likes."

"And how's the likes of me to get near the King?" The rag and bone man laughed hopelessly.

"Oh, that's easily done," said the inn-keeper airily. "Every one in the country has the right to see the King. When you get in there, just ask where he lives, any one can tell you."

"Hm, I know that myself," said Lars Peter with assurance. "I was once nearly taken for the guards myself—for the palace. If it hadn't been for having flat feet, then——"

"Well, it isn't quite as easy as you think; he's got so many mansions. The King's got no-one to associate with, you see, as there's only one King in every land, and talk to his wife always, no man could stand—the King as little as we others. That's why he gets bored, and moves from one castle to another, and plays at making a visitor of himself. So you'd better make inquiries. 'Twouldn't come amiss to get some one to speak for you either. You've got money, I suppose?"

"I've got goods on the cart for over a hundred crowns," said Lars Peter with pride.

"That's all right, because in the Capital nearly all the doors need oiling before they are opened. Maybe the castle gate will creak a little, but then——" The inn-keeper rubbed one palm against the other.

"Then we'll oil it," said Lars Peter, with a wave of his arm as he got up.

He had plenty of courage now, and hummed as he harnessed the horse and got into the cart. Now he knew what to do, and he was anxious to act. Day and night he had been faced with the question of getting Sörine out of prison, but how? It was no good trying to climb the prison wall at night, and fetch her out, as one read of in books. But he could go to the King! Had he not himself nearly been taken into the King's service as a guardsman? "He's got the height and the build," they had said. Then they had noticed his flat feet and rejected him; but still he had said he almost——

CHAPTER III
LARS PETER SEEKS THE KING

Lars Peter Hansen knew nothing of the Capital. As a boy he had been there with his father, but since then no opportunity had arisen for a trip to Copenhagen. He and Sörine had frequently spoken of taking their goods there and selling direct to the big firms, instead of going the round of the small provincial dealers, but nothing had ever come of it beyond talk. But today the thing was to be done. He had seen posters everywhere advertising: "The largest house in Scandinavia for rags and bones and old metals," and "highest prices given." It was the last statement which had attracted him.

Lars Peter sat reckoning up, as he drove along the Lyngby road towards the eastern end of the city. Going by prices at home he had a good hundred crowns' worth of goods on the cart; and here it ought to fetch at least twenty-five crowns more. That would perhaps pay for Sörine's release. This was killing two birds with one stone, getting Sörine out—and making money on the top of it! All that was necessary was to keep wide awake. He lifted his big battered hat and ran his hand through his tousled mop of hair—he was in a happy mood.

At Trianglen he stopped and inquired his way. Then driving through Blegdamsvej he turned into a side street. Over a high wooden paling could be seen mountains of old rusty iron: springs and empty tins, bent iron beds, dented coal-boxes red with rust, and pails. This must be the place. On the signboard stood: *Levinsohn & Sons, Export.*

The rag and bone man turned in through the gateway and stopped bewildered as he came into the yard. Before him were endless erections of storing-places and sheds, one behind the other, and inclosures with masses of rags, dirty cotton-wool and rusty iron and tin-ware. From every side other yards opened out, and beyond these more again. If he and Klavs went gathering rags until Doomsday, they would never be able to fill one yard. He sat and gazed, overwhelmed. Involuntarily he had taken his hat off, but then, gathering himself together, he drove into one of the sheds and jumped down from the cart. Hearing voices, he opened the door. In the darkness sat some young girls sorting some filth or other, which looked like blood-stained rags.

"Well, well, what a dove-cote to land in," broke out Lars Peter in high spirits. "What's that you're doing, sorting angels' feathers?" The room was filled with his good-humored chuckles.

As quick as lightning one of the girls grasped a [Pg 205] bundle and threw it at him. He only just escaped it by bending his head, and the thing brought up against the door-post. It was cotton-wool covered with blood and matter—from the hospital dust-bins. He knew that there was a trade in this in the Capital. "Puh!" he said in disgust, and hurried out. "Filthy, pish!" A shout of laughter went up from the girls.

From the head-office a little spectacled gentleman came tripping towards him. "What—what are you doing here?" he barked from afar, almost falling over himself in his eagerness. "It—it's no business of yours prying in here!" He was dreadfully dirty and unshaven, his collar and frock-coat looked as if they had been fished up from a ragbag. No, the trade never made Lars Peter as dirty as that; why, the dirt was in layers on this old man. But of course—this business was ever so much bigger than his own! Good-naturedly, he took off his hat.

"Are you Mr. Levinsohn?" asked he, when the old man had finished. "I've got some goods."

The old man stared at him speechless with surprise that any one could be so impudent as to take him for the head of the firm. "Oh, you're looking for Mr. Levinsohn," he said searchingly, "indeed?"

"Ay, I've got some goods I want to sell."

Now the old man understood. "And you must see him, himself—it's a matter of life and death—eh? No one else in the whole world can buy those goods from you, or the shaft'll break and the rags'll fall out and [Pg 206] break to pieces, and Heaven knows what! So you must see Mr. Levinsohn himself." He looked the rag and bone man up and down, almost bursting with scorn.

"Well, I shouldn't mind seeing him himself," Lars Peter patiently said.

"Then you'd better drive down to the Riviera with your dust-cart, my good man."

"What, where?"

"Yes, to the Riviera!" The old man rubbed his hands. He was enjoying himself immensely. "It's only about fourteen hundred miles from here—over there towards the south. The best place to find him is Monte Carlo—between five and seven. And his wife and daughters—I suppose you want to see them too? Perhaps a little flirtation? A little walk—underneath the palm-trees, what?"

"Good Lord! is he a grand sort like that," said Lars Peter, crestfallen. "Well—maybe I can trade with you?"

"At your service, Mr. Jens Petersen from—Sengeløse; if you, sir, will condescend to deal with a poor devil like me."

"I may just as well tell you that my name is Lars Peter Hansen—from Sand."

"Indeed—the firm feels honored, highly honored, I assure you!" The old man bustled round the cartload, taking in the value at a glance, and talking all the time. Suddenly he seized the nag by the head, but [Pg 207] quickly let go, as Klavs snapped at him. "We'll drive it down to the other yard," said he.

"I think we'd better leave the goods on the cart, until we've agreed about the price," Lars Peter thought; he was beginning to be somewhat suspicious.

"No, my man, we must have the whole thing emptied out, so that we can see what we're buying," said the old man in quite another tone. "That's not our way."

"And I don't sell till I know my price. It's all weighed and sorted, Lars Peter's no cheat."

"No, no, of course not. So it's really you? Lars Peter Hansen—and from Sand too—and no cheat. Come with me into the office then."

The rag and bone man followed him. He was a little bewildered, was the man making a fool of him, or did he really know him? Round about at home Lars Peter of Sand was known by every one; had his name as a buyer preceded him?

He had all the weights in his head, and gave the figures, while the old man put them down. In the midst of this he suddenly realized that the cart had disappeared. He rushed out, and down in the other yard found two men engaged in unloading the cart. For the second time today Lars Peter lost his temper. "See and get those things on to the cart again," he shouted, picking up his whip. The two men hastily took his measure; then without a word reloaded the cart. [Pg 208]

He was no longer in doubt that they would cheat him. The cursed knaves! If they had emptied it all out on to the heap, then he could have whistled for his own price. He drove the cart right up to the office door, and kept the reins on his arm. The old fox stood by his desk, looking at him out of the corners of his eyes. "Were they taking your beautiful horse from you?" he asked innocently.

"No, 'twas something else they wanted to have their fingers in," growled Lars Peter; he would show them that he could be sarcastic too. "Now then, will you buy the goods or not?"

"Of course we'll buy them. Look here, I've reckoned it all up. It'll be exactly fifty-six crowns—highest market price."

"Oh, go to the devil with your highest market price!" Lars Peter began mounting the cart again.

The old man looked at him in surprise through his spectacles: "Then you won't sell?"

"No, that I won't. I'd rather take it home again—and get double the price."

"Well, if you say so of course—Lars Peter Hansen's no cheat. But what are we to do, my man? My conscience won't allow me to send you dragging those things home again—it would be a crime to this beautiful horse." He approached the nag as if to pat it, but Klavs laid back his ears and lashed his tail. This praise of his horse softened Lars Peter, and the end of it was that he let the load go for ninety crowns. A cigar was thrown into the bargain. "It's from the cheap box, so please don't light it until you get outside the gate," said the impudent old knave. "Come again soon!"

Thanks! It would be some time before he came here again—a pack of robbers! He asked the way to an inn in Vestergade, where people from his neighborhood generally stayed, and there he unharnessed.

The yard was full of vehicles. Farmers with pipes hanging from their lips and fur-coats unbuttoned were loading their wagons. Here and there between the vehicles were loiterers, with broad gold chains across their chest and half-closed eyes. One of them came up to Lars Peter. "Are you doing anything tonight?" said he. "There's a couple of us here—retired farmers—going to have a jolly evening together. We want a partner." He drew a pack of cards from his breast-pocket, and began shuffling them.

No, Lars Peter had no time. "All the same, thanks." "Who are those men?" he asked the stable-boy.

"Oh, they help the farmers to find their way about town, when it's dark," answered the man, laughing.

"Are they paid for that then?" asked Lars Peter thoughtfully.

"Oh, yes—and sometimes a good deal. But then they fix up other things besides—lodging for the night and everything. Even a wife they'll get for you, if you like."

"Well, I don't care about that. If they'd only help a man to get hold of his own wife!"

"I don't think they do that. But you can try."

No, Lars Peter would not do that. He realized these were folk it was better to avoid. Then he sauntered out into the town. At Hauserplads there was an inn kept by a man he knew—he would look him up. Maybe he could give him a little help in managing the affair.

The street-lamps were just being lit, although it was not nearly dark; evidently there was no lack of money here. Lars Peter clattered in his big boots down towards Frue Plads, examining the houses as he went. This stooping giant, with faded hat and cape, looked like a wandering piece of the countryside. When he asked the way his voice rang through the street—although it was not loud for him. People stopped and laughed. Then he laughed back again and made some joke or other, which, though he did not mean it, sounded like a storm between the rows of houses. Gradually a crowd of children and young people gathered and followed in his wake. When they shouted after him he took it with good humor, but was not altogether at his ease until he reached the tavern. Here he took out his red pocket handkerchief and wiped the perspiration from his forehead.

"Hullo! Hans Mattisen," he shouted down into the dark cellar. "D'you know an old friend again, what?" His joy over having got so far made his voice sound still more overpowering than usual; there was hardly room for it under the low ceiling.

"Not so fast, not so fast!" came from a jolly voice behind the counter, "wait until I get a light."

When the gas was lit, they found they did not know each other at all. Hans Mattisen had left years ago. "Don't you worry about that," said the inn-keeper, "sit down." After Lars Peter had seated himself, he was given some lobscouse and a small bottle of wine, and soon felt at peace with the world.

The inn-keeper was a pleasant man with a keen sense of humor. Lars Peter was glad of a talk with him, and before he was aware of it, had poured out all his troubles. Well, he had come down here to get advice; and he had not gone far wrong either.

"Is that all?" said the inn-keeper, "we'll soon put that right. We've only to send a message to the Bandmaster."

"Who's that?" asked Lars Peter.

"Oh, he has the cleverest head in the world; there's not a piece of music but he can manage it. Curious fellow—never met one like him. For example, he can't bear dogs, because once a police-dog took him for an ordinary thief. He never can forget that. Therefore, if he asks, you've only to say that dogs are a damned nuisance—almost as loathsome as the police. He can't stand them either. Hi! Katrine," he called into the kitchen, "get hold of the Bandmaster quick, and tell him to come along—give him plenty of drink too, for he must be thawed before you get anything out of him."

"No fear about that," said Lars Peter airily, putting a ten-crown piece on the table, which the inn-keeper quickly pocketed. "That's right, old man—that's doing the thing properly," said he appreciatively. "I'll see to the whiskey. You're a gentleman, that's certain—you've got a well-filled pocketbook, I suppose?"

"I've got about a hundred crowns," answered Lars Peter, fearing it would not suffice.

"You shall see your wife!" shouted the inn-keeper, shaking Lars Peter's hand violently. "You shall see your wife as certain as I'm your friend! Perhaps she'll be with you tonight. What do you think of that, eh, old man?" He put his arm round Lars Peter's shoulders, shaking him jovially.

Lars Peter laughed and was moved—he almost had tears in his eyes. He was a little overcome by the warmth of the room and the whiskey.

A tall thin gentleman came down into the cellar. He wore a black frock-coat, but was without waistcoat and collar—perhaps because he had been sent for in such a hurry. He had spectacles on, and looked on the whole a man of authority. He had a distinguished appearance, somewhat like a town-crier or a conjurer from the market-place. His voice was shrill and cracked, and he had an enormous larynx.

The inn-keeper treated him with great deference. [Pg 213] "G'day, sir," said he, bowing low—"here's a man wants advice. He's had an accident, his wife's having a holiday at the King's expense."

The conductor glanced rather contemptuously at the rag and bone man's big shabby figure. But the inn-keeper winked one eye, and said, "I mustn't forget the beer-man." He went behind the desk and wrote on a slate, "100." The Bandmaster glanced at the figure and nodded to himself, then sat down and began to question Lars Peter—down to every detail. He considered for a few minutes, and then said, turning towards the inn-keeper, "Alma must tackle this—she's playing with the *princess*, you know."

"Yes, of course!" shouted the inn-keeper, delightedly. "Of course Alma can put it right, but tonight——?" He looked significantly at the Bandmaster.

"Leave it to me, my dear friend. Just you leave it to me," said the other firmly.

Lars Peter tried hard to follow their conversation. They were funny fellows to listen to, although the case itself was serious enough. He began to feel drowsy with the heat of the room—after his long day in the fresh air.

"Well, my good man, you wish to see the King?" said the Bandmaster, taking hold of the lapel of his coat. Lars Peter pulled himself together.

"I'd like to try that way, yes," he answered with strained attention. [Pg 214]

"Very well, then listen. I'll introduce you to my niece, who plays with the princess. This is how it stands, you see—but it's between ourselves—the *princess* rather runs off the lines at times, she gets so sick of things, but it's incognito, you understand—unknowingly, we say—and then my niece is always by her side. You'll meet her—and the rest you must do yourself."

"H'm, I'm not exactly dressed for such fine society," said Lars Peter, looking down at himself. "And I'm out of practice with the womenfolk—if it had been in my young days, now——!"

"Don't worry about that," said his friend, "people of high degree often have the most extraordinary taste. It would be damned strange if the *princess* doesn't fall in love with you. And if she once takes a fancy to you, you may bet your last dollar that your case is in good hands."

The inn-keeper diligently refilled their glasses, and Lars Peter looked more and more brightly at things. He was overcome by the Bandmaster's grand connections, and his ability in finding ways and means—exceedingly clever people he had struck upon. And when Miss Alma came, full-figured and with a curled fringe, his whole face beamed. "What a lovely girl," said he warmly, "just the kind I'd have liked in the old days."

Miss Alma at once wanted to sit on his knee, but Lars Peter kept her at arms' length. "I've got a wife," said [Pg 215] he seriously. Sörine should have no grounds for complaint. A look from the Bandmaster made Alma draw herself up.

"Just wait until the *princess* comes, then you'll see a lady," said he to Lars Peter.

"She's not coming. She's at a ball tonight," said Miss Alma with resentment.

"Then we'll go to the palace and find her." The Bandmaster took his hat, and they all got up.

Outside in the street, a half-grown girl ran up and whispered something to him.

"Sorry, but I must go," said he to Lars Peter—"my mother-in-law is at death's door. But you'll have a good time all right."

"Come along," cried Miss Alma, taking the rag and bone man by the arm. "We two are going to see life!"

"Hundred—er—kisses, Alma! don't forget," called the Bandmaster after them. His voice sounded like a market crier's.

"All right," answered Miss Alma, with a laugh.

"What's that he says?" asked Lars Peter wonderingly.

"Don't you bother your head about that fool," she answered, and drew him along.

Next morning Lars Peter woke early—as usual. There was a curious illumination in the sky, and with terror he tumbled quickly out of bed. Was the barn on [Pg 216] fire? Then suddenly he remembered that he was not at home; the gleam of light on the window-panes came from the street lamps, which struggled with the dawn of day.

He found himself in a dirty little room, at the top of the house—as far as he could judge from the roofs all round him. How in the name of goodness had he got here?

He seated himself on the edge of the bed, and began dressing. Slowly one thing after another began to dawn on him. His head throbbed like a piston rod—headache! He heard peculiar sounds: chattering women, hoarse rough laughter, oaths—and from outside came the peal of church bells. Through all the noise and tobacco smoke came visions of a fair fringe, and soft red lips—the *princess*! But how did he come to be here, in an iron bed with a lumpy mattress, and ragged quilt?

He felt for his watch to see the time—the old silver watch had vanished! Anxiously he searched his inner pocket—thank Heaven! the pocketbook was there alright. But what had happened to his watch? Perhaps it had fallen on the floor. He hurried into his clothes, to look for it—the big leather purse felt light in his pocket. It was empty! He opened his pocketbook—that too was empty!

Lars Peter scrambled downstairs, dreading lest any one should see him, slipped out into one of the side streets, and stumbled to the inn, harnessed the nag and set off. He began to long for the children at home—yes, and for the cows and pigs too.

Not until he was well outside the town, with a cold wind blowing on his forehead, did he remember Sörine. And, suddenly realizing the full extent of his disaster, he broke down and sobbed helplessly.

He halted at the edge of the wood—just long enough for Klavs to have a feed. He himself had no desire for food then. He was on the highroad again, and sat huddled up in the cart, while the previous evening's debauch sang through his head.

At one place a woman came running towards him. "Lars Peter!" she shouted, "Lars Peter!" The nag stopped. Lars Peter came to himself with a jerk; without a word he felt in his waistcoat pocket, gave her back her coin, and whipped up the horse.

On the highroad, some distance from home, a group of children stood waiting. Ditte had not been able to manage them any longer. They were cold and in tears. Lars Peter took them up into the cart, and they gathered round him, each anxious to tell him all the news. He took no notice of their chatter. Ditte sat quietly, looking at him out of the corners of her eyes.

When he was seated at his meal, she said, "Where're all the things you were to buy for me?" He looked up startled, and began stammering something or other—an excuse—but stopped in the middle.

"How was mother getting on?" asked Ditte then. She was sorry for him, and purposely used the word "mother" to please him.

For a few moments his features worked curiously. Then he buried his face in his hands.

CHAPTER IV
LITTLE MOTHER DITTE

At first, Lars Peter told them nothing of his visit to the Capital. But Ditte was old enough to read between the lines, and drew her own conclusions. At all events, her commission had not been executed. Sörine, for some reason or other, he had not seen either, as far as she could understand; and no money had been brought home. Apparently it had all been squandered—spent in drink no doubt.

"Now he'll probably take to getting drunk, like Johansen and the others in the huts," she thought with resignation. "Come home and make a row because there is nothing to eat—and beat us."

She was prepared for the worst, and watched him closely. But Lars Peter came home steady as usual. He returned even earlier than before. He longed for children and home when he was away. And, as was his custom, he gave an account of what he had made and spent. He would clear out the contents of his trouser-pockets with his big fist, spreading the money out over the table, so that they could count it together and lay their plans accordingly. But now he liked a glass with his meals! Sörine had never allowed him this, there was no need for it—said she—it was a waste of money. Ditte gave it willingly, and took care to have it ready for him—after all, he was a man!

Lars Peter was really ashamed of his trip to town, and not least of all that he had been made such a fool of. The stupid part of it was that he remembered so little of what had happened. Where had he spent the night—and in what society? From a certain time in the evening until he woke the following morning in that filthy bedroom, all was like a vague dream—good or bad, he knew not. But in spite of his shame he felt a secret satisfaction in having for once kicked over the traces. He had seen life. How long had he been out? Jolting round from farm to farm, he would brood on the question, would recall some parts of the evening and suppress others—to get as much pleasure out of it as possible. But in the end he was none the wiser.

However, it was impossible for him to keep any secret for long. First one thing, then another, came out, and eventually Ditte had a pretty good idea of what had happened, and would discuss it with him. In the evenings, when the little ones were in bed, they would talk it over.

"But don't you think she was a real princess?" asked Ditte each time. She always came back to this—it appealed to her vivid imagination and love of adventure.

"The Lord only knows," answered her father thoughtfully. He could not fathom how he could have been such a fool; he had managed so well with the Jews in the stable-yard. "Ay, the Lord only knows!"

"And the Bandmaster," said Ditte eagerly, "he must have been a wonderful man."

"Ay, that's true—a conjurer! He made I don't know how many drinks disappear without any one seeing how it was done. He held the glass on the table in his left hand, slapped his elbow with his right—and there it was empty."

To Ditte it was a most exciting adventure, and incidents that had seemed far from pleasant to Lars Peter became wonders in Ditte's version of the affair. Lars Peter was grateful for the child's help, and together they spoke of it so long, that slowly, and without his being aware of it, the whole experience assumed quite a different aspect.

It certainly had been a remarkable evening. And the princess—yes, she must have been there in reality, strange though it sounded that a beggar like him should have been in such company. But the devil of a woman she was to drink and smoke. "Ay, she was real enough—or I wouldn't have been so taken with her," admitted he.

"Then you've slept with a real princess—just like the giant in the fairy tale," broke out Ditte, clapping her hands in glee. "You have, father!" She looked beamingly at him.

Lars Peter was silent with embarrassment, and sat blinking at the lamp—he had not looked upon it in the innocent light of a fairy tale. To him it seemed—well, something rather bad—it was being unfaithful to Sörine.

"Ay, that's true," said he. "But then, will Mother forgive it?"

"Oh, never mind!" answered Ditte. "But it was a good thing you didn't cut yourself!"

Lars Peter lifted his head, looking uncertainly at her.

"Ay, because there must have been a drawn sword between you—there always is. You see, princesses are too grand to be touched."

"Oh—ay! that's more than likely." Lars Peter turned this over in his mind. The explanation pleased him, and he took it to himself; it was a comforting idea. "Ay, 'tis dangerous to have dealings with princesses, even though a man doesn't know it at the time," said he.

Lars Peter thought no more of visiting Sörine in prison. He would have liked to see her and clasp her hand, even though it were only through an iron grating; but it was not to be. He must have patience until she had served her time.

To him the punishment was that they had to live apart in the coming years. He lacked imagination to comprehend Sörine's life behind prison walls, and therefore he could not think of her for long at a time. But unconsciously he missed her, so much so that he felt depressed.

Lars Peter was no longer eager to work—the motive power was lacking. He was too easily contented with things as they were; there was no-one to taunt him with being poorer than others. Ditte was too good-natured; she was more given to taking burdens on her own shoulders.

He had grown quieter, and stooped more than ever. He played less with the children, and his voice had lost some of its ring. He never sang now, as he drove up to the farms to trade; he felt that people gossiped about him and his affairs, and this took away his confidence. It made itself felt when housewives and maids no longer smiled and enjoyed his jokes or cleared out all their old rubbish for him. He was never invited inside now—he was the husband of a murderess! Trade dwindled away—not that he minded—it gave him more time with the children at home.

At the same time there was less to keep house on. But, thanks to Ditte, they scraped along; little as she was, she knew how to make both ends meet, so they did not starve.

There was now plenty of time for Lars Peter to build. Beams and stones lay all round as a silent reproach to him.

"Aren't you going to do anything with it?" Ditte would ask. "Folk say it's lying there wasting."

"Where did you hear that?" asked Lars Peter bitterly.

"Oh—at school!"

So they talked about that too! There was not much where he was concerned which was not torn to pieces. No, he had no desire to build. "We've got a roof over our heads," said he indifferently. "If any one thinks our hut's not good enough, let them give us another." But the building materials remained there as an accusation; he was not sorry when they were overgrown with grass.

What good would it do to build? The Crow's Nest was, and would remain, the Crow's Nest, however much they tried to polish it up. It had not grown in esteem by Sörine's deed. She had done her best to give them a lift up in the world—and had only succeeded in pushing them down to the uttermost depth. Previously, it had only been misfortune which clung to the house, and kept better people away; now it was crime. No-one would come near the house after dusk, and by day they had as little as possible to do with the rag and bone man. The children were shunned; they were the offspring of a murderess, and nothing was too bad to be thought of them.

The people tried to excuse their harshness, and justified their behavior towards the family, by endowing them with all the worst qualities. At one time it was reported that they were thieves. But that died down, and then they said that the house was haunted. Old Maren went about searching for her money; first one, then another, had met her on the highroad at night, on her way to the Crow's Nest.

The full burden of all this fell on the little ones. It was mercilessly thrown in their faces by the other children at school; and when they came home crying, Lars Peter of course had to bear his share too. No-one dared say anything to him, himself—let them try if they dared! The rag and bone man's fingers tingled when he heard all this backbiting—why couldn't he and his be allowed to go in peace. He wouldn't mind catching one of the rogues red-handed. He would knock him down in cold blood, whatever the consequences might be.

Kristian now went to school too, in the infants' class. The classes were held every other day, and his did not coincide with Ditte's, who was in a higher class. He had great difficulty in keeping up with the other children, and could hardly be driven off in the mornings. "They call me the young crow," he said, crying.

"Then call them names back again," said Ditte; and off he had to go.

But one day there came a message from the schoolmaster that the boy was absent too often. The message was repeated. Ditte could not understand it. She had a long talk with the boy, and got out of him that he often played truant. He made a pretense of going to school, hung about anywhere all day long, and only returned home when school-time was over. She said nothing of this to Lars Peter—it would only have made things worse.

The unkindness from outside made them cling more closely to one another. There was something of the hunted animal in them; Lars Peter was reserved in his manner to people, and was ready to fly out if attacked. The whole family grew shy and suspicious. When the children played outside the house, and saw people approaching on the highroad, they would rush in, peeping at them from behind the broken window-panes. Ditte watched like a she-wolf, lest other children should harm her little brothers and sister; when necessary, she would both bite and kick, and she could hurl words at them too. One day when Lars Peter was driving past the school, the schoolmaster came out and complained of her—she used such bad language. He could not understand it; at home she was always good and saw that the little ones behaved properly. When he spoke of this, Ditte hardened.

"I won't stand their teasing," said she.

"Then stay at home from school, and then we'll see what they'll do."

"We'll only be fined for every day; and then one day they'll come and fetch me," said Ditte bitterly.

"They won't easily take you away by force. Somebody else would have something to say to that." Lars Peter nodded threateningly.

But Ditte would not—she would take her chance. "I've just as much right to be there as the others," she said stubbornly.

"Ay, ay, that's so. But it's a shame you should suffer for other people's wickedness."

Lars Peter seldom went out now, but busied himself cultivating his land, so that he could be near the children and home. He had a feeling of insecurity; people had banded themselves together against him and his family, and meant them no good. He was uneasy when away from home, and constantly felt as if something had happened. The children were delighted at the change.

"Are you going to stay at home tomorrow too, Father?" asked the two little ones every evening, gazing up at him with their small arms round his huge legs. Lars Peter nodded.

"We must keep together here in the Crow's Nest," said he to Ditte as if in excuse. "We can't get rid of the 'rag and bone man'—or the other either; but no-one can prevent us from being happy together."

Well, Ditte did not object to his staying at home. As long as they got food, the rest was of no consequence.

Yes, they certainly must keep together—and get all they could out of one another, otherwise life would be too miserable to bear. On Sundays Lars Peter would harness the nag and drive them out to Frederiksvaerk, or to the other side of the lake. It was pleasant to drive, and as long as they possessed a horse and cart, they could not be utterly destitute.

Their small circle of acquaintances had vanished, but thanks to Klavs they found new friends. They were a cottager's family by the marsh—people whom no-one else would have anything to do with. There were about a dozen children, and though both the man and his wife went out as day laborers, they could not keep them, and the parish had to help. Lars Peter had frequently given them a hand with his cart, but there had never been much intercourse as long as Sörine was in command of the Crow's Nest. But now it came quite naturally. Birds of a feather flock together—so people said.

To the children it meant play-fellows and comrades in disgrace. It was quite a treat to be asked over to Johansens on a Sunday afternoon, or even more so to have them at the Crow's Nest. There was a certain satisfaction in having visitors under their roof, and giving them the best the house could provide. For days before they came Ditte would be busy making preparations: setting out milk for cream to have with the coffee, and buying in all they could afford. On Sunday morning she would cut large plates of bread-and-butter, to make it easier for her in the afternoon. As soon as the guests arrived, they would have coffee, bread-and-butter and home-made cakes. Then the children would play "Touch," or "Bobbies and Thieves." Lars Peter allowed them to run all over the place, and there would be wild hunting in and outside the Crow's Nest. In the meanwhile the grown-ups wandered about in the fields, looking at the crops. Ditte went with them, keeping by the side of Johansen's wife, with her hands under her apron, just as she did.

At six o'clock they had supper, sandwiches with beer and brandy; then they would sit for a short time talking, before going home. There was the evening work to be done, and every one had to get up early the next morning.

They were people even poorer than themselves. They came in shining wooden shoes, and in clean blue working clothes. They were so poor that in the winter they never had anything to eat but herrings and potatoes, and it delighted Ditte to give them a really good meal: sandwiches of the best, and bottles of beer out of which the cork popped and the froth overflowed.

CHAPTER V
THE LITTLE VAGABOND

Lars Peter stood by the water-trough where Klavs was drinking his fill. They had been for a long trip, and both looked tired and glad to be home again.

At times a great longing for the highroad came over the rag and bone man, and he would then harness the nag and set off on his old rounds again. The road seemed to ease his trouble, and drew him further and further away, so that he spent the night from home, returning the following day. There was not much made on these trips, but he always managed to do a little—and his depression would pass off for the time being.

He had just returned from one of these outings, and stood in deep thought, happy to be home again, and to find all was well. Now there should be an end to these fits of wandering. Affairs at home required a man.

Povl and his sister Else hurried out to welcome him; they ran in and out between his legs, which to them were like great thick posts, singing all the while. Sometimes they would run between the nag's legs too, and the wise creature would carefully lift its hoofs, as though afraid of hurting them—they could stand erect between their father's legs.

Ditte came out from the kitchen door with a basket on her arm. "Now, you're thinking again, father," said she laughingly, "take care you don't step on the children."

Lars Peter pulled himself together and tenderly stroked the rough little heads. "Where are you off to?" asked he.

"Oh, to the shop. I want some things for the house."

"Let Kristian go, you've quite enough to do without that."

"He hasn't come home from school yet—most likely I'll meet him on the way."

"Not home yet?—and it's nearly supper-time." Lars Peter looked at her in alarm. "D'you think he can be off on the highroad again?"

Ditte shook her head. "I think he's been kept in—I'm sure to meet him. It's a good thing too—he can help me to carry the things home," she added tactfully.

But Lars Peter could no longer be taken in. He had just been thanking his stars that all was well on his return, and had silently vowed to give up his wanderings—and now this! The boy was at his old tricks again, there was no doubt about that—he could see it in the girl's eyes. It was in his children's blood, it seemed, and much as he cared for them—his sins would be visited on them. For the little ones' sake he was struggling to overcome his own wandering bent, and now it cropped out in them. It was like touching an open wound—he felt sick at heart.

Lars Peter led the horse into its stall, and gave it some corn. He did not take off the harness. Unless the boy returned soon, he would go and look for him. It had happened before that Lars Peter and Klavs had spent the night searching. And once Ditte had nearly run herself off her legs looking for the boy, while all the time he was quite happy driving round with his father on his rounds. He had been waiting for Lars Peter on the highroad, telling him he had a holiday—and got permission to go with his father. There was no trusting him.

When Ditte got as far as the willows, she hid the basket in them. She had only used the shop as an excuse to get away from home and look for the boy, without the father knowing anything was wrong. A short distance along the highroad lived some of Kristian's school-fellows, and she went there to make inquiries. Kristian had not been at school that day. She guessed as much—he had been in such a hurry to get off in the morning! Perhaps he was in one of the fields, behind a bush, hungry and wornout; it would be just like him to lie there until he perished, if no-one found him in the meanwhile.

She ran aimlessly over the fields, asking every one she met if they had seen her brother. "Oh, is it the young scamp from the Crow's Nest?" people asked. "Ay, he's got vagabond's blood in him."

Then she ran on, as quickly as she could. Her legs gave way, but she picked herself up and stumbled on. She couldn't think of going home without the boy; it would worry her father dreadfully! And Kristian himself—her little heart trembled at the thought of his being out all night.

A man on a cart told her he had seen a boy seven or eight years old, down by the marsh. She rushed down—and there was Kristian. He stood outside a hut, howling, the inhabitants gathered round him, and a man holding him firmly by his collar.

"Come to look for this young rascal?" said he. "Ay, we've caught him, here he is. The children told he'd shirked his school, and we thought we'd better make sure of him, to keep him out of mischief."

"Oh, he's all right," said Ditte, bristling, "he wouldn't do any harm." She pushed the man's hand away, and like a little mother drew the boy towards her. "Don't cry, dear," said she, drying his wet cheeks with her apron. "Nobody'll dare to touch you."

The man grinned and looked taken aback. "Do him harm?" said he loudly. "And who is it sets fire to other folk's houses and sets on peaceful womenfolk, but vagabonds. And that's just the way they begin."

But Ditte and Kristian had rushed off. She held him by his hand, scolding him as they went along. "There, [Pg 234] you can hear yourself what the man says! And that's what they'll think you are," said she. "And you know it worries Father so. Don't you think he's enough trouble without that?"

"Why did Mother do it?" said Kristian, beginning to cry.

He was worn out, and as soon as they got home Ditte put him quickly to bed. She gave him camomile tea and put one of her father's stockings—the left one—round his throat.

During the evening she and her father discussed what had happened. The boy lay tossing feverishly in bed. "It's those mischievous children," said Ditte with passion. "If I were there, they wouldn't dare to touch him."

"Why does the boy take any notice of it?" growled Lars Peter. "You've been through it all yourself."

"Ay, but then I'm a girl—boys mind much more what's said to them. I give it them back again, but when Kristian's mad with rage, he can't find anything to say. And then they all shout and laugh at him—and he takes off his wooden shoe to hit them."

Lars Peter sat silent for a while. "We'd better see and get away from here," said he.

Kristian popped his head over the end of the bed. "Yes, far, far away!" he shouted. This at all events he had heard.

"We'll go to America then," said Ditte, carefully covering him up. "Go to sleep now, so that you'll be [Pg 235] quite well for the journey." The boy looked at her with big, trusting eyes, and was quiet.

"'Tis a shame, for the boy's clever enough," whispered Lars Peter. "'Tis wonderful how he can think a thing out in his little head—and understand the ins and outs of everything. He knows more about wheels and their workings than I do. If only he hadn't got my wandering ways in his blood."

"That'll wear off in time!" thought Ditte. "At one time I used to run away too."

The following day Kristian was out again, and went singing about the yard. A message had been sent to school that he was ill, so that he had a holiday for a few days—he was in high spirits. He had got hold of the remains of an old perambulator which his father had brought home, and was busy mending it, for the little ones to ride in. Wheels were put on axles, now only the body remained to be fixed. The two little ones stood breathlessly watching him. Povl chattered away, and wanted to help, every other moment his little hands interfered and did harm. But sister Else stood dumbly watching, with big thoughtful eyes. "She's always dreaming, dear little thing," said Ditte, "the Lord only knows what she dreams about."

Ditte, to all appearance, never dreamed, but went about wide awake from morning till night. Life had already given her a woman's hard duties to fulfil, and she had met them and carried them out with a certain sturdiness. To the little ones she was the strict house-wife [Pg 236] and mother, whose authority could not be questioned, and should the occasion arise, she would give them a little slap. But underneath the surface was her childish mind. About all her experiences she formed her own opinions and conclusions, but never spoke of them to any one.

The most difficult of all for her to realize was that Granny was dead, and that she could never, never, run over to see her any more. Her life with Granny had been her real childhood, the memory of which remained vivid—unforgettable, as happy childhood is when one is grown up. In the daytime the fact was clear enough. Granny was dead and buried, and would never come back again. But at night when Ditte was in bed, dead-beat after a hard day, she felt a keen desire to be a child again, and would cuddle herself up in the quilt, pretending she was with Granny. And, as she dropped off, she seemed to feel the old woman's arm round her, as was her wont. Her whole body ached with weariness, but Granny took it away—wise Granny who could cure the rheumatism. Then she would remember Granny's awful fight with Sörine. And Ditte would awaken to find Lars Peter standing over her bed trying to soothe her. She had screamed! He did not leave her until she had fallen asleep again—with his huge hand held against her heart, which fluttered like that of a captured bird.

At school, she never played, but went about all alone. The others did not care to have her with them, and she [Pg 237] was not good at games either. She was like a hard fruit, which had had more bad weather than sunshine. Songs and childish rhymes sounded harsh on her lips, and her hands were rough with work.

The schoolmaster noticed all this. One day when Lars Peter was passing, he called him in to talk of Ditte. "She ought to be in entirely different surroundings," said he, "a place where she can get new school-fellows. Perhaps she has too much responsibility at home for a child of her age. You ought to send her away."

To Lars Peter this was like a bomb-shell. He had a great respect for the schoolmaster—he had passed examinations and things—but how was he to manage without his clever little housekeeper? "All of us ought to go away," he thought. "There're only troubles and worries here."

No, there was nothing to look forward to here—they could not even associate with their neighbors! He had begun to miss the fellowship of men, and often thought of his relations, whom he had not seen, and hardly heard of, for many years. He longed for the old homestead, which he had left to get rid of the family nickname, and seriously thought of selling the little he had, and turning homewards. Nicknames seemed to follow wherever one went. There was no happiness to be found here, and his livelihood was gone. "Nothing seems to prosper here," thought he, saving of course the blessed children—and they would go with him.

The thought of leaving did not make things better. Everything was at a standstill. It was no good doing anything until he began his new life—whatever that might be.

He and Ditte talked it over together. She would be glad to leave, and did not mind where they went. She had nothing to lose. A new life offered at least the chance of a more promising future. Secretly, she had her own ideas of what should come—but not here; the place was accursed. Not exactly the prince in Granny's spinning-song, she was too old for that—princes only married princesses. But many other things might happen besides that, given the opportunity. Ditte had no great pretensions, but "forward" was her motto. "It must be a place where there're plenty of people," said she. "Kind people," she added, thinking most of her little brothers and sister.

Thus they talked it over until they agreed that it would be best to sell up as soon as possible and leave. In the meantime, something happened which for a time changed their outlook altogether, and made them forget their plans.

CHAPTER VI
THE KNIFE-GRINDER

One afternoon, when the children were playing outside in the sunshine, Ditte stood just inside the open kitchen door, washing up after dinner. Suddenly soft music was heard a short distance away—a run of notes; even the sunshine seemed to join in. The little ones lifted their heads and gazed out into space; Ditte came out with a plate and a dishcloth in her hands.

Up on the road just where the track to the Crow's Nest turned off stood a man with a wonderful-looking machine; he blew, to draw attention—on a flute or clarionet, whatever it might be—and looked towards the house. When no-one appeared in answer to his call, he began moving towards the house, pushing the machine in front of him. The little ones rushed indoors. The man left his machine beside the pump and came up to the kitchen door. Ditte stood barring the way.

"Anything want grinding, rivetting or soldering, anything to mend?" he gabbled off, lifting his cap an inch from his forehead. "I sharpen knives, scissors, razors, pitchforks or plowshares! Cut your corns, stick pigs, flirt with the mistress, kiss the maids—and never say no to a glass and a crust of bread!" Then he screwed up his mouth and finished off with a song.

"Knives to grind, knives to grind! Any scissors and knives to grind? Knives and scissors to gri-i-ind!" he sang at the top of his voice.

Ditte stood in the doorway and laughed, with the children hanging on to her skirt. "I've got a bread-knife that won't cut," said she.

The man wheeled his machine up to the door. It was a big thing: water-tank, grindstone, a table for rivetting, a little anvil and a big wheel—all built upon a barrow. The children forgot their fear in their desire to see this funny machine. He handled the bread-knife with many flourishes, whistled over the edge to see how blunt it was, pretended the blade was loose, and put it on the anvil to rivet it. "It must have been used to cut paving-stories with," said he. But this was absurd; the blade was neither loose nor had it been misused. He was evidently a mountebank.

He was quite young; thin, and quick in his movements; he rambled on all the time. And such nonsense he talked! But how handsome he was! He had black eyes and black hair, which looked quite blue in the sunshine.

Lars Peter came out from the barn yawning; he had been having an after-dinner nap. There were bits of clover and hay in his tousled hair. "Where do you come from?" he cried gaily as he crossed the yard.

"From Spain," answered the man, showing his white teeth in a broad grin.

"From Spain—that's what my father always said when any one asked him," said Lars Peter thoughtfully. "Don't come from Odsherred by any chance?"

The man nodded.

"Then maybe you can give me some news of an Amst Hansen—a big fellow with nine sons?... The rag and bone man, he was called." The last was added guiltily.

"I should think I could—that's my father."

"No!" said Lars Peter heartily, stretching out his big hand. "Then welcome here, for you must be Johannes—my youngest brother." He held the youth's hand, looking at him cordially. "Oh, so that's what you look like now; last time I saw you, you were only a couple of months old. You're just like mother!"

Johannes smiled rather shyly, and drew his hand away; he was not so pleased over the meeting as was his brother.

"Leave the work and come inside," said Lars Peter, "and the girl will make us a cup of coffee. Well, well! To think of meeting like this. Ay, just like mother, you are." He blinked his eyes, touched by the thought.

As they drank their coffee, Johannes told all the news from home. The mother had died some years ago and the brothers were gone to the four corners of the earth. The news of his mother's death was a great blow to Lars Peter. "So she's gone?" said he quietly. "I've not seen her since you were a baby. I'd looked forward to seeing her again—she was always good, was mother."

"Well," Johannes drawled, "she was rather grumpy."

"Not when I was at home—maybe she was ill a long time."

"We didn't get on somehow. No, the old man for me, he was always in a good temper."

"Does he still work at his old trade?" asked Lars Peter with interest.

"No, that's done with long ago. He lives on his pension!" Johannes laughed. "He breaks stones on the roadside now. He's as hard as ever and will rule the roost. He fights with the peasants as they pass, and swears at them because they drive on his heap of stones."

Johannes himself had quarrelled with his master and had given him a black eye; and as he was the only butcher who would engage him over there, he had left, crossing over at Lynoes—with the machine which he had borrowed from a sick old scissor-grinder.

"So you're a butcher," said Lars Peter. "I thought as much. You don't look like a professional grinder. You're young and strong; couldn't you work for the old man and keep him out of the workhouse?"

"Oh, he's difficult to get on with—and he's all right where he is. If a fellow wants to keep up with the rest—and get a little fun out of life—there's only enough for one."

"I dare say. And what do you think of doing now? Going on again?"

Yes, he wanted to see something of life—with the help of the machine outside.

"And can you do all you say?"

Johannes made a grimace. "I learned a bit from the old man when I was a youngster, but it's more by way of patter than anything else. A fellow's only to ramble on, get the money, and make off before they've time to look at the things. It's none so bad, and the police can't touch you so long as you're working."

"Is that how it is?" said Lars Peter. "I see you've got the roving blood in you too. 'Tis a sad thing to suffer from, brother!"

"But why? There's always something new to be seen! 'Tis sickening to hang about in the same place, forever."

"Ay, that's what I used to think; but one day a man finds out that it's no good thinking that way! Nothing thrives when you knock about the road to earn your bread. No home and no family, nothing worth having, however much you try to settle down."

"But you've got both," said Johannes.

"Ay, but it's difficult to keep things together. Living from hand to mouth and nothing at your back—'tis a poor life. And the worst of it is, we poor folk *have* to turn that way; it seems better not to know where your bread's to come from day by day and go hunting it here, there and everywhere. It's that that makes us go a-roving. But now you must amuse yourself for a couple of hours; I've promised to cart some dung for a neighbor!"

During Lars Peter's absence Ditte and the children showed their uncle round the farm. He was a funny fellow and they very soon made friends. He couldn't be used to anything fine, for he admired everything he saw, and won Ditte's confidence entirely. She had never heard the Crow's Nest and its belongings admired before.

He helped her with her evening work, and when Lars Peter returned the place was livelier than it had been for many a day. After supper Ditte made coffee and put the brandy bottle on the table, and the brothers had a long chat. Johannes told about home; he had a keen sense of humor and spared neither home nor brothers in the telling, and Lars Peter laughed till he nearly fell off his chair.

"Ay, that's right enough!" he cried, "just as it would have been in the old days." There was a great deal to ask about and many old memories to be refreshed; the children had not seen their father so genial and happy for goodness knows how long. It was easy to see that his brother's coming had done him good.

And they too had a certain feeling of well-being—they had got a relation! Since Granny's death they had seemed so alone, and when other children spoke of their relations they had nothing to say. They had got an uncle—next after a granny this was the greatest of all relations. And he had come to the Crow's

Nest in the most wonderful manner, taking them unawares—and himself too! Their little bodies tingled with excitement; every other minute they crept out, meddling with the wonderful machine, which was outside sleeping in the moonlight. But Ditte soon put a stop to this and ordered them to bed.

The two brothers sat chatting until after midnight, and the children struggled against sleep as long as they possibly could, so as not to lose anything. But sleep overcame them at last, and Ditte too had to give in. She would not go to bed before the men, and fell asleep over the back of a chair.

Morning came, and with it a sense of joy; the children opened their eyes with the feeling that something had been waiting for them by the bedside the whole night to meet them with gladness when they woke—what was it? Yes, over there on the hook by the door hung a cap—Uncle Johannes was here! He and Lars Peter were already up and doing.

Johannes was taken with everything he saw and was full of ideas. "This might be made a nice little property," he said time after time. "'Tis neglected, that's all."[Pg 246]

"Ay, it's had to look after itself while I've been out," answered Lars Peter in excuse. "And this trouble with the wife didn't make things better either. Maybe you've heard all about it over there?"

Johannes nodded. "That oughtn't to make any difference to you, though," said he.

That day Lars Peter had to go down to the marsh and dig a ditch, to drain a piece of the land. Johannes got a spade and went with him. He worked with such a will that Lars Peter had some difficulty in keeping up with him. "'Tis easy to see you're young," said he, "the way you go at it."

"Why don't you ditch the whole and level it out? 'Twould make a good meadow," said Johannes.

Ay, why not? Lars Peter did not know himself. "If only a fellow had some one to work with," said he.

"Do you get any peat here?" asked Johannes once when they were taking a breathing space.

"No, nothing beyond what we use ourselves; 'tis a hard job to cut it."

"Ay, when you use your feet! But you ought to get a machine to work with a horse; then a couple of men can do ever so many square feet in a day."

Lars Peter became thoughtful. Ideas and advice had been poured into him and he would have liked to go thoroughly through them and digest them one by one. But Johannes gave him no time.

The next minute he was by the clay-pit. There was uncommonly fine material for bricks, he thought.[Pg 247]

Ay, Lars Peter knew it all only too well. The first summer he was married, Sörine had made bricks to build the outhouse and it had stood all kinds of weather. But one pair of hands could not do everything.

And thus Johannes went from one thing to the other. He was observant and found ways for everything; there was no end to his plans. Lars Peter had to attend; it was like listening to an old, forgotten melody. Marsh, clay-pit and the rest had said the same year after year, though more slowly; now he had hardly time to follow. It was inspiriting, all at once to see a way out of all difficulties.

"Look here, brother," said he, as they were at dinner, "you put heart into a man again. How'd you like to stay on here? Then we could put the place in order together. There's not much in that roving business after all."

Johannes seemed to like the idea—after all, the highroad was unsatisfactory as a means of livelihood!

During the day they talked it over more closely and agreed how to set about things; they would share as brothers both the work and what it brought in. "But what about the machine?" said Lars Peter. "That must be returned."

"Oh, never mind that," said Johannes. "The man can't use it; he's ill."

"Ay, but when he gets up again, then he'll have nothing to earn his living; we can't have that on our conscience. I'm going down to the beach tomorrow [Pg 248] for a load of herrings, so I'll drive round by Hundested and put it off there. There's sure to be a fisherman who'll take it over with him. I'd really thought of giving up the herring trade; but long ago I bound myself to take a load, and there should be a good catch these days."

At three o'clock next morning Lars Peter was ready in the yard to drive to the fishing village; at the back of the cart was the wonderful machine. As he was about to start, Johannes came running up, unwashed and only half awake; he had just managed to put on his cap and tie a handkerchief round his neck. "I think I'll go with you," he said with a yawn.

Lars Peter thought for a minute—it came as a surprise to him. "Very well, just as you like," said he at last, making room. He had reckoned on his brother beginning the ditching today; there was so little water in the meadow now.

"Do me good to get out a bit!" said Johannes as he clambered into the cart.

Well—yes—but he had only just come in. "Don't you want an overcoat?" asked Lars Peter. "There's an old one of mine you can have."

"Oh, never mind—I can turn up my collar."

The sun was just rising; there was a white haze on the shores of the lake, hanging like a veil over the rushes. In the green fields dewdrops were caught by millions in the spiders' webs, sparkling like diamonds in the first rays of sunshine.

Lars Peter saw it all, and perhaps it was this which turned his mind; at least, today, he thought the Crow's Nest was a good and pretty little place; it would be a sin to leave it. He had found out all he wanted to know about his relations and home and what had happened to every one in the past years and his longing for home had vanished; now he would prefer to stay where he was. "Just you be thankful that you're away from it all!" Johannes had said. And he was right—it wasn't worth while moving to go back to the quarreling and jealousies of relations. As a matter of fact there was no inducement to leave: no sense in chasing your luck like a fool, better try to keep what there was.

Lars Peter could not understand what had happened to him—everything looked so different today. It was as if his eyes had been rubbed with some wonderful ointment; even the meager lands of the Crow's Nest looked beautiful and promising. A new day had dawned for him and his home.

"'Tis a glorious morning," said he, turning towards Johannes.

Johannes did not answer. He had drawn his cap down over his eyes and gone to sleep. He looked somewhat dejected and his mouth hung loosely as if he had been drinking. It was extraordinary how he resembled his mother! Lars Peter promised himself that he would take good care of him.

CHAPTER VII
THE SAUSAGE-MAKER

Nothing was done to the land round the Crow's Nest this time; it was a fateful moment when Johannes, instead of taking his spade and beginning the ditching, felt inclined to go with his brother carting herrings. On one of the farms where they went to trade, a still-born calf lay outside the barn; Johannes caught sight of it at once. With one jump he was out of the cart and beside it.

"What do you reckon to do with it?" asked he, turning it over with his foot.

"Bury it, of course," answered the farm-lad.

"Don't folks sell dead animals in these parts?" asked Johannes when they were in the cart again.

"Why, who could they sell them to?" answered Lars Peter.

"The Lord preserve me, you're far behind the times. D'you know what, I've a good mind to settle down here as a cattle-dealer."

"And buy up all the still-born calves?" Lars Peter laughed.

"Not just that. But it's not a bad idea, all the same; the old butcher at home often made ten to fifteen crowns out of a calf like that."

"I thought we were going to start in earnest at home," said Lars Peter.

"We'll do that too, but we shall want money! Your trade took up all your time, so everything was left to look after itself, but cattle-dealing's another thing. A hundred crowns a day's easily earned, if you're lucky. Let me drive round once a week, and I'll promise it'll give us enough to live on. And then we've the rest of the week to work on the land."

"Sounds all right," said Lars Peter hesitatingly. "There's trader's blood in you too, I suppose?"

"You may be sure of that, I've often earned hundreds of crowns for my master at home in Knarreby."

"But how'd you begin?" said Peter. "I've got fifty crowns at the most, and that's not much to buy cattle with. It's put by for rent and taxes, and really oughtn't to be touched."

"Let me have it, and I'll see to the rest," said Johannes confidently.

The very next day he set off in the cart, with the whole of Lars Peter's savings in his pocket. He was away for two days, which was not reassuring in itself. Perhaps he had got into bad company, and had the money stolen from him—or frittered it away in poor trade. The waiting began to seem endless to Lars Peter. Then at last Johannes returned, with a full load and singing at the top of his voice. To the back of the cart was tied an old half-dead horse, so far gone it could hardly move.

"Well, you seem to have bought something young!" shouted Lars Peter scoffingly. "What've you got under the sacks and hay?"

Johannes drove the cart into the porch, closed the gates, and began to unload. A dead calf, a half-rotten pig and another calf just alive. He had bought them on the neighboring farms, and had still some money left.

"Ay, that's all very well, but what are you going to do with it all?" broke out Lars Peter amazed.

"You'll see that soon enough," answered Johannes, running in and out.

There was dash and energy in him, he sang and whistled, as he bustled about. The big porch was cleared, and a tree-stump put in as a block; he lit a wisp of hay to see if there was a draught underneath the boiler. The children stood open-mouthed gazing at him, and Lars Peter shook his head, but did not interfere.

He cut up the dead calf, skinned it, and nailed the skin up in the porch to dry. Then it was the sick calf's turn, with one blow it was killed, and its skin hung up beside the other.

Ditte and Kristian were set to clean the guts, which they did very unwillingly.

"Good Lord, have you never touched guts before?" said Johannes.

"A-a-y. But not of animals that had died," answered Ditte.

"Ho, indeed, so you clean the guts while they're alive, eh? I'd like to see that!"

They had no answer ready, and went on with their work—while Johannes drew in the half-dead horse, and went for the ax. As he ran across the yard, he threw the ax up into the air and caught it again by the handle; he was in high spirits.

"Takes after the rest of the family!" thought Lars Peter, who kept in the barn, and busied himself there. He did not like all this, although it was the trade his race had practised for many years, and which now took possession of the Crow's Nest; it reminded him strongly of his childhood. "Folk may well think us the scum of the earth now," thought he moodily.

Johannes came whistling into the barn for an old sack.

"Don't look so grumpy, old man," said he as he passed. Lars Peter had not time to answer before he was out again. He put the sack over the horse's head, measured the distance, and swung the ax backwards; a strange long-drawn crash sounded from behind the sack, and the horse sank to the ground with its skull cracked. The children looked on, petrified.

"You'll have to give me a hand now, to lift it," shouted Johannes gaily. Lars Peter came lingeringly across the yard, and gave a helping hand. Shortly afterwards the horse hung from a beam, with its head downwards, the body was cut up and the skin folded back like a cape.

Uncle Johannes' movements became more and more mysterious. They understood his care with the skins, these could be sold; but what did he want with the guts and all the flesh he cut up? That evening he lit the fire underneath the boiler, and he worked the whole night, filling the place with a disgusting smell of bones, meat and guts being cooked.

"He must be making soap," thought Lars Peter, "or cart grease."

The more he thought of it the less he liked the whole proceeding, and wished that he had let his brother go as he had come. But he could do nothing now, but let him go on.

Johannes asked no one to help him; he kept the door of the outhouse carefully closed and did his work with great secrecy. He was cooking the whole night, and the next morning at breakfast he ordered the children not to say a word of what he had been doing. During the morning he disappeared and returned with a mincing-machine, he took the block too into the outhouse. He came to his meals covered with blood, fat and scraps of meat. He looked dreadful and smelled even worse. But he certainly worked hard; he did not even allow himself time to sleep.

Late in the afternoon he opened the door of the outhouse wide: the work was done.

"Here you are, come and look!" he shouted. From a stick under the ceiling hung a long row of sausages, beautiful to look at, bright and freshly colored; no-one would guess what they were made of. On the big washing-board lay meat, cut into neat joints and bright red in color—this was the best part of the horse. And there was a big pail of fat, which had not quite stiffened. "That's grease," said Johannes, stirring it, "but as a matter of fact it's quite nice for dripping. Looks quite tasty, eh?"

"It shan't come into our kitchen," said Ditte, making a face at the things.

"You needn't be afraid, my girl; sausage-makers never eat their own meat," answered Johannes.

"What are you going to do with it now?" asked Lars Peter, evidently knowing what the answer would be.

"Sell it, of course!" Johannes showed his white teeth, as he took a sausage. "Just feel how firm and round it is."

"If you think you can sell them here, you're very much mistaken. You don't know the folks in these parts."

"Here? of course not! Drive over to the other side of the lake where no-one knows me, or what they're made of. We often used to make these at my old place. All the bad stuff we bought in one county, we sold in another. No-one ever found us out. Simple enough, isn't it?"

"I'll have nothing to do with it," said Lars Peter determinedly.

"Don't want you to—you're not the sort for this work. I'm off tomorrow, but you must get me another horse. If I have to drive with that rusty old threshing-machine in there, I shan't be back for a whole week. Never saw such a beast. If he was mine I'd make him into sausages."

"That you shall never do," answered Lars Peter offendedly. "The horse is good enough, though maybe he's not to your liking."

The fact was they did not suit each other—Johannes and Klavs; they were like fire and water. Johannes preferred to fly along the highroad; but soon found out it wouldn't do. Then he expected that the nag—since it could no longer gallop and was so slow to set going—should keep moving when he jumped off. As a butcher he was accustomed to jump off the cart, run into a house with a piece of meat, catch up with the cart and jump on again—without stopping the horse. But Klavs did not feel inclined for these new tricks. The result was they clashed. Johannes made up his mind to train the horse, and kept striking it with the thick end of the whip. Klavs stopped in amazement. Twice he kicked up his hind legs—warningly, then turned round, broke the shafts, and tried to get up into the cart. He showed his long teeth in a grin, which might mean: Just let me get you under my hoofs, you black rascal! This happened on the highroad the day he had gone out to buy [Pg 257] cattle. Lars Peter and the children knew that the two were enemies. When Johannes entered the barn, Klavs at once laid back his ears and was prepared to both bite and fight. There was no mistaking the signs.

Next morning, before Johannes started out, Kristian was sent over with the nag to a neighbor who lived north of the road, and got their horse in exchange.

"It belonged to a butcher for many years, so you ought to get on with it," said Lars Peter as they harnessed it.

It was long and thin, just the sort for Johannes. As soon as he was in the cart, the horse knew what kind of man held the reins. It set off with a jerk, and passed the corner of the house like a flash of lightning. The next minute they were up on the highroad, rushing along in a whirl of dust. Johannes bumped up and down on the seat, shouted and flourished his whip, and held the reins over his head. They seemed possessed by the devil.

"He shan't touch Klavs again," mumbled Lars Peter as he went in.

The next day Johannes came back with notes in his pocketbook and a mare running behind the cart. It was the same kind of horse as the one he drove, only a little more stiff in its movements; he had bought it for next to nothing—to be killed.

"But it would be a sin to kill it; it's not too far gone to enjoy life yet, eh, old lady?" said he, slapping its back. The mare whinnied and threw up its hind legs. [Pg 258]

"'Tis nigh on thirty," said Lars Peter, peering into its mouth.

"It may not be up to much, but the will's there right enough, just look at it!" He cracked his whip and the old steed threw its head back and started off. It didn't get very far, however, its movements were jerky and painful.

"Quite a high flier," said Lars Peter laughingly, "it looks as if a breath of air would blow it up to heaven. But are you sure it's not against the law to use it, when it's sold to be killed?"

Johannes nodded. "They won't know it when I've finished with it," said he.

As soon as he had had a meal, and got into his working clothes, he started to remodel the horse. He clipped its mane and tail, and cropped the hair round its hoofs.

"It only wants a little brown coloring to dye the gray hair—and a couple of bottles of arsenic, and then you'll see how smart and young she'll be. The devil himself wouldn't know her again."

"Did you learn these tricks from your master?" asked Lars Peter.

"No, from the old man. Never seen him at it?"

Lars Peter could not remember. "It must have been after my time," said he, turning away.

"'Tis a good old family trick," said Johannes.

That there was money to be made from the new [Pg 259] business was soon evident, and Lars Peter got over his indignation. He let Johannes drive round buying and selling, while he himself remained at home, making sausages, soap and grease from the refuse. He had been an apt pupil, it was the old family trade.

The air round the Crow's Nest stank that summer. People held their noses and whipped up their horses as they passed by. Johannes brought home money in plenty and they lacked for nothing. But neither Lars Peter nor the children were happy. They felt that the Crow's Nest was talked about more even than before. And the worst of it was, they no longer felt this to be an injustice. People had every right to look down on them now; there was not the consolation that their honor was unassailable.

Johannes did not care. He was out on the road most of the time. He made a lot of money, and was proud of it too. He often bought cattle and sold them again. He was dissipated, so it was said—played cards with fellows of his own kidney, and went to dances. Sometimes after a brawl, he would come home with a wounded head and a black eye. Apparently he spent a great deal of money; no-one could say how much he made. That was his business, but he behaved as if he alone kept things going, and was easily put out. Lars Peter never interfered, he liked peace in the house.

One day, however, they quarreled in earnest. Johannes had always had his eye on the nag, and one day when Lars Peter was away, he dragged it out of [Pg 260] the stall and tied it up, he was going to teach it to behave, he said to the children. With difficulty he harnessed it to the cart, it lashed its tail and showed its teeth, and when Johannes wanted it to set off, refused to stir, however much it was lashed. At last, beside himself with temper, he jumped off the cart, seized a shaft from the harrow, and began hitting at its legs with all his might. The children screamed. The horse was trembling, bathed in perspiration, its flanks heaving violently. Each time he jumped up to it, the nag kicked up its hind legs, and at last giving up the fight, Johannes threw away his weapon and went into his room.

Ditte had tried to throw herself between them, but had been brushed aside; now she went up to the horse. She unharnessed it, gave it water to drink, and put a wet sack over its wounds, while the little ones stood round crying and offering it bread. Shortly afterwards Johannes came out; he had changed his clothes. Quickly, without a look at any one, he harnessed and drove off. The little ones came out from their hiding-place and gazed after him.

"Is he going away now?" asked sister Else.

"I only wish he would, or the horse bolt, so he could never find his way back again, nasty brute," said Kristian. None of them liked him any longer.

A man came along the footpath down by the marsh, it was their father. The children ran to meet him, and all started to tell what had happened. Lars Peter stared at them for a moment, as if he could not take in what they had said, then set off at a run; Ditte followed him into the stable. There stood Klavs, looking very miserable; the poor beast still trembled when they spoke to it; its body was badly cut. Lars Peter's face was gray.

"He may thank the Lord that he's not here now!" he said to Ditte. He examined the horse's limbs to make sure no bones were broken; the nag carefully lifted one leg, then the other, and moaned.

"Blood-hound," said Lars Peter, softly stroking its legs, "treating poor old Klavs like that."

Klavs whinnied and scraped the stones with his hoofs. He took advantage of his master's sympathy and begged for an extra supply of corn.

"You should give him a good beating," said Kristian seriously.

"I've a mind to turn him out altogether," answered the father darkly. "'Twould be best for all of us."

"Yes, and d'you know, Father? Can you guess why the Johansens haven't been to see us this summer? They're afraid of what we'll give them to eat; they say we make food from dead animals."

"Where did you hear that, Ditte?" Lars Peter looked at her in blank despair.

"The children shouted it after me today. They asked if I wouldn't like a dead cat to make sausages."

"Ay, I thought as much," he laughed miserably. "Well, we can do without them,—what the devil do I want with them!" he shouted so loudly that little Povl began to cry.

"Hush now, I didn't mean to frighten you," Lars Peter took him in his arms. "But it's enough to make a man lose his temper."

Two days afterwards, Johannes returned home, looking as dirty and rakish as he possibly could. Lars Peter had to help him out of the cart, he could hardly stand on his legs. But he was not at loss for words. Lars Peter was silent at his insolence and dragged him into the barn, where he at once fell asleep. There he lay like a dead beast, deathly white, with a lock of black hair falling over his brow, and plastered on his forehead—he looked a wreck. The children crept over to the barn-door and peered at him through the half dark; when they caught sight of him they rushed out with terror into the fields. It was too horrible.

Lars Peter went to and fro, cutting hay for the horses. As he passed his brother, he stopped, and looked at him thoughtfully. That was how a man should look to keep up with other people: smooth and polished outside, and cold and heartless inside. No-one looked down on him just because he had impudence. Women admired him, and made some excuse to pass on the highroad in the evenings, and as for the men—his dissipation and his fights over girls probably overwhelmed them.

Lars Peter put his hand into his brother's pocket and took out the pocketbook—it was empty! He had taken 150 crowns with him from their joint savings—to be used for buying cattle, it was all the money there was in the house; and now he had squandered it all.

His hands began to tremble. He leant over his brother, as if to seize him; but straightened himself and left the barn. He hung about for two or three hours, to give his brother time to sleep off the drink, then went in again. This time he would settle up. He shook his brother and wakened him.

"Where's the money to buy the calf?" asked he.

"What's that to you?" Johannes threw himself on his other side.

Lars Peter dragged him to his feet. "I want to speak to you," said he.

"Oh, go to hell," mumbled Johannes. He did not open his eyes, and tumbled back into the hay.

Lars Peter brought a pail of ice-cold water from the well.

"I'll wake you, whether you like it or not!" said he, throwing the pailful of water over his head.

Like a cat Johannes sprang to his feet, and drew his knife. He turned round, startled by the rude awakening; caught sight of his brother and rushed at him. Lars Peter felt a stab in his cheek, the blade of the knife struck against his teeth. With one blow he knocked Johannes down, threw himself on him, wrestling for the knife. Johannes was like a cat, strong and quick in his movements; he twisted and turned, used his teeth, and tried to find an opening to stab again. He was foaming at the mouth. Lars Peter warded off the attacks with his hands, which were bleeding already from several stabs. At last he got his knee on his brother's chest.

Johannes lay gasping for breath. "Let me go!" he hissed.

"Ay, if you'll behave properly," said Lars Peter, relaxing his grip a little. "You're my youngest brother, and I'm loth to harm you; but I'll not be knocked down like a pig by you."

With a violent effort Johannes tried to throw off his brother. He got one arm free, and threw himself to one side, reaching for the knife, which lay a good arm's length away.

"Oh, that's your game!" said Lars Peter, forcing him down on to the floor of the barn with all his weight, "I'd better tie you up. Bring a rope, children!"

The three stood watching outside the barn-door; one behind the other. "Come on!" shouted the father. Then Kristian rushed in for Ditte, and she brought a rope. Without hesitation she went up to the two struggling men, and gave it to her father. "Shall I help you?" said she.

"No need for that, my girl," said Lars Peter, and laughed. "Just hold the rope, while I turn him over."

He bound his brother's hands firmly behind his back, then set him on his feet and brushed him. "You look like a pig," said he, "you must have been rolling on the muddy road. Go indoors quietly or you'll be sorry for it. No fault of yours that you're not a murderer today."

Johannes was led in, and set down in the rush-bottomed armchair beside the fire. The children were sent out of doors, and Ditte and Kristian ordered to harness Uncle Johannes' horse.

"Now we're alone, I'll tell you that you've behaved like a scoundrel," said Lars Peter slowly. "Here have I been longing for many a year to see some of my own kin, and when you came it was like a message from home. I'd give much never to have had it now. All of us saw something good in you; we didn't expect much, so there wasn't much for you to live up to. But what have you done? Dragged us into a heap of filth and villainy and wickedness. We've done with you here—make no mistake about that. You can take the one horse and cart and whatever else you can call your own, and off you go! There's no money to be got; you've wasted more than you've earned."

Johannes made no answer, and avoided his brother's eyes.

The cart was driven up outside. Lars Peter led him out, and lifted him like a child on to the seat. He loosened the rope with his cut and bleeding hands; the blood from the wound on his cheek ran down on to his chin and clothes. "Get off with you," said he threateningly, wiping the blood from his chin, "and be smart about it."

Johannes sat for a moment swaying in the cart, as if half asleep. Suddenly he pulled himself together, and with a shout of laughter gathered up the reins and quickly set off round the corner of the house up to the highroad.

Lars Peter stood gazing after the horse and cart, then went in and washed off the blood. Ditte bathed his wounds in cold water and put on sticking-plaster.

For the next few days they were busy getting rid of all traces of that summer's doings. Lars Peter dug down the remainder of the refuse, threw the block away, and cleaned up. When some farmer or other at night knocked on the window-panes with his whip, shouting: "Lars Peter, I've got a dead animal for you!" he made no answer. No more sausage-making, no more trading in carrion for him!

CHAPTER VIII
THE LAST OF THE CROW'S NEST

Ditte went about singing at her work; she had no-one to help her, and ran about to and fro. One eye was bound up, and each time she crossed the kitchen she lifted the bandage and bathed her eye with something brown in a cup. The eye was bloodshot, and hurt, and showed the colors of the rainbow, but all the same she was happy. Indeed, it was the sore eye which put her in such a happy mood. They were going away from the Crow's Nest, right away and forever, and it was all on account of her eye.

Lars Peter came home; he had been out for a walk. He hung up his stick behind the kitchen door. "Well, how's the eye getting on?" he asked, as he began to take off his boots.

"Oh, it's much better now. And what did the schoolmaster say?"

"Ay, what did he say? He thought it good and right that you should stand up for your little brothers and sister. But he did not care to be mixed up in the affair, and after all 'tis not to be wondered at."

"Why not? He knows how it all happened—and he's so truthful!"

"Hm—well—truthful! When a well-to-do farmer's son's concerned, then——. He's all right, but he's got his living to make. He's afraid of losing his post, if he gets up against the farmers, and they hang together like peas in a pod. He advised me to let it drop—especially as we're leaving the place. Nothing would come of it but trouble and rows again. And maybe it's likely enough. They'd get their own back at the auction—agree not to bid the things up, or stay away altogether."

"Then you didn't go to the police about it?"

"Ay, but I did. But he thought too there wasn't much to be made of the case. Oh, and the schoolmaster said you needn't go to school for the rest of the time—he'd see it was all right. He's a kind man, even if he is afraid of his skin."

Ditte was not satisfied. It would have done the big boy good to be well punished. He had been the first to attack Kristian, and had afterwards kicked her in her eye with his wooden shoe, because she had stood up for her brother. And she had been certain in her childish mind that this time they would get compensation—for the law made no difference whoever the people were.

"If I'd been a rich farmer's daughter, and he had come from the Crow's Nest, what then?" she asked hoarsely.

"Oh, he'd have got a good thrashing—if not worse!" said the father. "That's the way we poor people are treated, and can only be thankful that we don't get fined into the bargain."

"If you meet the boy, won't you give him a good thrashing?" she asked shortly afterwards.

"I'd rather give it to his father—but it's better to keep out of it. We're of no account, you see!"

Kristian came in through the kitchen door. "When I'm bigger, then I'll creep back here at night and set fire to his farm," said he, with flashing eyes.

"What's that you say, boy—d'you want to send us all to jail?" shouted Lars Peter, aghast.

"'Twould do them good," said Ditte, setting to work again. She was very dissatisfied with the result of her father's visit.

"When're you going to arrange about the auction?" she said stiffly.

"They'll see to that," answered Lars Peter quickly, "I've seen the clerk about it. He was very kind." Lars Peter was grateful for this, he did not care to go to the magistrate.

"Ay, he's glad to get rid of us," said Ditte harshly. "That's what they all are. At school they make a ring and sing about a crow and an owl and all ugly birds! and the crow and his young steal the farmer's chickens, but then the farmer takes a long stick and pulls down the Crow's Nest. Do you think I don't know what they mean?"

Lars Peter was silent, and went back to his work. He too felt miserable now.

But in the evening, as they sat round the lamp, talking of the future, all unpleasantness was forgotten. Lars Peter had been looking round for a place to settle down in, and had fixed on the fishing-hamlet where he used to buy fish in the old days. The people seemed to like him, and had often asked him why he didn't settle down there. "And there's a jolly fellow there, the inn-keeper, he can do anything. He's rough till you get to know him, but he's got a kind heart. He's promised to find me a couple of rooms, until we can build a place for ourselves—and help me to a share in a boat. What we get from the auction ought to be enough to build a house."

"Is that the man you told us about, who's like a dwarf?" asked Ditte with interest.

"Ay, he's like a giant and a dwarf mixed together—so to say—he might well have had the one for a father and the other for a mother. He's hunch-backed in front and behind, and his face as black as a crow's, but he can't help that, and otherwise he's all right. He's a finger in everything down there."

Ditte shuddered. "Sounds like a goblin!" said she.

Lars Peter was going in for fishing now. He had had a great deal to do in this line during his life, but he himself had never gone out; his fingers itched to be at it. Ditte too liked the thought of it. Then she would be near the sea again, which she dimly remembered from her childhood with Granny. And they would have done with everything here, and perhaps get rid of the rag and bone name, and shake off the curse.

Then they had to decide what to take with them. Now that it came to the point, it was dreadful to part with one's possessions. When they had gone through things together, and written on Kristian's slate what was to be sold, there wasn't much put down. They would like to take it all with them.

"We must go through it again—and have no nonsense," said Lars Peter. "We can't take the whole bag of tricks with us. Money'll be needed too—and not so little either."

So they went over the things again one by one. Klavs was out of the question. It would be a shame to send him to strangers in his old age; they could feed him on the downs. "It's useful to have," thought Lars Peter; "it gives a man a better standing. And we can make a little money by him too." This was only said by way of comfort. Deep down in his heart, he was very anxious about the nag. But no-one could face the thought of being parted from it.

The cow, on the other hand, there was quite a battle about. Lars Peter wished to take it too. "It's served us faithfully all this while," said he, "and given the little ones their food and health. And it's good to have plenty of milk in the house." But here Ditte was sensible. If they took the cow, they would have to take a field as well.

Lars Peter laughed: Ay, that was not a bad idea, if only they could take a lump of meadow on the cart—and piece of the marsh. Down there, there was nothing but sand. Well, he would give up the cow. "But the pig we'll keep—and the hens!"

Ditte agreed that hens were useful to keep, and the pig could live on anything.

The day before the auction they were busily engaged in putting all in order and writing numbers on the things in chalk. The little ones helped too, and were full of excitement.

"But they're not all matched," said Ditte, pointing at the different lots Lars Peter had put up together.

"That doesn't matter," answered Lars Peter—"folks see there's a boot in one lot, bid it up and then buy the whole lot. Well, then they see the other boot in another lot—and bid that up as well. It's always like that at auctions; folks get far more than they have use for—and most of it doesn't match."

Ditte laughed: "Ay, you ought to know all about it!" Her father himself had the bad habit of going to auctions and bringing home a great deal of useless rubbish. It could be bought on credit, which was a temptation.

How things collected as years went by, in attics and outhouses! It was a relief to get it all cleared away. But it was difficult to keep it together. The children had a use for it all—as soon as they saw their opportunity, [Pg 273] they would run off with something or other—just like rats.

The day of the auction arrived—a mild, gray, damp October day. The soft air hung like a veil over everything. The landscape, with its scattered houses and trees, lay resting in the all-embracing wet.

At the Crow's Nest they had been early astir. Ditte and Lars Peter had been running busily about from the house to the barn and back again. Now they had finished, and everything was in readiness. The children were washed and dressed, and went round full of expectation, with well-combed heads and faces red from scrubbing and soap. Ditte did not do things by halves, and when she washed their ears, and made their eyes smart with the soap, weeping was unavoidable. But now the disagreeable task was over, and there would be no more of it for another week; childish tears dry quickly, and their little faces beamingly met the day.

Little Povl was last ready. Ditte could hardly keep him on the chair, as she put the finishing touches—he was anxious to be out. "Well, what d'you say to sister?" she asked, when he was done, offering her mouth.

"Hobble!" said he, looking roguishly at her; he was in high spirits. Kristian and Else laughed.

"No, now answer properly," said Ditte seriously; she did not allow fun when correcting them. "Say, 'thank you, dear'—well?" [Pg 274]

"Thank you, dear lump!" said the youth, laughing immoderately.

"Oh, you're mad today," said Ditte, lifting him down. He ran out into the yard to the father, and continued his nonsense.

"What's that he says?" shouted Lars Peter from outside.

"Oh, it's only something he's made up himself—he often does that. He seems to think it's something naughty."

"You, lumpy, lump!" said the child, taking hold of his father's leg.

"Mind what you're doing, you little monkey, or I'll come after you!" said Lars Peter with a terrible roar.

The boy laughed and hid behind the well.

Lars Peter caught him and put him on one shoulder, and his sister on the other. "We'll go in the fields," said he.

Ditte and Kristian went with him, it would be their last walk there; involuntarily they each took hold of his coat. Thus they went down the pathway to the clay-pit, past the marsh and up on the other side. It was strange how different everything looked now they were going to lose it. The marsh and the clay-pit could have told their own tale about the children's play and Lars Peter's plans. The brambles in the hedges, the large stone which marked the boundary, the stone behind which they used to hide—all spoke to them in their own way today. The winter seed was in the earth, and [Pg 275] everything ready for the new occupier, whoever he might be. Lars Peter did not wish his successor to have anything to complain of. No-one should say that he had neglected his land, because he was not going to reap the harvest.

"Ay, our time's up here," said he, when they were back in the house again. "Lord knows what the new place'll be like!" There was a catch in his voice as he spoke.

A small crowd began to collect on the highroad. They stood in groups and did not go down to the Crow's Nest, until the auctioneer and his clerk arrived. Ditte was on the point of screaming when she saw who the two men were; they were the same who had come to fetch her mother. But now they came on quite a different errand, and spoke kindly.

Behind their conveyance came group after group of people, quite a procession. It looked as if no-one wanted to be the first to put foot on the rag and bone man's ground. Where the officials went, they too could follow, but the auctioneer and his clerk were the only ones to shake hands with Lars Peter; the others hung aimlessly about, and put their heads together, keeping up a whispering conversation.

Lars Peter summed up the buyers. There were one or two farmers among them, mean old men, who had come in the hope of getting a bargain. Otherwise they were nearly all poor people from round about, cottagers and laborers who were tempted by the chance of buying [Pg 276] on credit. They took no notice of him, but rubbed up against the farmers—and made up to the clerk; they did not dare to approach the auctioneer.

"Ay, they behave as if I were dirt," thought Lars Peter. And what were they after all? Most of them did not even own enough ground to grow a carrot in. A good thing he owed them nothing! Even the cottagers from the marsh, whom he had often helped in their poverty, followed the others' example and looked down on him today. There was no chance now of getting anything more out of him.

After all, it was comical to go round watching people fight over one's goods and chattels. They were not too grand to take the rag and bone man's leavings—if only they could get it on credit and make a good bargain.

The auctioneer knew most of them by name, and encouraged them to bid. "Now, Peter Jensen Hegnet, make a good bid. You haven't bought anything from me for a whole year!" said he suddenly to one of the cottagers. Or, "Here's something to take home to your wife, Jens Petersen!" Each time he named them, the man he singled out would laugh self-consciously and make a bid. They felt proud at being known by the auctioneer.

"Here's a comb, make a bid for it!" shouted the auctioneer, when the farm implements came to be sold. A wave of laughter went through the crowd; it was an old harrow which was put up. The winnowing-machine he called a coffee-grinder. He had something funny to say about everything. At times the jokes were such that the laughter turned on Lars Peter, and this was quickly followed up. But Lars Peter shook himself, and took it as it came. It was the auctioneer's profession to say funny things—it all helped on the sale!

The poor silly day laborer, Johansen, was there too. He stood behind the others, stretching his neck to see what was going on—in ragged working clothes and muddy wooden shoes. Each time the auctioneer made a remark, he laughed louder than the rest, to show that he joined in the joke. Lars Peter looked at him angrily. In his house there was seldom food, except what others were foolish enough to give him—his earnings went in drink. And there he stood, stuck-up idiot that he was! And bless us, if he didn't make a bid too—for Lars Peter's old boots. No-one bid against him, so they were knocked down to him for a crown. "You'll pay at once, of course," said the auctioneer. This time the laugh was against the buyer; all knew he had no money.

"I'll pay it for him," said Lars Peter, putting the crown on the table. Johansen glared at him for a few minutes; then sat down and began putting on the boots. He had not had leather footwear for years and years.

Indoors, a table was set out with two large dishes of sandwiches and a bottle of brandy, with three glasses round. At one end of the table was a coffee-pot. Ditte kept in the kitchen; her cheeks were red with excitement in case her preparations should not be appreciated. She had everything ready to cut more sandwiches as soon as the others gave out; every other minute she peeped through the door to see what was going on, her heart in her mouth. Every now and then a stranger strolled into the room, looking round with curiosity, but passed out without eating anything. A man entered—he was not from the neighborhood, and Ditte did not know him. He stepped over the bench, took a sandwich, and poured himself out a glass of brandy. Ditte could see by his jaws that he was enjoying himself. Then in came a farmer's wife, drew him away by his arm, whispering something to him. He got up, spat the food out into his hand, and followed her out of doors.

When Lars Peter came into the kitchen, Ditte lay over the table, crying. He lifted her up. "What's the matter now?" he asked.

"Oh, it's nothing," sniffed Ditte, struggling to get away. Perhaps she wanted to spare him, or perhaps to hide her shame even from him. Only after much persuasion did he get out of her that it was the food. "They won't touch it!" she sobbed.

He had noticed it himself.

"Maybe they're not hungry yet," said he, to comfort her. "And they haven't time either."

"They think it's bad!" she broke out, "made from dog's meat or something like that."

"Don't talk nonsense!" Lars Peter laughed strangely. "It's not dinner-time either."

"I heard a woman telling her husband myself—not to touch it," she said.

Lars Peter was silent for a few minutes. "Now, don't worry over it," said he, stroking her hair. "Tomorrow we're leaving, and then we shan't care a fig for them. There's a new life ahead of us. Well, I must go back to the auction; now, be a sensible girl."

Lars Peter went over to the barn, where the auction was now being held. At twelve o'clock the auctioneer stopped. "Now we'll have a rest, good people, and get something inside us!" he cried. The people laughed. Lars Peter went up to the auctioneer. Every one knew what he wanted; they pushed nearer to see the rag and bone man humiliated. He lifted his dented old hat, and rubbed his tousled head. "I only wanted to say"—his big voice rang to the furthermost corners—"that if the auctioneer and his clerk would take us as we are, there's food and beer indoors—you are welcome to a cup of coffee too." People nudged one another—who ever heard such impudence—the rag and bone man to invite an auctioneer to his table, and his wife a murderess into the bargain! They looked on breathlessly; one farmer was even bold enough to warn him with a wink.

The auctioneer thanked him hesitatingly. "We've brought something with us, you and your clever little girl have quite enough to do," said he in a friendly manner. Then, noticing Lars Peter's crestfallen appearance, and the triumphant faces of those around, he understood that something was going on in which he was expected to take part. He had been here before—on an unpleasant errand—and would gladly make matters easier for these honest folk who bore their misfortune so patiently.

"Yes, thanks very much," said he jovially, "strangers' food always tastes much nicer than one's own! And a glass of brandy—what do you say, Hansen?" They followed Lars Peter into the house, and sat down to table.

The people looked after them a little taken aback, then slunk in one by one. It would be fun to see how such a great man enjoyed the rag and bone man's food. And once inside, for very shame's sake they had to sit down at the table. Appetite is infectious, and the two of them set to with a will. Perhaps people did not seriously believe all the tales which they themselves had both listened to and spread. Ditte's sandwiches and coffee quickly disappeared, and she was sent for by the auctioneer, who praised her and patted her cheeks. This friendly act took away much of her bitterness of mind, and was a gratifying reward for all her trouble.

"I've never had a better cup of coffee at any sale," said the auctioneer.

When they began again, a stranger had appeared. He nodded to the auctioneer, but ignored everybody else, and went round looking at the buildings and land. He was dressed like a steward, with high-laced boots. But any one could see with half an eye that he was no countryman. It leaked out by degrees that he was a tradesman from the town, who wished to buy the Crow's Nest—probably for the fishing on the lake—and use it as a summer residence.

Otherwise, there was little chance of many bids for the place, but his advent changed the outlook. It really could be made into a good little property, once all was put in order. When the Crow's Nest eventually was put up for sale, there was some competition, and Lars Peter got a good price for the place.

At last the auction was over, but the people waited about, as if expecting something to happen. A stout farmer's wife went up to Lars Peter and shook his hand. "I should like to say good-by to you," said she, "and wish you better luck in your new home than you've had here. You've not had much of a time, have you?"

"No, and the little good we've had's no thanks to any one here," said Lars Peter.

"Folks haven't treated you as they ought to have done, and I've been no better than the rest, but 'tis our way. We farmers can't bear the poor. Don't think too badly of us. Good luck to you!" She said good-by to all the children with the same wish. Many of the people made off, but one or two followed her example, and shook hands with them.

Lars Peter stood looking after them, the children by his side. "After all, folk are often better than a man gives them credit for," said he. He was not a little moved.

They loaded the cart with their possessions, so as to make an early start the next morning. It was some distance to the fishing-hamlet, and it was better to get off in good time, to settle down a little before night. Then they went to bed; they were tired out after their long eventful day; they slept on the hay in the barn, as the bedclothes were packed.

The next morning was a wonderful day to waken up to. They were dressed when they wakened, and had only to dip their faces in the water-trough in the yard. Already they felt a sensation of something new and pleasant. There was only the coffee to be drunk, and the cow to be taken to the neighbor's, and they were ready to get into the cart. Klavs was in the shafts, and on top of the high load they put the pig, the hens and the three little ones. It was a wonderful beginning to the new life.

Lars Peter was the only one who felt sad. He made an excuse to go over the property again, and stood behind the barn, gazing over the fields. Here he had toiled and striven through good and bad; every ditch was dear to him—he knew every stone in the fields, every crack in the walls. What would the future bring? Lars Peter had begun afresh before, but never with less inclination than now. His thoughts turned to bygone days.

The children, on the contrary, thought only of the future. Ditte had to tell them about the beach, as she remembered it from her childhood with Granny, and they promised themselves delightful times in their new home.

CHAPTER IX
A DEATH

The winter was cold and long. Lars Peter had counted on getting a share in a boat, but there seemed to be no vacancy, and each time he reminded the inn-keeper of his promise, he was put off with talk. "It'll come soon enough," said the inn-keeper, "just give it time."

Time—it was easy to say. But here he was waiting, with his savings dwindling away—and what was he really waiting for? That there might be an accident, so he could fill the place—it was not a pleasant thought. It had been arranged that the inn-keeper should help Lars Peter to get a big boat, and let him manage it; at least, so Lars Peter had understood before he moved down to the hamlet. But it had evidently been a great misunderstanding.

He went about lending a hand here and there, and replacing any one who was ill. "Just wait a little longer," said the inn-keeper. "It'll be all right in the end! You can get what you want at the store." It was as if he were keeping Lars Peter back for some purpose of his own.[Pg 285]

At last the spring came, heralded by furious storms and accidents round about the coast. One morning Lars Jensen's boat came in, having lost its master; a wave had swept him overboard.

"You'd better go to the inn-keeper at once," said his two partners to Lars Peter.

"But wouldn't it be more natural to go to Lars Jensen's widow?" asked Lars Peter. "After all, 'tis she who owns the share now."

"We don't want to be mixed up in it," said they cautiously. "Go to whoever you like. But if you've money in the house, you should put it into the bank—the hut might easily catch fire." They looked meaningly at each other and turned away.

Lars Peter turned this over in his mind—could that be the case? He took the two thousand crowns he had put by from the sale to build with, and went up to the inn-keeper.

"Will you take care of some money for me?" he said in a low voice. "You're the savings bank for us down here, I've been told."

The inn-keeper counted the money, and locked it up in his desk. "You want a receipt, I suppose?" said he.

"No-o, it doesn't really matter," Lars Peter said slowly. He would have liked a written acknowledgment, but did not like to insist on it. It looked as if he mistrusted the man.

The inn-keeper drew down the front of the desk—it [Pg 286] sounded to Lars Peter like earth being thrown on a coffin. "We can call it a deposit on the share in the boat," said he. "I've been thinking you might take Lars Jensen's share."

"Oughtn't I to have arranged it with Lars Jensen's widow, and not with you?" said Lars Peter. "She owns the share."

The inn-keeper turned towards him. "You seem to know more about other people's affairs in the hamlet than I do, it appears to me," said he.

"No, but that's how I understood it to be," mumbled Lars Peter.

Once outside, he shrugged his shoulders. Curse it, a fellow was never himself when with that hunch-backed dwarf. That he had no neck—and that huge head! He was supposed to be as strong as a lion, and there was brain too. He made folk dance to his piping, and got his own way. There was no getting the better of *him*. Just as he thought of something cutting which would settle him, the inn-keeper's face would send his thoughts all ways at once. He was not satisfied with the result of his visit, but was glad to get out again.

He went down to the beach, and informed the two partners of what he had done. They had no objection; they liked the idea of getting Lars Peter as a third man: he was big and strong, and a good fellow. "Now, you'll have to settle with the widow," said they.[Pg 287]

"What, that too?" broke out Lars Peter. "Good Lord! has the share to be paid for twice?"

"You must see about that yourself," they said; "we don't want to be mixed up in it!"

He went to see the widow, who lived in a little hut in the southern part of the hamlet. She sat beside the fireplace eating peas from a yellow bowl; the tears ran down her cheeks, dropping into the food. "There's no-one to earn money for me now," she sobbed.

"Ay, and I'm afraid I've put my foot in it," said Lars Peter, crestfallen. "I've paid the inn-keeper two thousand crowns for the share of the boat, and now I hear that it's yours."

"You couldn't help yourself," said she, and looked kindly at him.

"Wasn't it yours then?"

"My husband took it over from the inn-keeper about a dozen years ago, and paid for it over and over again, he said. But it's hard for a poor widow to say anything, and have to take charity from others. It's hard to live, Lars Peter! Who'll shelter me now? and scold me and make it up again?" She began to cry afresh.

"We'll look you up as often as we can, and as to food, we'll get over that too. I shouldn't like to be unfair to any one, and least of all to one who's lost her bread-winner. Poor folks must keep together."

"I know you won't let me want as long as you have anything yourself. But you've got your own family [Pg 288] to provide for, and food doesn't grow on the downs here. If only it doesn't happen here as it generally does—that there's the will but not the means."

"Ay, ay—one beggar must help the other. You shan't be forgotten, if all goes well. But you must spit three times after me when I've gone."

"Ay, that I will," said the widow, "and I wish you luck."

Here was an opportunity for him to work. A little luck with the catch, and all would be well. He was glad Lars Jensen's widow wished him no ill in his new undertaking. The curse of widows and the fatherless was a heavy burden on a man's work.

Now that Lars Peter was in the hamlet, he found it not quite what he had imagined it to be; he could easily think of many a better place to settle down in. The whole place was poverty-stricken, and no-one seemed to have any ambition. The fishermen went to sea because they were obliged to. They seized on any excuse to stay at home. "We're just as poor whether we work hard or not," said they.

"Why, what becomes of it all?" asked Lars Peter at first, laughing incredulously.

"You'll soon see yourself!" they answered, and after a while he began to understand.

That they went to work unwillingly was not much to be wondered at. The inn-keeper managed everything. He arranged it all as he liked. He paid for all repairs when necessary, and provided all new implements. He took care that no-one was hungry or cold, and set up a store which supplied all that was needed—on credit. It was all entered in the books, no doubt, but none of them ever knew how much he owed. But they did not care, and went on buying until he stopped their credit for a time. On the other hand, if anything were really wrong in one of the huts, he would step in and help.

That was why they put up with the existing condition of things, and even seemed to be content—they had no responsibilities. When they came ashore with their catch, the inn-keeper took it over, and gave them what he thought fit—just enough for a little pocket-money. The rest went to pay off their debts—he said. He never sent in any bills. "We'd better not go into that," he would say with a smile, "do what you can." One and all of them probably owed him money; it would need a big purse to hold it all.

They did not have much to spend. But then, on the other hand, they had no expenses. If their implements broke or were lost at sea, the inn-keeper provided new ones, and necessaries had only to be fetched from the store. It was an extraordinary existence, thought Lars Peter; and yet it appealed to one somehow. It was hard to provide what was needed when a man was on his own, and tempting to become a pensioner as it were, letting others take the whole responsibility.

But it left no room for ambition. It was difficult for him to get his partners to do more than was strictly necessary; what good was it exerting themselves? They went about half asleep, and with no spirit in their work. Those who did not spend their time at the inn drinking and playing cards had other vices; there was no home life anywhere.

Lars Peter had looked forward to mixing with his fellow-men, discussing the events of the day, and learning something new. Many of the fishermen had been abroad in their young days, on merchant vessels or in the navy, and there were events happening in other countries which affected both him and them. But all their talk was of their neighbors' affairs—the inn-keeper always included. He was like a stone wall surrounding them all. The roof of his house—a solid building down by the coast, consisting of inn, farm and store—could be seen from afar, and every one involuntarily glanced at it before anything was said or done. With him, all discussions ended.

No-one had much good to say for him. All their earnings went to him in one way or other—some spent theirs at the inn, others preferred to take it out in food—and all cursed him in secret.

Well, that was their business. In the end, people are treated according to their wisdom or stupidity. Lars Peter did not feel inclined to sink to the level of the others and be treated like a dumb animal. His business was to see that the children lacked for nothing and led a decent life.

CHAPTER X
THE NEW WORLD

Ditte stood in the kitchen, cutting thick slices of bread and dripping for the three hungry little ones, who hung in the doorway following her movements eagerly with their eyes. She scolded them: it was only an hour since dinner, and now they behaved as if they had not tasted food for a week. "Me first, me first!" they shouted, stretching out their hands. It stopped her washing up, and might waken her father, who was having a nap up in the attic—it was ridiculous. But it was the sea that gave them such enormous appetites.

The more she hushed them, the more noise they made, kicking against the door with their bare feet. They could not wait; as soon as one got a slice of bread, he made off to the beach to play. They were full of spirits—almost too much so indeed. "You mind the king of the cannibal islands doesn't catch sight of you," she shouted after them, putting her head out of the door, but they neither heard nor saw.

She went outside, and stood gazing after them, as they tore along, kicking up the sand. Oh dear, Povl had dropped his bread and dripping in the sand—but he picked it up again and ran on, eating as he went. "It'll clean him inside," said Ditte, laughing to herself. They were mad, simply mad—digging in the sand and racing about! They had never been like this before.

She was glad of the change herself. Even if there had been any opportunity, she could not play; all desires had died long ago. But there was much of interest. All these crooked, broken-down moss-grown huts, clustered together on the downs under the high cliffs, each surrounded by its dust-heap and fish-refuse and implements, were to Ditte like so many different worlds; she would have liked to investigate them all.

It was her nature to take an interest in most things, though, unlike Kristian, she didn't care to roam about. He was never still for a moment; he had barely found out what was behind one hill, before he went on to the next. He always wanted to see beyond the horizon, and his father always said, he might travel round the whole world that way, for the horizon was always changing. Lars Peter often teased him about this; it became quite a fairy tale to the restless Kristian, who wanted to go over the top of every new hill he saw, until at last he fell down in the hamlet again—right down into Ditte's stew-pan. He had often been punished for his roaming—but to no good. Povl wanted to pick everything to pieces, to see what was inside, or was busy with hammer and nails. He was already [Pg 293] nearly as clever with his hands as Kristian. Most of what he made went to pieces, but if a handle came off a brush, he would quickly mend it again. "He only pulls things to pieces so as to have something to mend again," said his father. Sister stood looking on with her big eyes.

Ditte was always doing something useful, otherwise she was not happy. With Granny's death, all her interest in the far-off had vanished; that there was something good in store for her she never doubted, it acted as a star and took away the bitterness of her gloomy childhood. She was not conscious of what it would be, but it was always there like a gleam of light. The good in store for her would surely find her. She stayed at home; the outside world had no attractions for her.

Her childhood had fallen in places where neighbors were few and far between. The more enjoyment it was to her now to have the society of others.

Ditte took a keen interest in her fellow-beings, and had not been many days in the hamlet before she knew all about most people's affairs—how married people lived together, and who were sweethearts. She could grasp the situation at a glance—and see all that lay behind it; she was quick to put two and two together. Her dull and toilsome life had developed that sense, as a reward for all she had gone through. There was some spite in it too—a feeling of vengeance against all who looked down on the rag and bone man, although they themselves had little to boast about. [Pg 294]

The long, hunch-backed hut, one end of which the inn-keeper had let off to them, lay almost in the midst of the hamlet, just above the little bay. Two other families beside lived in the little hut, so they only had two small rooms and a kitchen to call their own, and Lars Peter had to sleep in the attic. It was only a hovel, "the workhouse" it was generally called, but it was the only place to be had, and they had to make the best of it, until Lars Peter could build something himself—and they might thank the inn-keeper that they had a roof above their heads. Ditte was not satisfied with the hut—the floors were rotten, and would not dry when she had washed them. It was no better than the Crow's Nest—and there was much less room. She looked forward to the new house that was to be built. It should be a real house, with a red roof glistening in the sun, and an iron sink that would not rot away.

But in spite of this she was quite happy. When she stood washing up inside the kitchen door, she could see the downs, and eagerly her eyes followed all who went to and fro. Her little brain wondered where they were going, and on what errand. And if she heard voices through the wall, or from the other end of the hut, she would stop in her work and listen breathlessly. It was all so exciting; the other families in the hut were always bustling and moving about—the old grandmother, who lay lame in bed on the other side of the wall, cursing existence, while the twins screamed at the top of their voices, and the Lord only knew where the daughter-in-law [Pg 295] was, and Jacob the fisherman and his daughter in the other end of the hut. Suddenly, as one stood thinking of nothing at all, the inn-keeper would come strolling over the downs, looking like a goblin, to visit the young wife next door; then the old grandmother thumped on the floor with her crutch, cursing everything and everybody.

There was much gossip in the hamlet—of sorrow and shame and crime; Ditte could follow the stories herself, often to the very end. She was quick to find the thread, even in the most difficult cases.

Her life was much happier now: there was little to do in the house, and no animals to look after, so she had more time of her own. Her schooldays were over, and she was soon to be confirmed. Even the nag, whom at first she had been able to keep her eye on from the kitchen window, needed no looking after now. The inn-keeper had forbidden them to let it feed on the downs, and had taken it on to his own farm. There it had been during the winter, and they only saw it when it was carting sea-weed or bringing a load of fish from the beach for the inn-keeper. It was not well-treated in its present home, and had all the hard tasks given it, so as to spare the inn-keeper's own animals. Tears came into Ditte's eyes when she thought of it. It became like a beast of burden in the fairy tale, and no-one there to defend it. It was long since it had pulled crusts of bread from her mouth with its soft muzzle.

Ditte lost her habit of stooping, and began to fill [Pg 296] out as she grew up. She enjoyed the better life and the children's happiness—the one with the other added to her well-being. Her hair had grown, and allowed itself the luxury of curling over her forehead, and her chin was soft and round. No-one could say she was pretty, but her eyes were beautiful—always on the alert, watching for something useful to do. Her hands were red and rough—she had not yet learned how to take care of them.

Ditte had finished in the kitchen, and went into the living room. She sat down on the bench under the window, and began patching the children's clothes; at the same time she could see what was happening on the beach and on the downs.

Down on the shore the children were digging with all their might, building sand-gardens and forts. To the right was a small hut, neat and well cared for, outside which Rasmus Olsen, the fisherman, stood shouting in through the window. His wife had turned him out—it always sounded so funny when he had words with his wife, he mumbled on loudly and monotonously as a preacher—it made one feel quite sleepy. There was not a scrap of bad temper in him. Most likely his wife would come out soon, and she would give it him in another fashion.

They were always quarrelling, those two—and always about the daughter. Both spoiled her, and each tried to get her over to their side—and came to blows over it. And Martha, the wretch, sided first with one and then [Pg 297] with the other—whichever paid her best. She was a pretty girl, slim but strong enough to push a barrow full of fish or gear through the loose sand on the downs, but she was wild—and had plenty to say for herself. When she had had a sweetheart for a short time, she always ended by quarreling with him.

The two old people were deaf, and always came outside to quarrel—as if they needed air. They themselves thought they spoke in a low voice, all the time shouting so loudly that the whole hamlet knew what the trouble was about.

Ditte could see the sea from the window—it glittered beneath the blazing sun, pale blue and wonderful. It was just like a big being, softly caressing—and then suddenly it would flare up! The boats were on the beach, looking like cattle in their stalls, side by side. On the bench, two old fishermen sat smoking.

Now all the children from the hamlet came rushing up from the beach, like a swarm of frightened bees. They must have caught sight of the inn-keeper! He did not approve of children playing; they ought to be doing something useful. They fled as soon as he appeared, imagining that he had the evil eye. The swarm spread over the downs in all directions, and suddenly vanished, as if the earth had swallowed them.

Then he came tramping in his heavy leather boots. His long arms reached to his knees. When he went through the loose sand, his great bony hands on his thighs, he looked as if he were walking on all fours. [Pg 298] His misshapen body was like a pair of bellows, his head resting between his broad shoulders, moved up and down like a buoy; every breath sounded like a steam-whistle, and could be heard from afar. Heavens, how ugly he looked! He was like a crouching goblin, who could make himself as big as he pleased, and see over all the huts in his search for food. The hard shut mouth was so big that it could easily swallow a child's head—and his eyes! Ditte shut her own, and shivered.

She quickly opened them, however; she must find out what his business was, taking care not to be seen herself.

The ogre, as the children called him, mainly because of his big mouth, came to a standstill at Rasmus Olsen's house. "Well, are you two quarreling again?" he shouted jovially. "What's wrong now—Martha, I suppose?"

Rasmus Olsen was silent, and shuffled off towards the beach. But his wife was not afraid, and turned her wrath on to the inn-keeper. "What's it to do with you?" she cried. "Mind your own business!" The inn-keeper passed on without taking any notice of her, and entered the house. Most likely he wanted to see Martha; she followed on his heels. "You can save yourself the trouble, there's nothing for you to pry into!" she screamed. Shortly afterwards he came out again, with the woman still scolding at his heels, and went across the downs. [Pg 299]

The fisherman's wife stood looking round, then catching sight of Ditte, she came over. She had not finished yet, and needed some object to go on with. "Here he goes round prying, the beastly hunch-back!" she screamed, still beside herself with rage, "walking straight into other people's rooms as if they were his own. And that doddering old idiot daren't throw him out, but slinks off. Ay, they're fine men here on the downs; a woman has to manage it all, the food and the shame and everything! If only the boy had lived." And throwing her apron over her head, she began to cry.

"Was he drowned?" asked Ditte sympathetically.

"I think of it all day long; I shall never forget him; there'll be no happiness in life for me. Maybe it's stupid to cry, but I can't help it—it's the mean way he met his death. If he had been struck down by illness, and the Lord had had a finger in it—'twould be quite another thing! But that he was strong and well—'twas his uncle wanted him to go out shooting wild duck. I tried to stop him, but the boy *would* go, and there was no peace until he did. 'But, Mother,' he said, 'you know I can handle a gun; why, I shoot every day.' Then they went out in the boat with two guns, and not ten minutes afterwards he was back again, lying dead in a pool of blood. That's why I can't bear to see wild ducks, or taste 'em either. Whenever I sit by the window, I can see them bringing him in—there they are [Pg 300] again. That's why my eyes are dimmed, I'm always crying: 'tis all over with me now."

The woman was overcome by grief. Her hands trembled, and moved aimlessly over the table and back again.

Ditte looked at her from a new point of view. "Hush, hush, don't cry any more," said she, putting her arms round her and joining in her tears. "Wait—I'll make a cup of coffee." And gradually she succeeded in comforting her.

"You've good hands," said the old woman, taking Ditte's hand gratefully. "They're rough and red because your heart's in the right place."

As they were having their coffee, Lars Peter returned. He had been to see the inn-keeper, to hear how the nag was being treated, and was out of humor. Ditte asked what was troubling him.

"Oh, it's the nag—they'll finish it soon," said he miserably.

The fisherman's wife looked at him kindly. "At least I can hear your voice, even though you're talking to some one else," said she. "Ay, he's taken your horse—and cart too! He can find a use for everything, honor and money—and food too! D'you go to the tap-room?"

"No, I haven't been there yet," said Lars Peter, "and I don't think to go there every day."

"No, that's just it: you're not a drinker, and such are treated worse than the others. He likes folks to [Pg 301] spend their money in the tap-room more than in the store—that's his way. He wants your money, and there's no getting out of it."

"How did he come to lord it over the place? It hasn't always been like this," said Lars Peter.

"How—because the folk here are no good—at all events here in the hamlet. If we've no-one to rule us, then we run about whining like dogs without a master until we find some one to kick us. We lick his boots and choose him for our master, and then we're satisfied. In my childhood it was quite different here, everybody owned their own hut. But then he came and got hold of everything. There was an inn here of course, and when he found he couldn't get everything his own way, he started all these new ideas with costly fishing-nets and better ways and gear, and God knows what. He gave them new-fangled things—and grabbed the catch. The fishermen get much more now, but what's the good, when he takes it all! I'd like to know what made you settle down here?"

"Round about it was said that he was so good to you fisher-people, and as far as I could see there was no mistake about it either. But it looks rather different now a man's got into the thing."

"Heavens! *good*, you say! He helps and helps, until a man hasn't a shirt left to his back. Just you wait; you'll be drawn in too—and the girl as well if she's pretty enough for him. At present he's only taking what you've got. Afterwards he'll help you till [Pg 302] you're so deep in debt that you'd like to hang yourself. Then he'll talk to you about God and Holy Scripture. For he can preach too—like the devil!"

Lars Peter stared hopelessly. "I've heard that he and his wife hold some kind of meetings, but we've never been; we don't care much for that sort of thing. Not that we're unbelievers, but so far we've found it best to mind our own affairs, and leave the Lord to look after His."

"We don't go either, but then Rasmus drinks—ay, ay, you'll go through it all yourself. And here am I sitting gossiping instead of getting home." She went home to get supper ready for the doddering idiot.

They sat silent for a few minutes. Then Ditte said: "If only we'd gone to some other place!"

"Oh, things are never as black as they're painted! And I don't feel inclined to leave my money and everything behind me," answered Lars Peter.

[Pg 303]

CHAPTER XI
GINGERBREAD HOUSE

Now that the children were surrounded by people, they felt as if they lived in an ant-hill. The day was full of happenings, all equally exciting—and the most exciting of it all was their fear of the "ogre." Suddenly, when they were playing hide-and-seek amongst the boats, or sat riding on the roof of the engine-house, he would appear, his long arms grasping the air, and if he caught hold of one of them, they would get something else to add to their fear. His breath smelt of raw meat, the children declared; they did not make him out better than he was. To run away from him, with their hearts thumping, gave zest to their existence.

And when they lay in bed at night listening, they heard sounds in the house, which did not come from any of their people. Then came steps in stocking-feet up in the attic, and they would look towards Ditte. Kristian knew what it meant, and they buried their heads underneath the bedclothes, whispering. It was Jacob, the fisherman, creeping about upstairs, listening to what they said. He always stole about, trying to find out [Pg 304] from the talk a certain *word* he could use to drive the devil out of the inn-keeper. The children worried over the question, because he had promised them sixpence if they could discover the word. And from the other side of the wall, they could hear the old grandmother's cough. She had dropsy, which made her fatter and fatter outside, but was hollow within. She coughed up her inside.

The son was on a long voyage, and seldom came home; but each time he returned, he found one of the children dead and his wife with a new baby to make up for it. She neglected her children, and in consequence they died. "Light come, light go!" said folk, and laughed. Now only the twins remained: there they lay in the big wooden cradle, screaming day and night, with a crust of bread as a comforter. The mother was never at home. Ditte looked after them, or they would have perished.

A short distance away on the downs, was a little house, quite different from the others. It was the most beautiful house the little ones had ever seen: the door and the window-panes were painted blue; the beams were not tarred as in the other huts, but painted brown; the bricks were red with a blue stripe. The ground round the house was neat: the sand was raked, and by the well it was dry and clean. A big elder—the only tree in the whole hamlet—grew beside the well. On the window-sill were plants, with red and blue flowers, and behind them sat an old woman peeping out. She [Pg 305] wore a white cap, and the old man had snow-white hair. When the weather was fine he was always pottering round the house. And occasionally the old woman appeared at the door, admiring his handiwork. "How nice you've made everything look, little father!" said she. "Ay, it's all for you, little mother," he answered, and they laughed at each other. Then he took hold of her hand, and they tripped towards the elder tree and sat down in the shade; they were like a couple of children, but she soon wanted to go back to her window, and it was said that she had not gone beyond the well for many a year.

The old people kept to themselves, and did not mix with the other inhabitants of the hamlet, but when Lars Peter's children passed, the old woman always looked out and nodded and smiled. They made some excuse to pass the house several times a day: there was something in the pretty little place and the two old people which attracted them. The same cleanness and order that ruled their house was apparent in their lives; no-one in the hamlet had anything but good to say of them.

Amongst themselves, the children called it Gingerbread House, and imagined wonderful things inside it. One day, hand in hand, the three went up and knocked on the door. The old man opened it. "What do you want, children?" he asked kindly, but blocking the door. Yes, what did they want—none of them knew. And there they stood open-mouthed. [Pg 306]

"Let them come inside, father," a voice said. "Come in then, children." They entered a room that smelt of flowers and apples. Everything was painted: ceiling, beams and walls; it all shone; the floor was painted white, and the table was so brightly polished that the window was reflected in it. In a softly cushioned armchair a cat lay sleeping.

The children were seated underneath the window, each with a plate of jelly. A waterproof cloth was put on the table, in case they spilled anything. The old couple trotted round them anxiously; their eyes gleamed with pleasure at the unexpected visit, but they were uneasy about their furniture. They were not accustomed to children, and Povl nearly frightened their lives out of them, the way he behaved. He lifted his plate with his little hands, nearly upsetting its contents, and said: "Potatoes too!" He thought it was jam. But sister helped him to finish, and then it was happily over. Kristian had gulped his share in a couple of spoonfuls, and stood by the door, ready to run off to the beach—already longing for something new. They were each given a red apple, and shown politely to the door; the old couple were tired. Povl put his cheek on the old woman's skirt. "Me likes you!" said he.

"God bless you, little one! Did you hear that, father?" she said, nodding her withered old head.

Kristian thought he too ought to show his appreciation. "If you want any errands done, only tell me," said he, throwing back his head. "I can run ever so [Pg 307] fast." And to show how clever he was on his legs, he rushed down the path. A little way down, he turned triumphantly. "As quick as that," he shouted.

"Yes, thanks, we'll remember," nodded the two old people.

This little visit was the introduction to a pleasant acquaintance. The old people liked the children, and even fetched them in when passing, and bore patiently with all their awkwardness. Not that they were allowed to tumble about—they could do that on the downs. The old man would tell them a story, or get his flute and play to them. The children came home with sparkling eyes, and quieter than usual, to tell Ditte all about it.

The following day, Ditte went about pondering how she could do the old people a service for their kindness towards the children, and, as she could think of nothing, she took Kristian into her confidence. He was so clever in finding ways out of difficulties.

It was the fisher-people's custom to put aside some of the catch before it was delivered to the inn-keeper, and one day Ditte took a beautiful thick plaice, and told Kristian to run with it to the old couple. "But they mustn't know that it is from us," said she. "They'll be having their after-dinner nap, so you can easily leave it without their seeing you." Kristian put it down on the little bench underneath the elder; but when later on he crept past, to see if it had been taken, only the tail and the fins remained—the cat had eaten it up. [Pg 308] Ditte scolded him well, and Kristian had to puzzle his brains once more.

"Father might get Klavs, and take them for a drive on Sunday," said he. "They never get anywhere—their legs are too old."

"You silly!—we've nothing to do with Klavs now," Ditte said sharply.

But now she knew what to do! She would scrub out the *little house* for them every night; the old woman had to kneel down to do it every morning. It was a sin she should have to do it. After the old people had gone to bed—they went to rest early—Ditte took a pail of water and a scrubbing brush, and some sand in her pinafore, and crept up. Kristian stood outside at home, waiting for her. He was not allowed to go with her, for fear of disturbing the old couple—he was so noisy.

"What d'you think they'll say when they come down in the morning and find it all so clean?" cried he, hopping first on one foot and then the other. He would have liked to stay up all night to see their surprise.

Next time the children visited the old people, the old man told them a story about a little fairy who came every night to scour and scrub, to save his little mother. Then Kristian laughed—he knew better.

"It was Ditte!" he burst out. He put his hand to his mouth next moment, but it was too late.

"But Ditte isn't a fairy!" broke out sister Else, [Pg 309] offended. They all three laughed at her until she began to cry, and had to be comforted with a cake.

On their way home, whom should they meet but Uncle Johannes, who was looking for their house. He was rigged out very smartly, and looked like a well-to-do tradesman. Lars Peter was pleased to see him. They had not met since their unfortunate parting in the Crow's Nest, and now all was forgotten. He had heard one or two things about him—Johannes kept the gossips busy. The two brothers shook hands as if no unpleasantness had come between them. "Sit down and have something to eat," said Lars Peter. "There's boiled cod today."

"Thanks, but I'm feeding up at the inn later on; we're a few tradesmen up there together."

"That'll be a grand dinner, I suppose?" Lars Peter's eyes shone; he had never been to a dinner party himself.

"Ay, that it will—they do things pretty well up there. He's a good sort, the inn-keeper."

"Some think so; others don't. It all depends how you look at him. You'd better not tell them you're my brother—it'll do you no good to have poor relations down here."

Johannes laughed: "I've told the inn-keeper—he spoke well of you. You were his best fisherman, he said."

"Really, did he say that?" Lars Peter flushed with pride. [Pg 310]

"But a bit close, he said. You thought codfish could talk reason."

"Well, now—what the devil did he mean by it? What nonsense! Of course codfish can't speak!"

"I don't know. But he's a clever man—he might have been one of the learned sort."

"You're getting on well, I hear," said Lars Peter, to change the subject. "Is it true you're half engaged to a farmer's daughter?"

Johannes smiled, stroking his woman-like mouth, where a small mustache was visible. "There's a deal of gossip about," was all he said.

"If only you keep her—and don't have the same bad luck that I had. I had a sweetheart who was a farmer's daughter, but she died before we were married."

"Is that true, Father?" broke out Ditte, proud of her father's standing.

"What do you think of him, my girl?" asked Lars Peter, when his brother had gone. "Picked up a bit, hasn't he?"

"Ay, he looks grand," admitted Ditte. "But I don't like him all the same."

"You're so hard to please." Lars Peter was offended. "Other folks seem to like him. He'll marry well."

"Ay, that may be. It's because he's got black hair—we women are mad on that. But I don't think he's good."

[Pg 311]

CHAPTER XII
DAILY TROUBLES

It was getting on towards Christmas, a couple of months after they had come to the hamlet, when one day Lars Peter was mad enough to quarrel with the inn-keeper. He was not even drunk and it was a thing unheard of in the hamlet for a sober man to give the inn-keeper a piece of his mind. But he had been more than stupid, every one agreed, and he himself too.

It was over the nag. Lars Peter could not get used to seeing the horse work for others, and it cut him to the heart that it should have to work so hard. It angered him, too, to be idle himself, in spite of the inn-keeper's promises—and there were many other things besides. One day he declared that Klavs should come home, and he would begin to drive round again. He went up to the farm and demanded his horse.

"Certainly!" The inn-keeper followed him out and ordered the horse to be harnessed. "Here's your horse, cart and everything belonging to it—is there anything more of yours?" [Pg 312]

Lars Peter was somewhat taken aback. He had expected opposition and here was the inn-keeper quite friendly, in fact almost fawning on him. "I wanted to cart some things home," said he, rather crestfallen.

"Certainly, Lars Peter Hansen," said the inn-keeper, preceding him into the shop. He weighed out all Lars Peter ordered, reminded him of one thing after another, laying the articles in a heap on the counter. "Have you raisins for the Christmas cakes?" he asked. "Ditte bakes herself." He knew every one's doings and was thoughtful in helping them.

When Lars Peter was about to carry the things out to the cart, he said smilingly, "That will be—let me see, how much do you owe for last time?"

"I'd like to let it wait a bit—till I get settled up after the auction!"

"Well, I'm afraid it can't. I don't know anything about you yet."

"Oh, so you're paying me out." Lars Peter began to fume.

"Paying you out? Not at all. But I like to know what sort of a man I'm dealing with before I can trust him."

"Oh, indeed! It's easy enough to see what sort of a fellow you are!" shouted Lars Peter and rushed out.

The inn-keeper followed him out to the cart. "You'll have a different opinion of me some day," said he gently, "then we can talk it over again. Never mind. But another thing—where'll you get food for the horse?"

"I'll manage somehow," answered Lars Peter shortly.

"And stabling? It's setting in cold now."

"You leave that to me!"

Lars Peter drove off at a walking pace. He knew perfectly well that he could find neither food nor stabling for the horse without the inn-keeper's help. Two or three days afterwards he sent Kristian with the horse and cart back to the farm.

He had done this once, but he was wiser now—or at all events more careful. When occasionally he felt a longing for the road and wanted to spend a day on it in company with Klavs, he asked politely for the loan of it, and he was allowed to have it. Then he and the horse were like sweethearts who seldom saw each other.

He was no wiser than before. The inn-keeper he couldn't make out—with his care for others and his desire to rule.

His partners and the other men he didn't understand either. He had spent his life in the country where people kept to themselves—where he had often longed for society. It looked cosy—as seen from the lonely Crow's Nest—people lived next door to each other; they could give a helping hand occasionally and chat with each other. But what pleasure had a man here? They toiled unwillingly, pushing responsibilities and troubles on to others, getting only enough for a meager meal from day to day and letting another man run off with their profits. It was extraordinary how that crooked devil scraped in everything with his long arms, without any one daring to protest. He must have an enormous hold on them somehow.

Lars Peter did not think of rebelling again. When his anger rose he had only to think of fisher-Jacob, who was daily before his eyes. Every one knew how he had become the wreck he was. He had once owned a big boat, and had hired men to work with him, so he thought it unnecessary to submit to the inn-keeper. But the inn-keeper licked him into shape. He refused to buy his fish, so that they had to sail elsewhere with it, but this outlet he closed for them too. They could buy no goods nor gear in the village—they were shunned like lepers, no one dared help them. Then his partners turned against him, blaming him for their ill-luck. He tried to sell up and moved to another place, but the inn-keeper would not buy his possessions and no-one else dared; he had to stay on—and learn to submit. Although he owned a boat and gear, he had to hire it from the inn-keeper. It told so heavily on him that he lost his reason; now he muddled about looking for a magic word to fell the inn-keeper; at times he went round with a gun, declaring he would shoot him. But the inn-keeper only laughed.

Ditte talked a great deal with the women. They all agreed that the inn-keeper had the evil eye. He was always in her mind; she went in an everlasting dread of him. When she saw him on the downs she almost screamed; Lars Peter tried to reason her out of it.

Little Povl came home from the beach one morning feeling ill. He was sick, and his head ached, he was hot one moment and cold the next. Ditte undressed him and put him to bed; then called her father, who was asleep in the attic.

Lars Peter hurried down. He had been out at sea the whole night and stumbled as he walked.

"Why, Povl, little man, got a tummy-ache?" asked he, putting his hand on the boy's forehead. It throbbed, and was burning hot. The boy turned his head away.

"He looks really bad," he said, seating himself on the edge of the bed, "he doesn't even know us. It's come on quickly, there was nothing the matter with him this morning."

"He came home a few minutes ago—he was all gray in the face and cold, and he's burning hot now. Just listen to the way he's breathing."

They sat by the bedside, looking at him in silence; Lars Peter held his little hand in his. It was black, with short stumpy fingers, the nails almost worn down into the flesh. He never spared himself, the little fellow, always ready; wide awake from the moment he opened his eyes. Here he lay, gasping. It was a sad sight! Was it serious? Was there to be trouble with the children again? The accident with his first children he had shaken off—but he had none to spare now! If anything happened to them, he had nothing more to live for—it would be the end. He understood now that they had kept him up—through the business with Sörine and all that followed. It was the children who gave him strength for each new day. All his broken hopes, all his failures, were dimmed in the cheery presence of the children; that was perhaps why he clung to them, as he did.

Suddenly Povl jumped up and wanted to get out of bed. "Povl do an' play, do an' play!" he said over and over again.

"He wants to go out and play," said Ditte, looking questioningly at her father.

"Then maybe he's better already," broke out Lars Peter cheerily. "Let him go if he wants to."

Ditte dressed him, but he drooped like a withered flower, and she put him to bed again.

"Shall I fetch Lars Jensen's widow?" she asked. "She knows about illness and what to do."

No—Lars Peter thought not. He would rather have a proper doctor. "As soon as Kristian comes home from school, he can run up to the inn, and ask for the loan of the nag," said he. "They can hardly refuse it when the child's ill."

Kristian came back without the horse and cart, but with the inn-keeper at his heels. He came in without knocking at the door, as was his custom.

"I hear your little boy's ill," he said kindly. "I thought I ought to come and see you, and perhaps give you a word of comfort. I've brought a bottle of something to give him every half hour; it's mixed with prayers, so at all events it can't do him any harm. Keep him well wrapped up in bed." He leaned over the bed, listening to the child's breathing. Povl's eyes were stiff with fear.

"You'd better keep away from the bed," said Lars Peter. "Can't you see the boy's afraid of you?" His voice trembled with restrained fury.

"There's many that way," answered the inn-keeper good-naturedly, moving away from the bed. "And yet I live on, and thrive—and do my duty as far as I can. Well, I comfort myself with the thought that the Lord has some reward in store. Perhaps it does folks no harm to be afraid of something, Lars Peter! But give him the mixture at once."

"I'd rather fetch the doctor," said Lars Peter, reluctantly giving the child the medicine. He would have preferred to throw it out of the window—and the inn-keeper with it.

"Ay, so I understood, but I thought I'd just have a talk to you first. What good's a doctor? It's only an expense, and he can't change God's purpose. Poor people should learn to save."

"Ay, of course, when a man's poor he must take things as they come!" Lars Peter laughed bitterly.

"Up at the inn we never send for the doctor. We put our lives in God's keeping. If so be it's His will, then——"

"It seems to me there's much that happens that's not His will at all—and in this place too," said Lars Peter defiantly.

"And yet I'll tell you that not even the smallest cod is caught—in the hamlet either—without the will of the Father." The inn-keeper's voice was earnest; it sounded like Scripture itself, but there was a look in his eyes, which made Lars Peter uncomfortable all the same. He was quite relieved when this unpleasant guest took his departure and disappeared over the downs.

Ditte came down from the attic, where she had hidden. "What d'you want to hide from that hunchback for?" shouted Lars Peter. He needed an outlet for his temper. Ditte flushed and turned away her face.

Soon afterwards a knock sounded on the wall. It was their lame neighbor. The daughter-in-law was at home, and sat with the twins in her arms.

"I heard he was in your house," said the old one—"his strong voice sounded through the walls. You be careful of him!"

"He was very kind," said Ditte evasively. "He spoke kindly to father, and brought something for little Povl."

"So he brought something—was it medicine? Pour it into the gutter at once. It can't do any harm there."

"But Povl's had some."

The old woman threw up her hands. "For the love of Jesus! for the love of Jesus! Poor child!" she wailed. "Did he say anything about death? They say in the village here every family owes him a death! Did he say he'd provide the coffin? He manages everything—he's always so good and helpful when anything's wrong. Ay, maybe he was good-tempered—and the child'll be allowed to live."

Ditte burst into tears; she thought it looked bad for little Povl, if his life depended on the innkeeper. He was vexed with them because the little ones were not sent to Sunday-school—perhaps he was taking his revenge.

But in a few days Povl recovered, and was as lively as ever, running about and never still for a minute, until suddenly he would fall asleep in the midst of his play. Lars Peter was cheerful again, and went about humming. Ditte sang at her washing up, following the little lad's movements with her motherly eyes. But for safety's sake she sent the children to Sunday-school.

CHAPTER XIII
DITTE'S CONFIRMATION

That autumn Ditte was to be confirmed. She found it very hard to learn by rote all the psalms and hymns. She had not much time for preparation, and her little brain had been trained in an entirely different direction than that of learning by heart; when she had finished her work, and brought out her catechism, it refused to stay in her mind.

One day she came home crying. The parson had declared that she was too far behind the others and must wait for the next confirmation; he dared not take the responsibility of presenting her. She was in the depths of despair; it was considered a disgrace to be kept back.

"Well,—there's no end of our troubles, it seems," broke out Lars Peter bitterly. "They can do what they like with folks like us. I suppose we should be thankful for being allowed to live."

"I know just as much as the others, it's not fair," sobbed Ditte.

"Fair—as if that had anything to do with it! If you did not know a line of your catechism, I'd like to see the girl that's better prepared to meet the Lord than you. You could easily take his housekeeping on your shoulders; and He would be pretty blind if He couldn't see that His little angels could never be better looked after. The fact is we haven't given the parson enough, they're like that—all of them—and it's the likes of them that have the keys of Heaven! Well, it can't be helped, it won't kill us, I suppose."

Ditte refused to be comforted. "I *will* be confirmed," she cried. "I won't go to another class and be jeered at."

"Maybe if we tried oiling the parson a little," Lars Peter said thoughtfully. "But it'll cost a lot of money."

"Go to the inn-keeper then—he can make it all right."

"Ay, that he can—there's not much he can't put right, if he's the mind to. But I'm not in his good books, I'm afraid."

"That doesn't matter. He treats every one alike whether he likes them or not."

Lars Peter did not like his errand; he was loth to ask favors of the man; however, it must be done for the sake of the child. Much to his surprise the inn-keeper received him kindly. "I'll certainly speak to the parson and have it seen to," said he. "And you can send the girl up here some day; it's the custom in the hamlet for *the ogre's* wife to provide clothes for girls going to be confirmed." His big mouth widened in a grin. Lars Peter felt rather foolish.

So Ditte was confirmed after all. For a whole week she wore a long black dress, and her hair in a thin plait down her back. In the church she had cried; whether it was the joy of feeling grown-up, or because it was the custom to cry, would be difficult to say. But she enjoyed the following week, when Lars Jensen's widow came and did her work, while she made calls and received congratulations. She was followed by a crowd of admiring girls, and small children of the hamlet rushed out to her shouting: "Hi, give us a ha'penny!" Lars Peter had to give all the halfpennies he could gather together.

The week over, she returned to her old duties. Ditte discovered that she had been grown-up for several years; her duties were neither heavier nor lighter. She soon got accustomed to her new estate; when they were invited out, she would take her knitting with her and sit herself with the grown-ups.

"Won't you go with the young people?" Lars Peter would say. "They're playing on the green tonight." She went, but soon returned.

Lars Peter was getting used to things in the hamlet; at least he only grumbled when he had been to the tap-room and was a little drunk. He no longer looked after the house so well; when Ditte was short of anything she had always to ask for it—and often more than once. It was not the old Lars Peter of the Crow's Nest, who used to say, "Well, how goes it, Ditte, got all you want?" Having credit at the store had made him careless. When Ditte reproached him, he answered: "Well, what the devil, a man never sees a farthing now, and must take things as they come!"

The extraordinary thing about the inn-keeper was, that he seemed to know everything. As long as Lars Peter had a penny left, the inn-keeper was unwilling to give him credit, and made him pay up what he owed before starting a new account. In this way he had stripped him of one hundred-crown note after the other, until by Christmas nothing was left.

"There!" said Lars Peter when the last note went, "that's the last of the Crow's Nest. Maybe now we'll have peace! And he can treat us like the others in the hamlet—or I don't know where the food's to come from."

But the inn-keeper thought differently. However often the children came in with basket and list, they returned empty-handed. "He seems to think there's still something to get out of us," said Lars Peter.

It was a sad lookout. Ditte had promised herself that they should have a really good time this Christmas; she had ordered flour, and things for cakes, and a piece of pork to be stuffed and cooked like a goose. Here she was empty-handed; all her beautiful plans had come to nothing. Up in the attic was the Christmas tree which the little ones had taken from the plantation; what good was it now, without candles and ornaments?

"Never mind," said Lars Peter, "we'll get over that too. We've got fish and potatoes, so we shan't starve!" But the little ones cried.

Ditte made the best of a bad job, and went down to the beach, where she got a pair of wild ducks that had been caught in the nets: she cleaned and dressed them—and thus their Christmas dinner was provided. A few red apples—which from time to time had been given her by the old couple at the Gingerbread House, and which she had not eaten because they were so beautiful—were put on the

Christmas tree. "We'll hang the lantern on the top, and then it'll look quite fine," she explained to the little ones. She had borrowed some coffee and some brandy—her father should not be without his Christmas drink.

She had scrubbed and cleaned the whole day, to make everything look as nice as possible; now she went into the kitchen and lit the fire. Lars Peter and the children were in the living room in the dusk—she could hear her father telling stories of when he was a boy. Ditte hummed, feeling pleased with everything.

Suddenly she screamed. The upper half of the kitchen door had opened. Against the evening sky she saw the head and shoulders of a deformed body, a goblin, in the act of lifting a parcel in over the door. "Here's a few things for you," he said, panting, pushing [Pg 325] the parcel along the kitchen-table. "A happy Christmas!" And he was gone.

They unpacked the parcel in the living room. It contained everything they had asked for, and many other things beside, which they had often wished for but had never dreamt of ordering: a calendar with stories, a pound of cooking chocolate, and a bottle of old French wine. "It's just like the Lord," said Ditte in whose mind there were still the remains of the parson's teaching—"when it looks blackest He always helps."

"Ah, the inn-keeper's a funny fellow, there we've been begging for things and got nothing but kicks in return; and then he brings everything himself! He's up to something, I'm afraid. Well, whatever it may be—the things'll taste none the worse for it!" Lars Peter was not in the least touched by the gift.

Whatever it might be—at all events it did not end with Christmas. They continued to get goods from the store. The inn-keeper often crossed off things from the list, which he considered superfluous, but the children never returned with an empty basket. Ditte still thought she saw the hand of Providence in this, but Lars Peter viewed it more soberly.

"The devil, he can't let us starve to death, when we're working for him," said he. "You'll see the rascal's found out that there's nothing more to be got out of us, he's a sharp nose, he has."

The explanation was not entirely satisfactory—even [Pg 326] to Lars Peter himself. There was something about the inn-keeper which could not be reckoned as money. He was anxious to rule, and did not spare himself in any way. He was always up and doing; he had every family's affairs in his head, knew them better than they did themselves, and interfered. There was both good and bad in his knowledge; no-one knew when to expect him.

Lars Peter was to feel his fatherly care in a new direction. One day the inn-keeper said casually: "that's a big girl, you've got there, Lars Peter; she ought to be able to pay for her keep soon."

"She's earned her bread for many a year, and more too!" answered Lars Peter. "I don't know what I'd have done without her."

The inn-keeper went on his way, but another time when Lars Peter was outside chopping wood he came again and began where he left off. "I don't like to see children hanging about after they've been confirmed," said he. "The sooner they get out the quicker they learn to look after themselves."

"Poor people learn that soon enough whether they are at home or out at service," answered Lars Peter. "We couldn't do without our little housekeeper."

"They'd like to have Ditte at the hill-farm next May—it's a good place. I've been thinking Lars Jensen's widow could come and keep house for you; she's a good worker and she's nothing to do. You might do worse than marry her." [Pg 327]

"I've a wife that's good enough for me," answered Lars Peter shortly.

"But she's in prison—and you're not obliged to stick to her if you don't want to."

"Ay, I've heard that, but Sörine'll want somewhere to go when she comes out."

"Well, that's a matter for your own conscience, Lars Peter. But the Scriptures say nothing about sharing your home with a murderess. What I wanted to say was, that Lars Jensen's wife takes up a whole house."

"Then perhaps we could move down to her?" said Lars Peter brightly. "It's not very pleasant living here in the long run." He had given up all hope of building himself.

"If you marry her, you can consider the house your own."

"I'll stick to Sörine, I tell you," shouted Lars Peter, thumping his ax into the block. "Now, you know it."

The inn-keeper went off, as quietly and kindly as he had come. Jacob the fisherman stood behind the house pointing at him with his gun; it was loaded with salt, he was only waiting for the *word* to shoot. The inn-keeper looked at him as he passed and said, "Well, are you out with your gun today?" Jacob shuffled out of the way.

The inn-keeper's new order brought sorrow to the little house. It was like losing a mother. What would [Pg 328] they do without their house-wife, Ditte, who looked after them all?

Ditte herself took it more quietly. She had always known that sooner or later she would have to go out to service—she was born to it. And all through her childhood it ran like a crimson thread; she must prepare herself for a future master and mistress. "Eat, child," Granny had said, "and grow big and strong and able to make the most of yourself when you're out amongst strangers!" And Sörine—when her turn came—had made it a daily saying: "You'd better behave, or no-one'll have you." The schoolmaster had interwoven it with his teachings, and the parson involuntarily turned to her when speaking of faithful service. She had performed her daily tasks with the object of becoming a clever servant—and she thought with a mixture of fear and expectation of the great moment when she should enter service in reality.

The time was drawing near. She was sorry, and more so for those at home. For herself—it was something that could not be helped.

She prepared everything as far as possible beforehand, taught sister Else her work, and showed her where everything was kept. She was a thoughtful child, easily managed. It was more difficult with Kristian. Ditte was troubled at the thought of what would happen, when she was not there to keep him in order. Every day she spoke seriously to him.

"You'll have to give up your foolish ways, and running off when you're vexed with any one," said she. "Remember, you're the eldest; it'll be your fault if Povl and sister turn out badly! They've nobody but you to look to now. And stop teasing old Jacob, it's a shame to do it."

Kristian promised everything—he had the best will in the world. Only he could never remember to keep his good resolutions.

There was no need to give Povl advice, he was too small. And good enough as he was. Dear, fat, little fellow! It was strange to think that she was going to leave him; several times during the day Ditte would hug him.

"If only Lars Jensen's widow'll be good to the children—and understand how to manage them!" she said to her father. "You see, she's never had children of her own. It must be strange after all!"

Lars Peter laughed.

"It'll be all right," he thought, "she's a good woman. But we shall miss you sorely."

"I'm sure you will," answered Ditte seriously. "But she's not wasteful—that's one good thing."

In the evening, when she had done her daily tasks and the children were in bed, Ditte went through drawers and cupboards so as to leave everything in order for her successor. The children's clothes were carefully examined—and the linen; clean paper was put in the drawers and everything tidied up. Ditte lingered over her work: it was like a silent devotion. The child was bidding farewell to her dear troublesome world, feeling grateful even for the toil and trouble they had given her.

When Lars Peter was not out fishing she would sit beside him under the lamp with some work or other in her hands, and they spoke seriously about the future, giving each other good advice.

"When you get amongst strangers you must listen carefully to everything that's said to you," Lars Peter would say. "Nothing vexes folks more than having to say a thing twice. And then you must remember that it doesn't matter so much how you do a thing, as to do it as they like it. They've all got their own ways, and it's hard to get into sometimes."

"Oh, I'll get on all right," answered Ditte—rather more bravely than she really felt.

"Ay, you're clever enough for your age, but it's not always that. You must always show a good-tempered face—whether you feel it or not. It's what's expected from folks that earn their bread."

"If anything happens, I'll just give them a piece of my mind."

"Ay, but don't be too ready with your mouth! The truth's not always wanted, and least of all from a servant: the less they have to say the better they get on. Just you keep quiet and think what you like—that no-one can forbid you. And then you know, you've always got a home here if you're turned out of your place. You must never leave before your term is up; it's a bad thing to do—whatever you do it for. Rather bear a little unfairness."

"But can't I stand up for my rights?" Ditte did not understand.

"Ay, so you ought—but what is your right? Anyone that's got the power gets the right on his side, that's often proved. But you'll be all right if you're sensible and put your back to the wall."

Then came the last night. Ditte had spent the day saying good-by in the different huts. She could have found a better way to spend these last precious hours, but it was a necessary evil, and if she did not do it they would talk of it behind her back. The three little ones followed close at her heels.

"You mustn't come in," said she. "We can't all go, there's too many, they'll think we want to be treated to something."

So they hid themselves nearby, while she was inside, and went with her to the next house; today they *would* be near her. And they had been so the whole day long. The walk along the beach out to the Naze, where they could see the hill-farm had come to nothing. It was too late, and Ditte had to retract her promise. It cost some tears. The farm where Ditte was going out to service played a strong part in their imagination. They were only comforted, when their father promised that on Sunday morning he would take them for a row.

"Out there you can see the hill-farm and all the land round about it, and maybe Ditte'll be standing there and waving to us," he said.

"Isn't it really further off than that?" asked Ditte.

"Oh, it's about fourteen miles, so of course you'd have to have good eyes," answered Lars Peter, trying to smile. He was not in the humor for fun.

Now at last the three little ones were in the big bed, sleeping peacefully, Povl at one end, sister and Kristian at the other. There was just room for Ditte, who had promised to sleep with them the last night. Ditte busied herself in the living room, Lars Peter sat by the window trying to read Sörine's last letter. It was only a few words. Sörine was not good at writing; he read and re-read it, in a half-whisper. There was a feeling of oppression in the room.

"When's Mother coming out?" asked Ditte, suddenly coming towards him.

Lars Peter took up a calendar. "As far as I can make out, there's still another year," he said quietly. "D'you want to see her too?"

Ditte made no answer. Shortly afterwards she asked him: "D'you think she's altered?"

"You're thinking of the little ones, I suppose. I think she cares a little more for them now. Want makes a good teacher. You must go to bed now, you'll have to be up early in the morning, and it's a long way. Let Kristian go with you—and let him carry your bundle as far as he goes. It'll be a tiresome way for you. I'm sorry I can't go with you!"

"Oh, I shall be all right," said Ditte, trying to speak cheerfully, but her voice broke, and suddenly she threw her arms round him.

Lars Peter stayed beside her until she had fallen asleep, then went up to bed himself. From the attic he could hear her softly moaning in her sleep.

At midnight he came downstairs again, he was in oilskins and carried a lantern. The light shone on the bed—all four were asleep. But Ditte was tossing restlessly, fighting with something in her dreams. "Sister must eat her dinner," she moaned, "it'll never do ... she'll get so thin."

"Ay, ay," said Lars Peter with emotion. "Father'll see she gets enough to eat."

Carefully he covered them up, and went down to the sea.

CPSIA information can be obtained
at www.ICGtesting.com
Printed in the USA
LVOW10s1500071216
516239LV00032B/1346/P